The Fur and Feathers Party

The Fur and Feathers Party

MAGGIE LAWRENCE

Published in 2021 by Margaret E Lawrence

A catalogue record for this
work is available from the
National Library of Australia

ISBN: 978-0-6451303-2-4 (pbk)

ISBN: 978-0-6451303-3-1 (e-bk)

This is a work of fiction. References to real people, events, establishments, organizations, or locales are intended only to provide a sense of authenticity, and are used fictitiously. All other characters and all incidents and dialogue, are drawn from the author's imagination, and are not to be construed as real.

Dedicated to all those who love and respect animals
and who care about the health and welfare
of our beautiful planet.

What if . . .

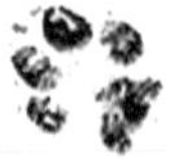

1

Pup

PUP LAY PANTING in a heap of bedraggled and sweaty fur at the edge of a busy highway. She looked more like a grubby tan-and-silver rug than anything remotely like an Australian silky-haired terrier. Her usual abundance of allure had disappeared faster than a delicious treat after a well-mannered walk. Her long silky mane, normally tumbling down her body like a gossamer waterfall, was now a dry and tangled mess.

The temperature on this late January day had climbed to a sizzling forty-six degrees Centigrade, making this the hottest day in the Hornsby Shire of New South Wales since records began.

Rugged national park covered more than two thirds of the area. Unrelenting green and grey eucalypts lined the road, their roots gasping for the rain that had not paid them a visit in months.

The weather bureau had labelled the fire risk 'Catastrophic'. Anyone caught lighting a fire would have a massive fine or end up behind bars.

A hot north wind had whipped up pieces of gravel from the edge of the road, turning them into small gritty tornados. They irritated the little terrier's eyes and skin.

The searing temperature had transformed the highway into a massive grey hotplate, suitable for a giant to fry eggs.

Pup could not have picked a worse day or time to be out in the open with no shelter, food or water. Even if she survived the trucks, cars and motorcycles that were belting along the highway, she would not last long in these conditions.

She was just two years old and had always tried to put her best paw forward. Pup was proud of the fact that she never left steaming putrid piles in the middle of a public pavement. She didn't have Stick Finding Obsession, Compulsive Yapping Disorder or Ball Throwing Syndrome. She never left her toys around for people to fall over. She tried to keep her barking and growling in check. The only time she'd ever woken David at night was to warn him that a possum was devouring the mangoes he'd left on the kitchen table.

As she lay panting on the boiling hot roadside, Pup wondered why David would have chosen her from all the other dogs at the shelter if he didn't want her?

She had only been with David for a year. That was a long time in a dog's life. He had managed to convince her that she was the most important creature in his life. He'd even allowed her to sleep on his bed, and often gave her little treats and toys. It was cruel of him to pretend that she had a happy and safe future if he intended to leave her with his neighbour, Mrs Beanie. The only time Pup had ever been near the old lady was when she had kicked her for smelling the wild roses that grew along the brick fence bordering Mrs Beanie's front garden.

For a little terrier with a strong sense of smell, it wasn't pleasant inhaling the stale musty smell coming from the old lady's clothes. Her garden was overgrown with weeds, and Pup wondered why a person, who clearly never cared for her flowers and shrubs, would be annoyed if she left a deposit there.

The heat was melting parts of the roadway. Burning hot bitumen stuck to the pads of Pup's silky-haired feet, but she was too sad to notice. Her joyful, adventurous, and playful nature had vanished.

If Pup had known the important role she was destined to play in improving the lives of the birds and animals, she would not want to give up her life so easily. She'd be so excited she would somersault down the road like tumbleweed in the desert. Every animal, bird and fish would know who she was, and be grateful to her. But how could this little terrier have known what was just around the corner? Dogs don't go to fortune-tellers.

In this moment the little silky-haired terrier no longer cared that dogs went weak at the paws when they saw her voluptuous tan-and-silver fur, her soft and pointy inquisitive ears, and warm brown expressive eyes.

Pup could only think of one thing: how could David just abandon her?

She drifted into a daydream, her mind re-living the events of just a few hours earlier that had changed her life forever.

~

David's living room was full of large taped-up cardboard boxes. He was busy filling a new box with Pup's belongings.

'Where are we moving to?' she barked excitedly. 'Does it

have a bigger garden with lots of interesting new smells?' David glanced at his little dog briefly, said nothing and continued packing the box.

Pup watched as her make-believe bone, her soft toy that made a noise like a cat mewing, and her sheepskin rug that caused her to drift into a long, and comfortable sleep, disappeared inside the box.

'Why are you in such a bad mood?' Pup barked. She decided to try and help David and dragged her special blanket, dumping it near him to add to the box containing the rest of her things.

He pushed her away, picking up the blanket and leaving it on the veranda.

'I don't understand why you are being like this David. If I've done something wrong, then please tell me what it is. I've never seen you like this before,' she barked.

'Shut up Pup,' David snapped.

A loud knock on the door shook the little terrier into dog protection mode. She barked as aggressively as she could manage for a small dog, and ran to see who was there.

A tall man with huge muscles, a large beer gut and covered in tattoos, stood on the other side of the wire security door. He didn't wait for David to invite him in. He just walked straight into the house, ignoring Pup's warning yap.

His attitude annoyed her. She growled in her most threatening tone and tried to bite him on the leg.

'Stop that!' David yelled. Pup was really confused. He'd never shouted at her before for protecting him. It was her job after all and she didn't like this man.

She could see a horrible dark aura creeping over his body like black mould on a shower wall. Pup didn't trust him. It was her job to let David know. The man might be planning to steal something from the house. But David just shook the man's hand like they were old friends.

Pup noticed how her master's aura didn't have its usual sparkle. There was a tinge of pale green and blue, but it lacked lustre. She'd seen this before in people who were sad.

'What could he be so sad about?' she thought.

Pup watched the man. He carried David's bed out the front door, loading it into the back of a large van.

'He's taking your bed David. What are you going to sleep on?' But he ignored her loud barking. He was busy securing the box containing Pup's things, with large sticky tape.

The man went in and out of the house carrying taped-up boxes and hurling them into the back of his van.

David glanced at Pup as he carried the box towards the front door. His look was strange and wistful. Almost like he was going to cry. He picked up her lead and attached it to her collar. He tied her to the front veranda fence. He placed her special blanket beside her on the floor.

Pup watched David scribble a hasty note on a piece of paper. He picked up the cardboard box containing the remainder of her belongings and walked away. She craned her neck to see where he was going and noticed him leaving the box on Mrs Beanie's front porch. He stuck the note under the front door mat.

'I wish I knew what he's written on that note,' Pup thought.

David returned and walked up to the little terrier. His angry mood seemed to have softened. He rubbed her on the back.

'Why are you tying me up like this David? Surely I am going with you?' But David didn't seem to understand her question.

He gently stroked her ears and she saw David's eyes welling up.

'Now you be a good dog, Pup. Mrs Beanie is going to take care of you. She will come and get you tonight.' He put a bowl of water near her.

Pup's tummy contracted into a tight ball of tension. She didn't want to have anything to do with Mrs Beanie. The one time she had attempted to pat her, it was more like a slap than a kindly stroke. In dog's years the old lady had to be at least sixteen, even twenty.

Pup watched horrified as David hurled suitcases and boxes into his car. He climbed into the driver's seat without looking back.

'Wait! I want to go with you. I don't want to be with Mrs Beanie. She doesn't even like me.'

Pup's fur stood on end as it began to sink in that David was not taking her with him.

David started up his bright red Holden Astra, following the van containing all his belongings down the street until Pup could no longer see them.

'Wait! David please come back,' Pup barked hysterically pulling furiously on her lead but it would not give way. She was determined she was going to escape before Mrs Beanie arrived home.

Her collar felt a bit loose. She angled her head and pulled backwards. She tried positioning her head in a different way. She pulled hard. The collar and leash eventually came off. She was free.

She ran as fast as silky-haired terrier legs would allow, but couldn't see David, or his red car anywhere. She dropped down on the side of the road sad, confused and exhausted.

~

Pup had been lying on the road for sometime and the pads on her silky-haired feet were now sore and cracked and burning from the heat. She licked her paws and they tasted salty increasing her thirst. But even the thought of finding some cool water to drink and a shady tree to sit under, did nothing to relieve her feelings of abandonment.

Pup no longer cared if she died from dehydration or got run over. She had lost the will to live.

2

Cracker Yellow-Crest

CRACKER FOUGHT HER WAY OUT of her egg. It seemed to have been laid in a layer of chewed wood dust, shredded from the inside of the limb of a eucalyptus tree. It was exactly thirty days after her egg had been deposited in the nest.

Two white-feathered faces were staring down at her. One had a soft and gentle expression. The other was spoiling for a fight. Above both faces Cracker noticed crests like bright yellow combs. She wondered if they were just vain and had put them there so they would always have well-combed feathers.

She touched her head with a tiny claw. All she could feel was a small bump covered in soft fluff.

'Strewth. Where the hell am I?' she squawked in her new little cockatoo voice, gazing at the broken pieces of shell around her, and the hollow tree trunk that was her new home.

'This is your home darling,' Cracker's mother Beryl said. She stroked her new baby cockatoo gently on her soft downy head.

Cracker gazed at her mother's white feathery face with the

odd looking yellow comb-like thing that moved backwards and forwards when her mother spoke to her. She seemed kind enough. But the baby cockatoo didn't like the look of the face that was staring at her with its mouth wide open. It looked annoyed as if it was about to bite her.

'And who are you?' Cracker asked.

'Clancy's the name, but you can call me dad,' he said adding, 'if you must.'

'Don't speak to our new baby in that tone Clancy,' Beryl said.

'Now you listen to me Beryl. I've been stuck here with you, sittin' on this little bugger's egg for way too long. I've got no time for your lectures. Do you have any idea how many lilly pilly bushes have been stripped clean of berries while I've been stuck here?'

Cracker wished she could climb back into the safety of the egg. Her father seemed to have an anger management problem.

'Geez you're a grouchy bastard,' Cracker spat.

'Well you'd be grouchy too if you'd been stuck keeping an egg warm, while the rest of your flock are having a bird of a time stripping fly screens off houses.'

Clancy was now hanging upside down from a branch of the tree.

'He doesn't mean to be so rude dear,' Beryl said. She stroked her little one gently on the tiny bump that would soon grow her golden crest. 'He's just a little tired from sitting on the eggs.'

'The eggs?' Cracker asked. She looked around but could not see any other eggs. There was only the broken shell from where she had emerged earlier.

Clancy pulled at a leaf, tasted it and immediately spat it out. Cracker thought he had dreadful manners, and a bad attitude.

'There would have been another egg, but your mother here managed to sit too hard on it and the rest is history,' Clancy said swinging aggressively on the branch near Cracker.

'I told her she needed to lose some weight before she got preggers. But the silly female didn't listen. It's a wonder you made it into the world to be honest.'

Cracker was beginning to wish she hadn't. She was surprised by the way he spoke to her mother. There didn't seem to be much love between them. She wondered how her mother could put up with such a rude mate. He seemed to have little respect for her.

The egg had been nice and warm. She'd liked being inside it. But now this new world was feeling very unwelcoming.

'Why don't you go and hang out with your flock for a while?' Beryl said. 'I would like some time alone with our baby. Maybe you can find us some juicy berries for our dinner later on.'

'Well you'll be lucky if I can find any berries. They've probably all been eaten. All right. I'll see ya later.'

Clancy flew off with a loud screech. Cracker tried to cover the holes on the side of her face. His voice was so loud and unpleasant; it had set off a ringing sound inside her head. She wondered if there would be a way she could stuff something inside the holes. She didn't want to listen to him anymore. The baby cockatoo hoped she wasn't going to sound like her father when she got older. She was relieved to be alone with her new mother. Beryl seemed quite nice.

'Open your beak,' her mother screeched.

Cracker found Beryl's tone was almost as loud as her father, and was also hurting her delicate little ears.

'What for?'

'I need to feed you.' Cracker opened her beak as wide as she could. She suddenly realized her tummy was rumbling and she was rather hungry.

Beryl regurgitated the food into the tiny bird's open beak. Cracker didn't enjoy the process much. She hoped she would get used to it.

'So what's my name then?' the small cockatoo asked.

'Oh well let's see.' Cracker was surprised that her mother had to think about it. Surely they had chosen a name. Maybe they'd argued all through her incubation period, and this had never been discussed.

Suddenly the branch Clancy had been swinging on made a loud cracking sound. It broke and fell onto the ground below. 'I think we will call you Cracker,' Beryl said.

~

The tree hollow that was their home had a lovely view of the creek below that was lined with river gums.

From her cosy nest, Cracker had a cockatoo-eye view of the kookaburra and his large family that lived in the next-door tree. They often woke her up at daybreak laughing loudly. She thought the jokes must be pretty funny as they went on laughing for a long time.

One day she saw the kookaburra swoop onto an unsuspecting snake it had spotted beneath its tree. She watched as the bird gathered the snake in its long beak, flying high into the air before sending its prey plummeting to the ground. The snake lay barely moving.

The kookaburra swooped down and once again carried the half-dead snake to the top of the tree, before letting it fall to the ground. It showed no signs of life.

Cracker felt so disturbed watching the way the kookaburra killed the snake; she felt she had to say something. 'You're a mean bird to pick on that snake like that. Couldn't you have just eaten some berries instead?' The kookaburra gazed at Cracker a moment. Then he opened his beak and let out a loud chuckle. The young cockatoo was not impressed.

From her tree home Cracker also saw various dogs trailing behind their owners on their walks. *I'm glad I was born a bird,* she thought. *Soon I will be able to test my wings and fly wherever I want. The last thing I want is to be dependent on a human being for food and for getting around. Humans fill my bush home with those objects they carry around. They seem to contain water, or other liquids they like to drink.*

'Those white things they use to carry food in often end up in the creek. Humans don't seem to care much about our home. It's a cruel world,' Cracker told her mother. 'How did I end up here?'

'You were conceived on the side of a busy road,' Beryl said.

'Crikey! Couldn't dad have found a more private place?'

'It wasn't the most pleasant experience I've had in my life,' Beryl said. 'I had hoped it would be over quickly. But now you have come into the world, I wouldn't change a thing.'

Cracker felt sorry for her mother. Clancy didn't appear to be much of a catch. The way he complained about the incubation of the eggs, it seemed he just wanted to hang out with his male friends.

The young cockatoo also wished her mother had been more careful with her roosting. She would like to have had a brother or a sister. 'It's a pity you had to sit so hard on the eggs,' Cracker said.

'Your father was making that story up darling. He was

screeching at me about how long the eggs were taking to hatch. He wanted to be off with his flock somewhere. I was so upset by the deafening noise right in my ear, I moved off the eggs for a minute to get away from him. The egg that would have been your brother or sister got bumped by a strong gust of wind, and rolled out of the tree.'

'Geez I hope I never end up with a mate like that. I dunno how you put up with him.'

'Well although he grumbled a lot at the time, he did share the incubation of your egg Cracker, and he's quite a good provider.'

'A good provider of rude remarks,' Cracker added chuckling at her own turn of phrase.

As Cracker got older, she observed how much her father seemed to dislike the female of the species. She'd overheard him telling her mother 'Females are only good for two things: laying eggs and finding food.'

She came to the conclusion that Clancy disliked female birds altogether preferring to fly around with his male companions.

Cracker witnessed a time when her mother had brought home some mulberries she'd found on a tree in someone's garden. Clancy had said: 'why don't you check the berries out for bruises before you bring them home Beryl. These are inedible.'

Cracker had hoped Beryl would give him the feather, but she just put up with his rude treatment, and said nothing.

I hope I don't get a mate like him, Cracker thought.

Day after day, when she was still very tiny, Cracker watched her father fly off with his larrikin friends to rip the guttering off houses, or to raid people's sunflower seeds. Clancy did little to feather their nest. While he was out creating mischief, Beryl was left to do all the nestwork.

It annoyed Cracker that Beryl put up with Clancy's bad behaviour. She wished her mother would stand up to him. Maybe then he would respect her a bit more.

Cracker was not allowed to leave the nest for six weeks. Her mother used this time to teach her about staying safe in the Australian bush.

'Always remain with the flock as much as you can Cracker, and listen out for their warning of any dangers when you are pecking around on the ground. The birds will keep an eye on you. They will watch out for snakes and foxes, and even the noisy fast-moving objects that travel along the roads.

'Your Auntie Birdsy and Uncle Claw were both wiped out by stupid people inside those moving boxes. The humans can get distracted talking on dark objects they hold up to their ears. You must be careful of that, Cracker.

'Lots of cockatoos fly right into those fast moving boxes because they are so busy looking at what their friends are doing, and don't realize how low they're flying.

'You must always listen out for the warning screech of your flock in case you need to fly higher, or to a nearby branch for safety.'

'I'm not stupid. I've got sharp claws and a very good take off speed. Nothing is gonna bother me.'

'Oh my goodness. You're sounding just like your father,' Beryl said with a loud sigh.

Cracker knew she got impatient easily, but there was no way she would ever want to be like her father. She began to wonder where her father was. He hadn't been around for a while. Not that she missed him at all. In fact she found it rather peaceful just being with her mother. But she was curious to know where he was.

'What's happened to dad?' Cracker asked her mother.

Her mother said nothing for a minute and began preening herself; something Cracker noticed she always did when she was trying to avoid answering a question.

'Well I was resting in a tree watching him berating another male cockatoo for eating his berries. He was on the side of the road and he didn't see the fast-moving box coming around a corner. He didn't have time to get out of the way,' Beryl said.

Cracker was surprised her mother didn't shed a tear telling the story, but it seemed she was just relieved Clancy was gone. She must have been happy she no longer had to deal with his verbal abuse.

The young cockatoo didn't miss her father much either. They had never really bonded. She did think her mother was a bit too much of a worrier and a pessimist. Cracker had no time for wallowing. She'd had to toughen up to deal with her father.

~

Cracker grew stronger. Her yellow crest began to take shape on top of her head. By the time she had turned seven she was feeling pressured to find a mate, but she wasn't ready for tying the beak.

Like her father, Cracker was a bit of a larrikin and enjoyed stripping fruit trees, and taking one peck out of each apple so none of them were left without her signature.

She didn't even like eating apples or fruit that much, but she loved berries. It was a fun game for Cracker to ensure every apple on a tree had at least one peck out of it. Cracker thought about the time she had been clocked on her crest by a fast moving ball when Mrs Thompson noticed her pecking at her nashi pears. 'Hey leave my fruit alone,' Mrs Thompson had yelled, hurling the ball at Cracker.

But even though her yellow crest had carried a bruise for weeks, Cracker still thought it was a good game and kind of funny.

The months passed in this way until, by her eighth summer, Cracker started getting ready to leave home. She was tired of her mother telling her what to do.

'Cracker dear, you need to learn compassion towards other creatures that may be less fortunate than you, especially those born without wings,' Beryl would say. 'Some can only crawl along on the dirty ground. The poor wombat lives in dark muddy burrows. They are so slow when crossing the road, they can easily be hit by one of those fast moving objects the humans seem to like being inside.'

'It's their karma,' Cracker said.

Once Cracker had heard a wise owl telling its young that it believed in reincarnation: being re-born again and again. Cracker was curious and asked Owl to elaborate.

'I believe I only got to be an owl in this life coz I had done some good deeds as another kind of bird in a past life,' the Owl told Cracker. 'I was probably a mynah bird and I didn't drive the other smaller birds away, or bother people who were trying to enjoy a picnic in the bush. So I was rewarded in this life with some good karma, like being extra wise. Now all the birds and animals look up to me for all kinds of things,' the Owl said.

Cracker had spent hours talking to Owl about the concept of karma and reincarnation. She thought it was rather cool, and wondered what she might have been before she was born a cockatoo.

She thought about the wombat crawling along the ground. 'Wombats must have done something bad in a past life to be born without wings. I'm not going to waste time feeling sorry for them. It's their own fault,' Cracker said.

Cracker noticed the sad look of resignation in Beryl's eyes. She knew her mother didn't approve of her strong opinions, but she would never be like her mother. She saw Beryl as weak and was glad to have inherited some of her father's strength and confidence.

As she matured, Cracker began to notice a nagging little voice deep inside her. It seemed to be saying she was destined to lead a most unusual life, and was going to contribute something of real value to the world. She had no idea what that could be. Finding a mate was becoming important to her.

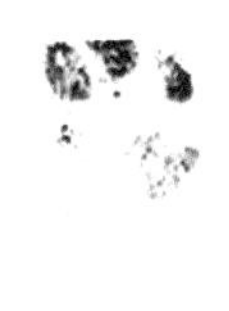

3

The U.S President

THE U.S. PRESIDENT pedalled away on his exercise bike in his private quarters. He thought about the amazing journey he'd been on to end up as the most powerful man in America, even the world.

He was nothing like some of the former presidents. He wasn't a famous actor or a reality TV star, or even just a businessman. He was just an ordinary man who had joined the Party to help out a bit.

If someone had told him that in a few years' time he would be the President of the United States, he would have thought they were delusional.

He was ready for his health drink and jumped off the bike. He walked across to his drinks cabinet and grabbed a long glass.

He filled it with some of the dark brown mixture that was waiting in his blender. He liked his health drinks and this mix of spinach, kale, parsley and prunes kept him feeling vibrant and regular.

People were always commenting on how young he looked for a man of fifty-six. He still had a good crop of dark hair on his head with only a few single strands of grey in his side burns.

He knew that he was a fine looking man with his large brown eyes, a full, kissable mouth and a toned athletic body. A woman had told him that he had a noble face, and she found the way his eyebrows met in the middle incredibly sexy.

Jim had his reasons for being a confirmed bachelor, but his looks and charismatic personality drove women crazy.

The door of his private quarters opened and his Chief of Staff came into the room holding a clipboard. 'I'd just like to go over a few things with you Mr President.'

The President noticed Hank's sudden nervous look as he gazed at the blender.

'Grab a glass Hank. This will put hairs where you don't already have them,' he chuckled.

Jim was aware that his Chief of Staff did not share his liking for these health drinks. But if this man would be working closely with him he would have to do something to maintain good health. The President didn't want to work with someone who was always coming down with whatever bugs were floating around.

'Thanks Mr President, but I might pass.'

'I insist, Hank, and will you please stop calling me Mr President. I don't like all this formality. Jim will be fine.'

'All right Mr Pres, ah Jim,' Hank said.

Jim filled Hank's glass with what was left of the thick brown mixture. He caught the look of resignation on Hank's face as he passed the glass to him. 'Down the hatch, Hank,' the President said with a mischievous twinkle in his eye.

He watched amused as his Chief of Staff shut his eyes and tried to swallow without tasting it. He waited until Hank had fully drained the glass before taking the now empty vessel, and putting it on a tray by the door with some other dirty dishes.

'Well done Hank. Now I want you to share this with me every day. You will thank me for it.'

'Yes Mr President.'

'Jim,' the President insisted.

'Jim. I am sure I will get to like it as much as you do.'

It was obvious Hank was lying but the President didn't mind.

'Of course you will.'

'You know Hank, when I became President of the United States, I told myself that I would never marry or get involved with anyone. I didn't want to end up like former presidents, if you know what I mean Hank?'

Jim realized that his determination to remain a bachelor made Hank uncomfortable, especially when there were so many women who wanted to be his partner.

He wondered if Hank was simply jealous because he was divorced, and wasn't as good looking, or as charismatic as Jim was. Hank was younger than Jim but was totally bald.

The President thought how lucky he was to still have a thick head of hair. He could tell that Hank tried to hide his baldness when he met women, by wearing a cap. He was also aware that, since his divorce, Hank had shown little interest in finding another partner.

'Jim there's the matter of the White House Christmas tree theme. Normally of course the First Lady would be the one choosing a theme but since - ' Jim cleared his throat nervously -

'there is no First Lady, would you like me to choose the theme sir?'

'Of course Hank. Do you have something in mind?'

'Well, Jim, I thought our Native North American animals might be something a little different.'

'I like your thinking Hank. Funnily enough, I was looking through a National Geographic the other day. There was a feature on some of our interesting animals. There were some lovely pictures of the white-tailed deer, the opossum and the pronghorn antelope. See if you can find someone who has created ornaments from these creatures. Oh, and don't forget the Bald Eagle.'

'I will get onto that Jim. Oh and – um I did want to go over your itinerary for the trip to Australia. Perhaps, if you don't mind me suggesting it Jim, you could think about taking some time off while you are there. Maybe you could have a bit of a holiday. They have funny animals there.'

The President climbed back onto his exercise bike and began pedalling furiously. 'Yes. Good idea Hank. Could you do some research for me on that? Find me a nice quiet out-of-the-way place to stay where I can chill out for a while?'

'I'll get right onto it, Jim. Of course, it will be summer over there so you'll get a nice break from our cold weather.'

'That will be welcome, Hank. I do find the winters hard to take over here. Oh, by the way Hank, you're coming with me to Australia.'

'But Jim, isn't that a little unusual? I mean who is going to be controlling the White House Office and overseeing all the policy development, amongst many other things if I am away?'

'You're my *gatekeeper*, Hank. It's a very short trip. We'll only be gone for about ten days. You can get Larry to run the show while we're away. He's always been an excellent personal aide. He was very competent at filling your shoes when you were off sick remember?'

'But Jim … I'

'There's nothing more to be said, Hank. I've already given Larry a heads-up. So go and brief him now on anything you think he should know before we leave.'

'But Jim, what about …'

'Hank, I know you're very important, but remember, I'm the President. I make the final decisions around here.'

'Yes Jim. I'll go and find Larry now.'

'Good, that's settled then.'

Hank nervously cleared his throat and left the room.

Jim continued his workout. As he pedalled away, he remembered how he didn't have anyone to accompany him to the Inaugural Ball. He thought about the way his Vice President had tried to get him to agree to be partnered by a friend of his wife. But Jim thought she was very pretentious and he made it quite clear to Elroy that he was perfectly happy to go to the Ball unaccompanied.

He had felt a little embarrassed when later the media made such a point that he was the only President to have gone to the Inaugural Ball without a partner. He wished they hadn't kept mentioning how many gorgeous and available women would have gladly gone with him to the event. He thought his voting public would be wondering what was wrong with him.

Jim stopped pedalling. *That's enough of a workout for one day*, he thought.

Hank came back into his private quarters, passing Jim a

fresh towel and a glass of purified water.

'Now, I wanted to talk to you about my getting a companion in the White House. It's no fun being a bachelor, Hank. I might be a very busy man, but I do get lonely at times.'

'I will see who I can introduce you to, Jim. I did meet a lovely woman the other night. She is very attractive, refined and politically savvy, and has been a governor for many years.'

'I'm not talking about a woman, Hank. I want a little dog!'

4

Tying the Beak

AUTUMN HAD ARRIVED and the mango season was drawing to an end. Cracker was making the most of the last edible fruit.

She was so busy enjoying the tangy yellow flesh that she didn't notice a cockatoo landing beside her. Without even wishing her a happy morning's peck, he launched into, 'Hey Cracker, you look like your feathers could do with a bit of a stroke.'

Cracker ignored him and kept pecking at the mango.

'How bout you hang out with me?'

Cracker stopped eating and turned to look at the male cockatoo. She noticed a wicked look in his beady eye.

'I'll put some fire in your crest,' he persisted.

Cracker was totally turned off. His approach reminded her of her father. 'I might pass on that flattering offer,' she told him. She finished eating the fruit and flew up onto a nearby branch. The male cockatoo gazed up at her with his beak open.

'You've obviously never been rejected before,' Cracker said. 'About time if you ask me. You're not going to get very far with females with that kind of an opening squawk,' she added.

The male bird gave her a feather flick and flew off, totally humiliated.

~

The sun was beginning to sleep in longer as winter approached. Cracker was having trouble reaching the biggest nashi pear on the top of Mrs Watkins pear tree. Her claws were stiff with the cold. She was balancing precariously on the spindly branch when she heard a friendly squawk.

'Why don't you let me help you with that?'

Standing on the ground at the foot of the tree was the most handsome cockatoo she'd ever seen. His pure white feathers shimmered in the sunlight. His eyes were an unusual shade of blue – they seemed warm and compassionate.

He flew up to the top of the tree and, with the ease of a circus acrobat, he grabbed at the juicy nashi pear with one claw, sending it plummeting to the ground. Its juice gushed out like a nashi pear hydrant.

Cracker was impressed. She could not control her crest. It seemed to be going backwards and forwards in an excited manner. She noticed this was causing the handsome bird's feathers to stand on end.

'I'm Henry,' he said, holding out a claw.

'That was masterful,' Cracker said, feeling her face flushing yellow. 'I wish I could balance on branches as well as you.'

'What's your name?' The male bird asked.

'Cracker.'

‘I will teach you, Cracker,’ Henry said. ‘You have a beautiful crest by the way.’ Cracker was smitten.

The two love birds were soon pecking holes in fruit together, seeing who could hang from the guttering of houses the longest, and enjoying the joke of startling humans getting dressed for work, when they suddenly appeared at their bedroom windows.

Under Henry’s expert tuition, Cracker had greatly improved her flying and fitness levels. She was able to balance on the most delicate of branches to reach the best fruit at the top of trees.

~

Cracker thought it was a huge joke to startle humans. One morning, as the mischievous cockatoo appeared at a woman’s bathroom window, she turned around to see where Henry was. She thought he had been keen to join her, but Henry was just sitting on the ground looking up at Cracker with an odd expression. She flew down beside him.

‘What’s up Henry?’

The bird said nothing. Cracker noticed he was trembling slightly.

‘Are you sick Henry?’

‘No. I’ve never been better, but there’s something I want to ask you?’

Cracker suddenly felt apprehensive. She hoped he wasn’t going to ask if she would be okay with him hanging out with another bird. Maybe he was tired of her company.

‘Will you fly up to that low branch and wait there please?’ Henry asked.

Cracker was now really worried. Maybe Henry was going to

say something that would make her really angry. Perhaps he wanted her well away from him so he could take off quickly before she tried to take a nip out of his crest.

She flew up to the branch. Henry looked up at Cracker and for a moment didn't seem able to screech. Then finally, with a wobble in his squawk, he said, 'I want you to be my bird. Will you marry me?'

Cracker was thrilled. She flew down beside him and, in her loudest and most screechy voice, answered 'YES'.

~

The two birds began planning to make their union official. Cracker wanted to look her best on the day, and stopped eating bread pieces that humans left for her on grass verges. She also cut back on her berry intake.

The excited cockatoo spent hours pecking at her feet. She wanted them to look wonderful when she took Henry's claw to screech their vows.

They set a day for the ceremony and Cracker was in bird heaven that soon she would be Henry's official mate.

'After the wedding I thought we might celebrate by spending a few days at Mr Johnson's strawberry farm,' Henry told Cracker excitedly.

'Oh that would be just bonza. I've been keen to have a peck at those strawberries, but I wanted to wait until I had a bird to accompany me. Mr Thompson has shot at birds like us, ya know Henry.'

'I wouldn't let anything happen to you Cracker. You'll have a great time eating your fill of the delicious fruit. I'll keep watch,' Henry added.

Cracker scratched her crest for a moment; she'd had a

thought and was wondering whether she should share it with Henry. She noticed he was staring at her with a questioning look, so she blurted it out; 'it's bad luck to see your bird-to-be before the wedding. So waddayasay I get to our chosen spot for our union, fifteen squawks ahead of you?'

'That sounds like a good idea,' Henry said. 'I'll be there right on the sixteenth squawk. I cannot wait.'

'Me too,' Cracker said.

Henry gave Cracker's crest a little friendly peck with his beak. Her crest shot backwards and forwards enjoying his affectionate touch. Cracker was crest over claws in love with her handsome friend.

~

The day arrived for the wedding. The air was crisp and still. The only sounds to interrupt the silent winter morning, were two butcherbirds learning a new song.

As the weak sun tried desperately to break through the covering of clouds, Cracker jumped in Mrs Taylor's birdbath to spruce up her feathers. She cleaned her claws until she could see her own reflection in them. She wanted to look her very best for her precious mate Henry.

The sun finally managed to put in an appearance and it was time for their ceremony.

Cracker flew to the spot she and Henry had chosen to say their vows underneath a shady pink peppercorn tree, on the edge of a crystal clear river. They had decided not to invite any other birds. This moment was going to be just for them.

The nervous bird-bride could feel a tightness developing in her stomach that she knew to be nerves. Soon they would make their union official, and they would be happily flying off to gorge on some of Mr Johnson's delicious strawberries. She couldn't wait.

Cracker began to count: one screech, two screeches, three screeches… and so on until she got to the appointed screech of fifteen. There was no sign of Henry.

'Come on Henry. It's not like you to be late,' Cracker said nervously pecking at her claws.

'Fifteen screeches, sixteen screeches, seventeen screeches.' Cracker stopped counting. She was beginning to get a little worried.

What are you doing Henry? This is a fine screech to choose to be late. Cracker flew up to the top of the pink peppercorn tree to see if she could see Henry coming. He was nowhere to be seen.

When forty screeches had gone by, Cracker was really concerned. If there was one thing she loved about Henry, he was a very good squawk-keeper. She forgot all about her desire for him not to see his bird-to-be before the wedding. Cracker decided to fly back to Henry's tree, to see what his excuse was for being late. Maybe he had just forgotten what screech they had agreed on to say their vows.

On arriving at Henry's personal eucalyptus tree, Cracker was disappointed to find no sign of him. She decided to ask around. Maybe another bird might know where he was.

Cracker tried hard to stay positive, but she couldn't help but think the worst. Something very significant must have happened to Henry to cause him to miss his own wedding. She knew him well enough to know he would have done everything bird-ably possible to be there as they had arranged.

The Cockatoo landed on a picnic table covered in food scraps that some human had left for the birds to enjoy.

'Have you seen Henry?' Cracker asked an African mynah bird, busy picking at the crumbs on the picnic table.

'Who is Henry?' the bird asked.

'Never mind. I'll leave you to your crumbs.' Cracker was annoyed. These birds were always sticking their beaks into other bird's business, and the one time she wanted one of them to actually know something, it didn't.

'Just my luck,' Cracker muttered to herself. She flew on a bit. She stopped when she saw a cockatoo trying to shred a fly-wire screen on the front door of a suburban house.

'Have you seen Henry?' Cracker asked the naughty bird.

'I saw him the other day. He was polishing off the last berry worth picking on my blackberry bush. I was really annoyed. But can't say I've seen him since then. Maybe he's hanging out in his tree with stomach pains from all the fruit he gobbled up.'

'Okay thanks.'

'I thought you two were going to tie the claw?' the cockatoo screeched. Cracker didn't answer. She flew off on wings that were now beginning to tremble with fear. She decided to do one more circuit of their bush home.

Cracker began to wonder if Henry had flown too low and hit a human box on the road. Or maybe he *was* lying ill somewhere from poisonous berries.

She gave herself a sharp peck. 'Enough of the negativity,' she muttered out loud. There had to be a very good reason why Henry had not turned up for their marriage vows.

Finally she decided to call a meeting of the flock.

~

Twenty cockatoos gathered underneath Cracker's private gum tree. 'Thank you all for coming,' Cracker told the flock. 'I called this meeting because my Henry is missing.' There wasn't a single squawk from the birds, just an unusual silence.

'So if any of you have seen him, or have any idea where he might be, will you please let me know.'

'Have you checked the roads?' a male cockatoo screeched.

Cracker gazed at her claws for a minute, trying to control her emotions. The birds waited for her response. She swallowed hard in an attempt to remove the lump that was building in her throat.

'Of course I've checked the roads. Henry had excellent road sense.'

'What about the wombat burrows? Maybe he's fallen down one of those. I almost did once,' a female cockatoo screeched.

'I doubt that very much. Henry was very good on his claws. But I will check.'

'We'll look out for him,' the cockatoo added. 'I hope you find him.'

Cracker could feel the lump in her throat growing. She wanted to end the meeting before her emotions got the better of her. She hoped this rare feeling would go away.

'I appreciate that you all came. Please ask the great bird in the sky to help me find Henry. You never know. It might help.'

Cracker didn't believe in this bird in the sky, but at times like this it didn't hurt to screech in his direction.

'Will do,' the birds all squawked in unison.

'Maybe ask Barn Owl if he's seen Henry,' another cockatoo called out. 'He's very wise. He might know something.'

'There's no way I am going to be disturbing Barny at this time of day. Anyway, how would he see Henry when he's in his tree with his eyes closed?'

Cracker flew off muttering to herself, 'Stupid bird.' She dropped onto the roof guttering of a house. She thought about how much fun she had enjoyed with Henry seeing how long they could hang there without it giving way. Then something happened to Cracker that caused her to be mortified: she shed a tear.

~

The nights were becoming longer as winter made its chilly presence felt. There was still no sign of Henry. Cracker noticed a wombat waddling slowly past the creek near her tree home.

'Excuse me Wombat. I'm Cracker and my mate Henry has disappeared. I just wondered if by any chance he might have fallen into your burrow?'

Cracker noticed the wombat now looked stunned.

'Believe me Cracker, if a cockatoo were to fall into my burrow it would be around the bush telegraph in no time. Sorry haven't seen him.'

Cracker watched the wombat waddling away very slowly and called after her.

'Okay well thank you, and I'm sorry you did some bad things in a past life, and haven't got wings this time around.'

The wombat turned around to gaze at the cockatoo again. Her mouth had dropped open. She finally spoke.

'What?' was all she could manage to say.

'It was just something I wondered after talking to an owl once about reincarnation. It's not important.'

Cracker sensed that the wombat was now thinking she had sunflower seeds for brains, and decided it was best not to say anymore. She flew off before she could cause any more trouble with the wombat. She'd seen a wombat try and attack a cockatoo once, but it was so slow on its feet that the bird got away before anything bad happened.

~

The cold months had really set in. Cracker was deeply upset to lose her Henry. Most of the berries were long since gone. But there was always a member of Cracker's flock determined to prove there were still berries to be found. Sulphur was one such resolute bird.

He was deep inside a prickly bush, hunting for the last remaining blackberries.

Cracker sat on a low branch washing her claws and keeping one eye on Sulphur.

'What's the matter Cracker? I thought you'd be battling with me for one last berry,' Sulphur said.

'I'm not really interested.'

'It's a pity about Henry,' Sulphur added.

Cracker didn't want to talk about him. She continued watching Sulphur who had now almost disappeared inside the blackberry bush.

Sulphur called out to her, 'Maybe Henry got cold claws about tying the beak.'

Cracker's yellow crest shot up with annoyance. She was incensed that Sulphur would dare suggest such a thing. She knew in her heart this was not like her Henry. He was crazy about her, and couldn't wait for them to join their claws in marriage.

'No I'm sure some human is behind Henry's disappearance,' Cracker spat. 'If ever I discover who they are, and what they did to Henry, I swear I will make sure they get their comeuppance. There is no way my clever Henry, with his masterful road sense, could just disappear from the face of the earth like that.'

5

Pup or Lavinia

PUP HAD A HAPPY ENTRY into the world. She was born at the dog breeder's house in Hornsby, a leafy suburb of Sydney. Pup was surrounded by the love and warmth of her mother, Muffin, and her five brothers and one sister.

The dog breeder, Corrina, was forty-five years old and lived in a large two-storey double brick house she had inherited from her parents. She was an only child and had tragically lost her mother and father in a car accident.

Corrina had given up her twenty-year government job as an administrative officer for the Ministry of Health. She was able to retire on a nice final pay out and, since the house had no mortgage, her overheads were not that high.

She took up breeding silky-haired terriers.

People loved the little terriers' responsive, inquisitive and friendly natures. They were a cross between a Yorkshire and Australian terrier and were always up for a challenge, or a new adventure. It was a good living for Corrina. Muffin had several litters and they all sold well to wonderful homes.

Initially, Corrina kept all the puppies from Muffin's last litter and enjoyed watching them playing together happily. But Pup sensed she was Corrina's favourite.

~

Pup played for hours in the large garden with her mother and the puppies. She loved the way Muffin would chase the family around and point out things they needed to learn.

The little terrier bonded with her mother better than the rest of the litter. She learned quickly how to mark out her territory, and how to recognise anything that could be dangerous: like snakes and certain spiders. She also learned what plants in the garden were poisonous to dogs.

The puppies were told the importance of protecting their master at all times, and how to growl and bark effectively. Muffin paid so much attention to Pup, that the little terrier felt very special. She developed a strong sense of self-worth. It didn't even bother her that she wasn't as big as other dogs.

'You need to understand that just because you are a little dog, doesn't mean you can't be as scary as the bigger dogs when you need to be,' Muffin told Pup, licking her head affectionately.

Shortly after Pup first opened her eyes, she asked her mother about her father.

'I hardly knew him. We made love and then he was taken away and I never saw him again.'

Muffin had clenched her teeth and Pup could tell this was not a topic she wanted to keep discussing.

Pup was a quick learner and she picked up how to tell by the inflection of the human voice what the person was saying to her. The first sentence that the little terrier mastered was 'Come on, we're going for a walk.' Very soon Pup had become so smart that, even when Corrina thought she was not revealing anything by spelling "w. a. l. k", Pup knew immediately what the sounds meant, and was racing up to her lead expectantly.

She loved living at Corrina's place. She never got tired of chasing her brothers and sister around the garden. Her favourite game was 'catch me if you can', followed closely by 'who is best at getting covered in mud?'. They were fun games and Pup loved having her family to play with.

The garden was filled with the most intoxicating aromas. It was a scintillating smellathon of Jasmine, Gardenia, Frangipani and Magnolia flowers. Pup enjoyed leaving her signature on as many enticing odours as she could manage.

As the house was on a half-acre block, there was plenty of room for the little terrier to test how fast her small legs could run.

Pup also liked to lie at Corrina's feet when she was watching the television.

One morning, when the 'Dawn Start' program was on television, Pup noticed a young man swimming with enormous fish. They had scary-looking teeth. She had no idea why, but she felt drawn to the man, and walked up to the TV screen for a closer look at him.

'That's David, the Weatherman,' Corrina told Pup. 'He is so handsome. The network is always getting him to do terrifying things. He doesn't look like he's enjoying swimming with those sharks. Honestly what those TV networks will make people do for the ratings!' Corrina said. 'Yesterday they had him plummeting off a tall building on a piece of rope. He looked absolutely terrified.'

'He's very brave to do that,' Pup barked. Corrina stared at her with a curious expression. 'I wish I knew what you were saying, Pup. We would have some good conversations.'

~

Twelve weeks went by and the puppies were growing fast. Pup was first to wait at the back door with her lead in her mouth for their usual morning walk. She knew that a world of exotic smells awaited her out in the street. She was anxious to get going and to leave her daily contribution at every possible opportunity. Normally the rest of the puppies would be waiting excitedly at the door with her. Pup wondered where they were.

An ominous feeling began creeping over her little silky-haired body. It soon became clear what this uncomfortable feeling was about: she watched terrified as, one by one, Corrina put her brothers and her only sister into a large dog carrier. Some of them were whimpering loudly. Other puppies seemed too confused to make any sounds at all.

One of her brothers seemed especially upset. Pup had named him 'Sniff' as he was such an expert at locating new and interesting smells to inhale.

Pup had learned the word "sniff" after an episode with Corrina's shoes. She had always enjoyed the smell of her sneakers, especially after she had been wearing them for a while. But one day when Pup had her nose deeply buried in a pair of her trainers, Corrina became angry. 'Will you please stop *sniffing* my shoes Pup?' she'd said. The little terrier never forgot what the word 'sniff' meant.

Sniff was barking a lot and he called out to Pup 'Where are we going? I'm scared. I want to stay with you.'

Pup ran up to the cage and tried her best to lick Sniff's face through the bars. He was distraught, but there was nothing she could say or do to comfort him. Pup knew that she had bonded better with Corrina than the rest of the litter, and she felt bad that she had been singled out to stay behind.

'Where are you taking them?' Pup barked. Corrina said nothing and carried the cage out of the house. Pup watched as Corrina loaded her family into the back of her yellow car. The noise of their barking and whimpering was deafening to her small terrier ears.

Pup ran up to Corrina, 'Can I come too?' she barked.

'No! Go back in the house,' Corrina shouted. Pup thought if she stood her ground maybe she would be allowed to join them. At least she would have a bit longer to say goodbye.

Corrina picked the sad little terrier up and put her back in the house, locking the door.

The car drove away and Pup's tears began to flow, as the sounds of scared puppy barks became fainter, and fainter, until she couldn't hear them anymore.

Pup's only consolation was that Corrina had not taken her mother away as well.

~

The winter chill had really arrived and Pup was chasing a ball around the back garden trying to stay warm. She noticed the back gate had blown open in the strong wind. Pup was tempted to go out and have a sniff around the electric light poles that often had such delectable scents left on them by other dogs out on walks.

Muffin appeared in the back garden and raced up to the open gate. 'Come on, Pup. Quick!' This is our chance to go outside without being on a lead.' Muffin raced through the gate, but for some reason the small terrier wasn't too keen to follow her. Pup had a sense of foreboding. She knew her mother would not go far, and would be able to find her way home okay, but her sixth sense was telling the little dog that something bad was about to happen. She couldn't quite put her paw on it, but it didn't feel good.

The little dog tried to distract her uncomfortable feeling by jumping around in the icy grass, and continuing to chase an orange ball around the garden. But the bad feeling would not leave her. There was no sign of Muffin when she checked the back gate.

Pup began to wonder if she should go and search for her mother. Maybe she was lost. She would be able to follow Muffin's scent fairly easily. But, just as she was about to go through the gate, Corrina came charging from outside into the garden. Tears were streaming down her face. She was carrying something wrapped in a blanket. It was her mother. Pup knew the smell of death.

Corrina kicked the back gate shut and, when Pup tried to run up to her, she shouted, 'No! Pup stay back.' She raced into the house leaving the little terrier trembling with fear.

Later that night Corrina sat crying on the sofa, cradling Muffin in a blanket.

Pup put her head on Corrina's lap and licked her hand as affectionately as she could. She wanted to also lick her mother, but she'd never been close to anything dead before, and Muffin was covered over by the blanket. 'Your mother had a wonderful life,' she told Pup, grabbing a tissue and blowing her nose loudly.

Pup blamed herself for not going with her mother. Muffin

could still be alive if she had been there to distract her. Perhaps she wouldn't have found that poisonous bone.

The next day, Pup watched Corrina burying her mother under the frangipani tree.

'Muffin is enjoying a well-earned rest,' Corrina told the little dog. Pup thought that was a strange thing for her to say. She hoped if she ate a poisonous bone, that no one would say that she was enjoying a well-earned rest in a dirty hole in the ground. She didn't think that would be something to look forward to. It would not be on her canine end-of-walks wish list.

That night Pup overheard Corrina talking to a friend on her phone. 'I won't be breeding any more silky-haired terriers. I get too attached to them. I cannot go through another experience like what happened yesterday with Muffin. But I will keep Pup,' she added. Pup felt relieved that she wasn't soon to be taken away in a cage like her brothers and sister.

~

The winter had decided to stay longer than normal and was exceptionally cold. The frangipani tree had lost all its leaves and flowers and had become a greenish-brown skeleton.

Corrina stayed indoors watching television for hours on end. Pup didn't get as many long walks as she'd been getting in the warmer months. She thought about her mother a lot. Life just wasn't the same without her. She was aware that Corrina felt bad that she wasn't paying as much attention to Pup as usual. But the little dog just couldn't get excited about anything. Even the thought of a walk didn't do much to improve the sadness she was feeling at losing Muffin, and the rest of her family.

'Pup, we're going for a walk in a different park today.

There'll be lots of new smells for you to enjoy there. Go and get your lead,' Corrina said.

Normally Pup would have jumped at the chance to show Corrina how clever she was at finding her lead, and dropping it at her feet. But there was a feeling in her body like a heavy, dark fog that she couldn't shift. Nothing seemed able to cheer her up. Even the thought of meeting some new dogs on a walk did little to lighten her mood.

'Oh come along Pup. You're making me very worried. What's wrong? Are you not well?'

Pup didn't want to cause her owner any more stress. She knew Corrina was very upset about what had happened to Muffin. So she forced herself to get up, and went to find her lead.

~

Weeks passed and soon it was spring again. The magpies were warbling their melodious song. Small buds were appearing on the frangipani tree. Bees and butterflies were beginning to dance around the jasmine that filled the air with its happy scent. The bright yellow wattle made its cheerful presence felt with splashes of brilliant gold, contrasting the various green shades of the ubiquitous eucalyptus trees.

Slowly, the dark heaviness hanging over the little terrier's head began to lift. Her old enthusiasm at going on a walk with her mother re-surfaced as the new season filled the bush with a refreshing blend of uplifting smells. The warmer spring days enhanced the fragrance of the lemon-scented and peppermint gums. It titillated Pup's little terrier senses, lifting her spirits.

Corrina took the small terrier to many new places where she met many different dogs. Some dogs looked strange to her.

One afternoon she met a particularly unusual dog that ambled along slowly towards her with an aloof, but dignified air. 'Greetings, little one. I'm a Chow Chow dog,' he said, shaking some water off his double coat of thick orange fur. 'What's your name?'

'Pup.'

'Hmmm highly original. Can't say I've heard that name before.' The Chow Chow chuckled to himself with a quiet grumble. Pup didn't think it was very funny, and a rude remark.

'And what's your name then?'

'Zhang Wei. It means 'great' in the human language. My master told me that. Would you like to sniff around with me for a bit?' The chow gazed at Pup with his deep-set eyes.

'No I don't think so,' Pup said, thinking *My goodness, he's got a blue tongue!*

She thought Zhang Wei was rather pompous. Pup had learned this English word after overhearing Corrina speaking about a man on the television in that way. She found this weird looking dog rather intimidating with its small ears, and huge head surrounded by a thick mane of orange fur. She thought he looked more like a bear than a dog. 'I really have to get back to my owner,' Pup added.

'Well enjoy your walk little dog. Don't run around too much or you will only exhaust yourself. Oh, and don't do anything I wouldn't do. That should give you plenty of room to do lots,' the Chow Chow chuckled.

Over the next few days Pup met many new dogs, but none quite as unusual as the Chow Chow. There was Wally the old Alsatian who told her stories about his life as a police dog sniffing for drugs and chasing after thieves; Sally a Foxhound who liked to hunt for foxes with horses; and Peter, the nutty little Jack Russell that attacked people who tried to leave the house, but was friendly to those who arrived.

That dog will never make a watchdog, Pup had thought at the time. *He's a real nutjob and is always running around in circles in a deranged kind of way. I'll bet he's been eating too many of those dog biscuits that taste funny.*

Then one unfortunate day, when the planets were not aligned very auspiciously for dogs, Lavinia arrived.

~

Lavinia was a two-year-old Burmese cat. Pup wondered how she managed to keep her chocolate brown short hair coat so smooth and shiny. It was as if she'd been regularly visiting Vidal Sassoon for cats. Lavinia's large green eyes had a permanent cunning expression. She seemed to have a bad attitude, considering herself superior to most other creatures.

It was obvious by the annoyed and surprised look she gave Pup when she first saw her that she'd been expecting to rule the roost at Corrina's house. The cat was clearly riled to find Pup already living there.

Whenever Corrina gave Pup a cuddle or a pat, it seemed to cause Lavinia's tail to lash from side to side. If it hadn't been for the mean way the cat hissed in her direction, Pup would have assumed that Lavinia's tail wagging was because she was happy. 'You have 'Little Dog Syndrome'. Your growling and barking really ruffles my fur,' Lavinia hissed. 'You're always trying to be bigger and more scary than you are. You even bark at your own tail when it moves.'

Lavinia's cat breath would have made a skunk run for cover. Once when Corrina was showing Pup some pictures of funny animals, she'd said 'Skunks are the nastiest smelling critters on the planet when they're mad.'

Pup assumed Lavinia smelled so bad because she ate revolting goo that came out of cans. It looked like something that the little terrier had deposited in the park one day when her stomach was upset. She was glad she didn't have to eat that stuff, and got to eat crunchy meaty bites that tasted delicious, and kept her gums healthy. Pup never needed to go to the dentist.

When they were all in the living room together at night, Pup was forced to watch stupid reality TV shows. She wondered if Corrina had something wrong with her nasal passages. She would allow Lavinia to sit close to her face, breathing on her with her stinking breath.

Pup thought they were stupid programs with female humans who seemed to have been selected by how much face paint they had on, and how blown up their lips were. Sometimes the females fought each other over one male human. They would do devious things to try and win him over. On other shows they were forced to eat things they obviously found disgusting. Pup assumed they did this for large amounts of pieces of paper she'd seen humans greedily stuffing into their pockets, after they had visited a hole in the wall. Perhaps they just wanted to have one up on someone who was not so heroic.

The little dog didn't like the way Lavinia would purr loudly and pretend to be enjoying the shows. *That cat will do anything to win Corrina over*, Pup thought.

'I'm a chocolate Burmese and that's a very special breed,' Lavinia would say. 'I can chase after a ball and bring it back in my mouth just like you can. So don't think you're smarter than me. All you do most days is smell things and yap. I could outsmart you any time I choose. You just watch.'

Pup's fur stood on end. She didn't want to put Lavinia to the test. She had seen how conniving the cat was when she wanted something. Lavinia would ingratiate herself by purring and rubbing on Corrina's legs, gazing up at her in an adoring, but smarmy way. In no time the sneaky cat would be rewarded with a saucer of milk.

That cat always gets what she wants, Pup thought.

She tried hard to get along with Lavinia but it just seemed that every time the cat opened her mouth, it was to say something nasty.

'I find the way you beg for food and walks is embarrassing. You're clueless about using your wiles to get what you want. My mother was a cat that never went without. She taught me the subtle art of feline manipulation. It's so uncool for an animal to be so fawning and dependent. Your open displays of affection are way too overindulgent for your own good. That's something I hate about you dogs. You're always so needy.'

Pup thought she was the most conniving creature she had ever met. She wished Corrina could understand the comments Lavinia habitually made to her. Maybe she wouldn't be so fond of the cat if she'd known what she was saying.

'Do you know what else I despise about dogs?'

'I don't really want to know,' Pup said, wishing Lavinia would fall into the toilet when she was trying to drink water out of the bowl. Maybe she could flush her away. She'd seen a cat do this on an American film Corrina had been watching a few weeks earlier.

One afternoon, as Pup was trying to get her ball that had

disappeared under an armchair, Lavinia followed close behind her. She hissed at her so loudly Pup's hair stood upright.

'I despise your disgusting toilet habits. You just do your business wherever the urge takes you. Even sometimes in the middle of a road or pavement where anyone could step on it. It would never occur to you dogs to cover it up.'

Pup tried to walk away but Lavinia sank a sharp claw into her tail. It really hurt and caused the little terrier to stop in her tracks.

'I haven't finished,' Lavinia said. 'And you greet another dog by sniffing them in private places. It's so unrefined and inappropriate. A well-brought-up cat would never do that. In fact I have never seen any cat resort to such undignified behaviour.'

'Would you mind stepping off my tail? You have sharp claws,' Pup said.

'I still haven't finished. I simply loathe the way you dogs only wash if your owner forces it on you. Us cats take a pride in our appearance. We are constantly washing and polishing our fur with our tongues. We always have lovely clean and shiny coats. There's a lot we could teach you dogs, that's for sure. But who could be bothered?'

Finally Lavinia lifted her paw off the little dog's tail. Pup ran out of the room. She couldn't stand being around this opinionated feline. Lavinia chased after, her hissing a final message. 'And one other thing Pup. I'm marking out my territory here, so don't you dare put your paws anywhere near my part of the house or garden.'

'You have a real cheek talking to me about bad behaviour. I've seen you race up the curtains in one of your crazy fits.

Then you just hang onto the torn pieces of fabric with your sharp claws. Soon the curtains look like the screen I've seen humans put on a horse's face to stop the flies from bothering them.'

'Well if you got a little more exercise around the house, maybe you wouldn't need to spend your whole life with your nose stuck in disgusting smells,' the snooty cat replied.

Pup hated the way Lavinia would sit on top of the door to the living room. She'd witnessed the mean cat waiting there patiently until Corrina opened the door, before launching like a feline firecracker with claws at the ready and landing with a painful thump on Corrina's bare shoulders.

'You never spare a thought for the pain you cause Corrina when you leap at her from the top of the door,' Pup said, the morning after one such incident.

'What are you yapping about now?'

'I've heard Corrina's loud scream. I've seen the scratches on her body.'

'Well, if I upset her so much, why doesn't she scold me?'

Pup knew this was true. It really made her mad that, even when Lavinia had just destroyed the curtains, she would still be stroked affectionately and allowed to sit on Corrina's lap.

Lavinia had a scratching pole but she preferred to sharpen her claws on unsuspecting visitors' legs. It was usually people who she sensed didn't like cats. It seemed to Pup that the nasty cat took great pleasure in finding someone who was afraid of cats, or disliked them. When one of Corrina's friends had come over for a meal, Pup had watched how Lavinia had wrapped herself around the girl's legs as if she was hoping for a pat. But the minute the unsuspecting girl began to stroke Lavinia's ears, she lashed out at her with her sharp claws, hissing loudly and leaving nasty red scratches on her legs.

It was hard for the little terrier to understand how Corrina failed to see through Lavinia's calculating ways. *How can she tolerate such bad behaviour?* Pup wondered.

'You're mummy's beautiful girl,' Corrina would say, lifting Lavinia up high in the air, and allowing her to climb onto her shoulders. Pup watched the conniving creature wrap itself around Corrina's neck, purring loudly and washing behind its ears while Corrina would get on with the housework.

'See how much she adores me,' Lavinia bragged. 'I'm definitely her favourite. You won't be here much longer. Just wait and see.'

Lavinia began to leave stinking deposits in corners of the living room. Eventually it became too much for Corrina. She decided Pup was freaking her cat out by being there.

'She chases me out of the house and whacks me across the face with her tail at every opportunity,' Lavinia lied with a look of terror she had been rehearsing for weeks. 'I can't even catnap for fear of being sat on. I'm sorry about the deposits, but I am so terrified of that dog, and so desperately tired, I haven't got the energy to even climb into my cat litter tray. My nine lives are disappearing very fast,' she said making sure that her large green eyes were wide with fright.

One particularly bad day, Lavinia had behaved appallingly, leaving messes in every room. Corrina was up half the night cleaning them up, and the other half listening to the cat's crying in feigned horror whenever Pup entered the room.

It was hard for the little dog to believe that Corrina would buy Lavinia's lies and decide that keeping a little silky-haired terrier in the house, was never going to work out. She thought it was so unfair. *Why should that cunning puss have been allowed to stay? It has stunk out Corrina's house with its deposits, its smelly dirt tray, and unpleasant breath.*

The very next day Corrina took Pup to the animal rescue centre.

6

Jim's Road to the White House

THE U.S. PRESIDENT had been born into a poor family. His father was a butcher. His mother worked part-time in a confectionery factory to help pay their bills, and cover the cost of their two boys' initial education.

Although his younger brother Paul had become a butcher like his dad, Jim wanted more from his life. Just after his eighteenth birthday he decided to break some big news to his father: 'I'm going to study Political Science dad.'

'And how is that gonna help you choose the best cuts of meat son?'

'I'm not interested in cuts of meat dad! I've watched how hard you and mum worked to put Paul and me through school. It's just not right that you've had to resort to food stamps, just so our family could have enough to eat. The only time you ever have a break is at Thanksgiving and Christmas.'

'It's our lot in life son.'

'Dad, we don't even have access to proper medical treatment. I've seen people living on the streets in places that were once affluent suburbs. It's getting harder and harder for families to pay for their children's education. Something has to be done about it. I don't want to have to struggle like this in life. I'm going to college.'

'Well we can't afford to put you through college son.'

'I'll pay my own way. Maybe work part-time cleaning houses.'

'And what kind of a job are you going to get once you finish your course? There are plenty of young people with degrees working in cafes making coffee. It's all they can get, son.'

'I'll worry about that when I graduate, dad. I want to do something where I can make a difference. Especially for those doing it tough. Who knows, I might even run for President.'

Jim's father stopped chopping up the piece of beef he was trimming. He put the knife down and stared at Jim for a minute with a stunned expression. He finally spoke: 'Isn't that a little unrealistic son?'

'Gee, I thought you might be just a little excited, for me dad.'

'Your grandfather would've thrown me out of the family if I'd said anything to him like that, son.'

'So, you're going to disown me for wanting to do something really significant with my life?'

'I didn't mean it like that, Jim. But be sensible son. If you're prepared to work hard to put yourself through college, that's very admirable, even if you do end up making cappuccinos for a living like all those out-of-work actors. But for your sake, I hope your stars are in the right place and you manage to pull off a proper job.'

Jim was so upset by his father's attitude; he walked out of

the butcher's shop without saying another word. He was determined he would prove his father wrong.

~

Jim paid his own way through college. It was tough juggling his studies and cleaning houses at night. But he finally graduated with excellent grades, and had a great new job.

He picked up his phone to call his father. He couldn't wait to tell him his exciting news.

'I've got a Policy Officer role in the Justice Department, dad. So you don't need to worry about me. I won't have to make coffees for a living.'

'Well, I'm happy to hear that son. Your mother and I have been concerned about you working so hard to put yourself through college. You've done well Jim.'

'Thanks Dad.'

'So does this mean you've given up your aspirations to be our next President?' his father said in a patronising tone.

'No, as a matter of fact I've joined the Democratic Party as a volunteer.'

For a minute, the phone was silent at the other end. Jim waited for his father to say something.

'Dad? Are you still there?'

'Yes son,' his father said with a heavy sigh.

'Look, I know you think I haven't got the slightest chance of pulling this off, but I've told the Party I'm prepared to do whatever it takes to prove I'm worthy of being their Presidential nominee.'

'That's a lot of work Jim. How are you going to manage that, and hold onto your new job?'

Jim felt let down. He was disappointed his father was not

being more supportive of his dreams. 'I don't know dad. But I am determined to do whatever it takes. I don't have a problem working real hard. I'm used to it.'

'Well good luck with that, son,' was all his father could say.

Jim heard the dial tone. 'It's good to know you have such a belief in me,' Jim said slamming his cell phone down on his computer desk.

~

It was an election year and Jim worked very hard at both his new job, and for the Party. His hard work eventually paid off, and he managed to receive the required number of delegates for the caucuses. When the primaries and caucuses were over, it was announced at the Party's National Convention that Jim was the Presidential nominee.

'I am beyond excited,' Jim said at his acceptance speech. 'I am deeply humbled. Thank you. This is an immense privilege, and I will do everything in my power to ensure our Party gets into Government.'

Jim travelled from state to state talking at rallies and debates where he explained his views to the general population.

'It's time something was done about gun control,' he told a cheering crowd at a rally in Los Angeles. 'I personally know a family who lost a young girl who was shot while innocently sitting in class listening to her English teacher,' he added.

'And our whole education system needs an overhaul. I plan to make sure that families can afford to educate their children properly. I want there to be jobs for them when they finish their studies.' Jim gazed at the crowd and was happy to see so many people waving flags, and banners of support.

It was exhausting for him trying to hold onto his day job,

and at the same time moving from state to state, outlining his thoughts and his plans to the public. He did many television and radio interviews, and visited people in hospitals and other health and educational institutions.

'I plan to introduce a national health scheme to make it possible for low-income people to have affordable healthcare,' he said during a television interview. And, at a rally in Cleveland Ohio, Jim stated 'I want to increase the minimum wage. I know how hard many of you struggle to find work. I grew up in a working class family. It's not always easy. I know. And for those of you in a job, some are paying way too much tax. I plan to change that.'

~

It was getting close to Election Day. Jim had just won the second televised debate when one of the Party members came up to him. 'You're going down well with audiences Jim,' he said giving him a high five.

'I hope you're right George. It's been an exhausting campaign.'

'Well, I think you're doing a wonderful job of convincing potential voters that you're a decent man who can do great things for America. Keep up the good work Jim, and I think you'll soon be giving your acceptance speech.'

Jim was happy about winning the debate, but he was concerned about one thing: 'I worry about climate change George,' Jim said. 'If we get into government, I'm not sure we will be doing enough to stop global warming.'

'I wouldn't be too concerned about that Jim,' the Party member said. 'We've got plans for reducing carbon emissions, and we're going to be considering more renewables. I think that's enough to convince the voters that we are serious about caring for the planet.'

'Elroy doesn't share my concerns.

'Don't worry about him. He's being careful to keep a low profile on that topic. He won't say, or do anything to upset the Party's success. His ego is way too big.'

'I hope you're right,' Jim replied.

When the votes were counted after Election Day, Jim was thrilled to discover he'd won the majority of votes in the Electoral College, as well as winning the popular vote.

He became the new President-elect and took part in the swearing-in ceremony where he took his oath of office: *"I do solemnly swear that I will faithfully execute the office of President of the United States, and will to the best of my ability, preserve, protect and defend the Constitution of the United States"*.

Jim delivered his inaugural address on the west front terrace of the Capitol building in Washington D.C. It was an eloquent and powerful speech. He'd included famous quotes from the most memorable addresses of past presidents; 1933 when Franklin D Roosevelt had said *"we have nothing to fear but fear itself"*, and in 1961 when John F. Kennedy had declared *"... ask not what your country can do for you – ask what you can do for your country"*.

Jim's speech was well received: The Chief Executive Officer of the National Organization of Women was moved to tears. The Attorney General of New Mexico was so over excited, he passed out and was taken to hospital.

Jim attended the Inaugural Luncheon. He watched the inaugural parade of ceremonial military regiments, citizens' groups, marching bands and floats as they passed the presidential reviewing stand. It was one official event after another. Then, shortly after the Inaugural Ball, Jim got a call from his father: 'Congratulations son. You've proved me wrong,' he said. 'I'm sorry I was not more supportive. Your mother and I are still pinching ourselves to make sure we're not just dreaming this, Jim. We're just thrilled that you have pulled this off.'

'Well I'm glad to hear that, dad,' Jim said.

~

Jim pedalled fast on his exercise bike. He'd been the U.S. President for just one month and was getting used to living in the White House. 'Thank goodness I've still got time for exercise,' Jim muttered to himself out loud.

Every day Jim scheduled in a good half hour at least twice a day, to stay fit. He used this time to reflect on things.

Although he rarely had any time to himself, Jim was finding he was lonely in the White House. He was determined he was going to find the right companion. A little dog would suit him nicely.

7

Pick Me

PUP HAD ONLY BEEN at the shelter for a couple of days. On one side of her cage she had an annoying cocker spaniel that liked the sound of his own bark, and a quiet and reserved Maltese terrier on the other.

'Have you been here long?' Pup asked the Maltese terrier.

'I dunno. No one seems to want me.' Pup felt her eyes begin to fill with water as she watched the Maltese terrier flop onto the ground. He buried his small, white and fluffy, fur-covered head into the blanket on the floor of his cage. Pup could hardly see his face anymore.

Gazing at this small sad animal took Pup right back to her feelings of abandonment when Corrina said goodbye to her at the shelter. She hadn't hung around for very long. She simply handed Pup to the Administrator along with her collar and lead, sheepskin mat, and her squeaky ball that she liked to play with. Then, after a quick pat to the little dog's head, Corrina raced off to her parked car, without looking back. Pup hoped, at the very least, that this hurried exit was because Corrina was trying to hide how upset she was feeling at saying goodbye to her.

Pup felt nothing but pity for the Maltese terrier. He seemed so certain that no one would choose him.

'Oh I'm sure someone would want you,' Pup said trying her best to reassure the little dog.

'I don't like humans much,' the terrier said. 'I ran away coz the man I lived with used to hit me all the time. He drank something out of a bottle that made him fall down after a while. He would often wake up on the floor the next morning.

'He only gave me dried biscuits to eat. They had about as much flavour as a dish of dirt. Sometimes he forgot to leave me any water and I couldn't sleep coz my mouth felt like sandpaper. I escaped one day when he accidentally left the front door open. I hoped he wouldn't come looking for me. Someone saw me running along the side of the road and brought me here. I didn't have a collar on. I'm scared he will come and get me and give me such a beating.'

'Oh that's awful,' Pup said.

'I just hope they put me down soon.'

'Put you down? What do you mean?'

'You don't know? That's what they do here if no one comes to take you away. You only have a short time to get a new owner and then it's well … I guess you go to some kind of paradise for dogs if you believe in that stuff.'

Pup was shocked. She had no idea she was on death row.

The door opened and Pup saw a nice-looking young man walking by all the cages checking out the animals one by one. She hoped he would be able to resist all the dogs that were gazing at him with longing eyes.

She liked the way he looked. He was obviously a man who cared about his appearance. His face wasn't covered in fur like he was trying to emulate a dog. He was well dressed in tailored blue jeans, and a white t-shirt with something written on the front in blue lettering that Pup didn't understand.

Her tummy felt as tight as an ill-fitting dog collar. She watched him walk past each dog, sometimes hurrying by as if he was trying to avoid a bad smell that had been planted in the air.

Pup began to pant furiously as he got closer to her cage. She noticed she wasn't the only one who liked the look of this man. The female administrator, who Pup thought was probably getting close to middle age for a human, was hot on his heels. Pup sensed by the way she was looking him up and down, that she was attracted to him.

The woman wore a low-cut sleeveless floral dress that revealed very tanned skin. Pup thought her hair looked funny with its short spikey bits that stood on end. It reminded the little dog of a porcupine when it had just met a predator.

The woman hobbled along on spindly high-heeled shoes that were wobbling precariously on the uneven floor. The man was getting closer to Pup's cage when the woman interrupted him.

'You're David Silk right? I saw you on 'Dawn Start' base-jumping off that building. I'm sorry you're no longer the weatherman. I loved watching you do all those crazy things. You were amazing. I'm Josephine, but my friends call me Josie,' she said. She held out a brown spotted hand with red coloured fingertips.

Pup was excited, realizing this was the weatherman she had

seen on television. But she felt sorry for this woman called Josephine. She could tell by the way David kept his hands firmly in the pockets of his pants, that he did not share her interest, and was wishing she would go away.

'Just part of the job,' David said. 'But I won't be expected to do daredevil things any longer thank goodness.' He put more distance between them.

'Yes I saw them announcing your new role the other day on the television. So you'll be one of the main presenters on the program now. You must be excited about that?'

'Sure am. I won't have to travel so much anymore and can get a small dog. Do you have anything?'

'Yes I do have some lovely small dogs. Follow me.' The administrator headed in the direction of Pup's cage and David followed, keeping a few paces away from her.

Pup jumped up and down excitedly. 'Over here! Pick me!' she barked.

'I'm going to miss watching you do all those crazy things you used to do as their weatherman. You were so brave. I mean that huge spider you allowed to crawl over your face. Unbelievable. You're a very courageous man.'

Josephine moved closer to David.

Pup cringed. She wished this woman would realize that David was not attracted to her. He hurried towards Pup's cage and gazed in at her. Josephine followed closely behind him.

'This is Pup, David. She's a silky-haired terrier only a year old. Her owner brought her here because she didn't get along with her cat.'

'The cat was a nightmare,' Pup barked. 'Always telling lies about me, and leaving horrible smells about the house.'

'Oh look, she's saying hello to you,' Josephine said in a saccharine voice. It annoyed the small terrier how humans often had no idea what she was saying. She had learned to understand so many of their human words, so why couldn't they understand her?

David put his hand through a gap in Pup's cage.

'She's a lovely natured little dog,' Josephine said. 'I'll get her out so you can pat her properly. Do you have a house with a garden?'

Pup raced out and jumped all over David. She liked the smell of his cologne. It reminded her of the lemon-scented gum that she loved in the Australian bush.

'Yes. I have a nice big house and huge garden with lots of trees.'

'It sounds charming. I'd love to have a garden. I live in a tiny apartment,' Josephine added with a look that said *and why don't you invite me over sometime to see your house?*

'Hello Pup,' David said patting her enthusiastically. She liked that he didn't use baby language as some humans do when speaking to dogs.

'I like you. I want to go home with you. Please take me away from here,' Pup pleaded. She was terrified her days might be numbered, after what the Maltese terrier had said.

'I'll take her,' David said. 'I don't want a really big dog, and she seems very friendly and affectionate.'

Pup was very excited, and relieved. But she caught sight of the Maltese terrier giving her a sad look, and she felt very sorry for the little dog.

Josephine got some papers for David to sign and put a lead on Pup. David took out his wallet and handed her some notes.

She grabbed hold of his hand but he pulled it away from her.

'Well I must get Pup to her new home. Thanks and um, goodbye.'

Pup saw the look of humiliation on Josephine's face. She felt her disappointment and was sorry that she couldn't take a hint.

She looked back at the sad face of the Maltese terrier. Pup felt guilty to have a nice new owner, while that poor little dog hadn't found anyone to love him. She wanted to offer him a word of hope so he would have something to cling to.

'I'm sure you will find someone kind who will want to take you home,' Pup said. 'You're a very lovely terrier.'

'Sure. You have a good life,' the dog said, turning his back on the little terrier and flopping with resignation onto the straw in the cage.

Pup felt really bad to be leaving him like that. 'Can't you find someone who would give him a happy home?' she barked at Josephine. He is desperately unhappy and he doesn't deserve to die.'

'Oh look, she is saying thank you to me for looking after her so well,' Josephine said. 'You are welcome little one. Enjoy your new home,' she added.

Pup just gave her an annoyed stare.

'Well I hope you and Pup will be very happy together. Maybe I could come and visit her sometime?'

Pup noticed the uncomfortable look on David's face and once again felt very sorry for this poor woman who just didn't get that he had no interest in her. *I'm glad I'm a dog and don't need to paint my nails, walk around in spindly-heeled shoes, or fuss over my fur to try and attract a mate.* Pup thought. David gave a small tug on her lead. 'I'm, ah going to be pretty busy with the new job. We'd better get on. Come along Pup.'

David headed out the door rather fast and Pup raced happily after him. Her new life was about to begin.

8

The Arrival of Rita

'I LOVE MY KENNEL' Pup barked to David. 'It even has my name on it.' Pup sank into the large padded dark blue cushion that David had given her to sleep on. 'It's really comfortable, and I am so happy you put my bed so close to your bedroom,' Pup barked.

'I hope you like your new kennel?' David asked. 'I put it near my bedroom so you won't feel too lonely,' he added.

Pup put her head on one side. She hoped this would communicate that she was frustrated he could not understand what she was saying. But he didn't seem to take much notice and just smiled at her, patting her on the head.

Pup heard a loud ringing sound that caused her head to spin. David picked up his smart phone and went into his bedroom.

He talks on that black thing he holds up to his head a lot, she thought. *But I don't mind. I can tell how much he loves me by the look in his large brown eyes.*

There were many things the little terrier loved about her new home with David. He'd created a large doggie door so she could go outside whenever she wanted. She enjoyed inhaling the scented flowers when the warm rays of the sun drew out their heady and delightful fragrance.

David's garden was bordered on two sides by a glorious hedge of gardenias and orange jasmine that filled the air with their exotic and heavenly aromas. There were two mango trees covered in the delicious sweet orange fruit; some native flowering bushes, and a beautifully scented pink frangipani tree.

The flowers attracted lots of bees and butterflies, and even dragonflies that Pup enjoyed trying to catch as they danced around the flowers and trees.

Every weekend when David wasn't working, he took Pup for a long walk in a park full of eucalyptus trees, and bright yellow wattle. It made her sneeze in the spring, but the subtle scents were intoxicating. Sometimes they even overpowered the various canine smells that had been left in the park. She found that annoying.

Pup made sure she had left her mark on every available spot for the next dog to enjoy. She met all kinds of dogs on her walk. It seemed everyone who lived in the area had a canine companion. Some were friendly and they would exchange sniffs. If the smells were mutually satisfying they would chase each other and play 'who can find the biggest stick'. Other dogs would give her a dirty look, or even try to attack her for being in what they considered was their exclusive territory.

She wasn't a huge fan of chasing balls and sticks. She'd seen the look of frustration on some human faces when their dogs had brought a stick back to be thrown for the twentieth time. She never wanted to bore David with Obsessive Canine Behaviour (OCB). One blue heeler, predictably named Blue, belonged to a woman who seemed to take a big fancy to David.

Blue was one of those dogs with Serious Stick Disorder. He saw every human he met as a potential repetitive stick hurler. Pup found Blue embarrassing. When he returned the stick it was covered in his slobber, and he was so demanding and pushy.

'Give it a rest,' she barked at Blue when he brought back the slimy stick for the fourth time, dumping it at David's feet.

'Don't tell me what to do, you little bitch,' Blue snapped.

Pup was mad now. How dare he speak to her in that tone of bark. She decided to show him there was nothing little about her and jumped at his throat, yapping and growling.

David pulled sharply on her collar and Pup felt her throat constricting. She could hardly breathe.

'I am so sorry,' David said to Blue's attractive female owner.

'Pup is normally very well behaved.'

'It's okay. I'm Penny,' she said holding out her hand. Pup thought she sounded different from other humans. But she'd heard women who sounded like her, when she'd been watching the television with David. They were called 'English women'.

Pup noticed David's face had gone the same shade of red as one of the roses she'd sniffed in his garden. He took the woman's hand and shook it.

'David.'

'Yes. Haven't I seen you on the Dawn Start program?' Pup could tell she was attracted to David. But it wasn't an over-the-top kind of attraction like she'd witnessed with Josephine at the animal shelter.

'Yep, used to be the weatherman,' David said.

Pup liked her voice and her pretty blonde hair, cut in a smart style. She thought if she were a female human being, she would like to have unblemished pale skin; rosy cheeks and huge green soulful eyes, just like this woman. She wondered what her doggie skin would look like if all her fur were removed. She'd seen a dog once that was totally bald. Its skin was a blotchy pattern of pink and grey: like plain fabric covered in beetroot splashes. She hoped she wouldn't look like that.

Pup was trying not to look, but she couldn't help but notice the woman's curvy body in her low cut t-shirt and shorts. She watched David closely. He was sneakily checking Penny out with an approving look.

The rest was history. Before long Penny was around nearly every night and, when she wasn't, David was at her house.

Initially Penny left Blue with a young guy who rented her spare room. He was a dog lover and walked Blue when Penny didn't have time to do it.

David and Penny spent a lot of time together and Pup wondered if they were going to tie the paw.

After a while when Pup had got to know Blue better, they began to get along. They played in David's garden for hours. Blue had stopped being so obsessed with finding sticks.

But then one night David slammed the phone down after talking to Penny, and went silently into his bedroom closing the door.

Pup tried to push the door open but it wouldn't budge. She barked at him, 'Please open the door. I am worried about you.' But he just shouted back 'Go away Pup.' She put her head on one side. What was wrong with him? He had never spoken to her like this before. She went to her kennel and flopped down despondently.

Pup was sorry that Penny stopped coming to see David. She had always been kind to the little dog. She wondered why any woman in her right mind would want to leave David. He was so good looking, kind and affectionate and he had a great job.

She overheard conversations David had with friends on his phone. It now became clear that her new owner had no idea that Penny had been two-timing him. But it wasn't long before David met another woman.

~

Pup met Rita for the first time in a cloud of strong smelling patchouli oil. The little dog's nose was so sensitive that she almost passed out from what she considered was an overpowering stink. Rita obviously thought that essential oil of patchouli was a turn on. It wasn't for the small terrier. She couldn't imagine how it could be for David either, but he seemed to really like this new woman.

Pup could tell right away that Rita didn't like dogs. Her aura turned red as soon as she saw the little terrier, a warning flag to a dog that a person is afraid of animals.

'I'm sorry, but I really can't be near dogs. I'm allergic to them. They make me sneeze,' Rita said. She held a tissue over her un-made up and overly tanned face; and backed away from Pup.

'Can you put her outside?'

Pup felt she wasn't a part of the conversation and was being completely ignored. Rita got right up her nose. Apart from her dreadful taste in perfume, she didn't think much of her taste in clothes either. Rita was a couple of years older than David and often wore long, unstylish Indian cotton dresses with paisley patterns, and loose cotton shirts that did nothing for the slim and shapely figure that seemed to be hiding underneath.

Pup hated Rita's loud scratchy voice, and the way she never stopped talking. She was clearly afraid to leave a gap in case someone else wanted to say something. David could hardly get a word in. And Rita wore dirty leather sandals that smelt of unwashed feet. When she was barefoot, she would leave the sandals around the house for people to trip over. She even wore them when it was raining, as if she couldn't afford any decent shoes.

The little terrier wondered if Rita ever washed. Her long, dark straggly hair was often tied up in a bun. Pup thought she dressed like the females she'd seen on television attending an outdoor music festival. Surely David could do better than this? She had always thought he looked so much nicer than some of the male humans she had seen walking their dogs in the park. They had worn dirty looking t-shirts, rubber shoes, and shorts that hung on them like an empty sack.

David had great taste in clothes, even when they were casual. On her walks with David the little dog had seen many women they passed in the park, turn back to look at him again.

Pup also noticed how many times David had to ask Rita to put used food containers in the yellow bin. She had understood that this was the bin for things that could be transformed into something else that a human might need in the future. She had heard David say that human rubbish often ended up in a large hole in the ground, clogging up space.

But Rita didn't seem to care about that and would throw everything into the same bin. Pup thought she was not showing any respect for the countryside, and was glad that David took a stand on this. A few times she'd heard David speaking to Rita about her habit of putting things in the wrong bin. It clearly annoyed him and he'd said 'Rita, I found a large plastic bag in the yellow bin again.'

'Well that's the bin for plastics isn't it?'

'Not plastic bags. I've told you before, they have to go in the main rubbish bin. And if you're going to put a TV dinner tray in the yellow bin, please make sure you wash it first.'

'Sorry honey,' she'd said.

Pup thought David put up with a lot from this woman but he didn't seem to mind. Often when Pup had been out on walks with him, he would pick up someone else's thrown away stuff and carry it to the nearest bin. But clearly Rita was about as interested in protecting the environment, as Pup was to smell her patchouli oil. She wondered what David could possibly see in her. She assumed, since they were often in the bedroom with the door closed for hours, that it had something to do with that.

Pup had overheard David say that Rita lived in Melbourne. She didn't know where that was, but decided it must be a long way away, as Rita only came to stay for a couple of days at a time, and always complained that she hated flying on planes.

David and Rita began to spend more time together, but Pup was always left outside no matter what the weather was like. David had moved her kennel onto the back veranda and even fed her out there to keep his new woman happy.

One day, when David had left the back door slightly ajar to get rid of the foul smell from the fish dish that Rita had cooked, Pup overheard their conversation. She watched them through a crack in the door.

'I've tried to get a transfer to Sydney but there's nothing

going,' Rita said. 'All this travelling to see you every weekend is beginning to stress me out. You know I hate flying.'

'Well I have something for us to celebrate.' David picked up a large black glass bottle and tore at the gold wrapping around its top. Something flew out of the bottle with a loud pop. The sound it made hurt Pup's ears and gave her a fright. She wondered what the bubbly stuff was that fizzed out of the bottle and into two glasses David was holding. She'd seen him opening one of these bottles before, and wondered why humans seemed to like this bubbling liquid so much. They always drank this glass of fizzy stuff with great gusto, especially when they appeared to be happy about something.

Humans certainly are strange, she thought. There was something about drinking the stuff inside this bottle that caused them to be friendlier. Sometimes if they had drunk more than a few glasses of the sparkling stuff, they would become very tired and have to lie down for a while.

David clinked his glass with Rita and took a long sip.

'I've been offered a position in the Melbourne office as a newsreader for prime time TV. It's a very big salary increase.'

'Oh, that's fab darling,' Rita said. 'We'll be able to see so much more of each other. Why don't you move in with me?'

'Well I'd have Pup, and you don't seem so keen on dogs.'

'It's not that I don't like them David, it's just that the last time I was at your house, I broke out in a rash, and got asthma.'

Pup thought she probably broke out in a rash from plastering herself in her foul smelling oil.

'I'll have to think about that,' David said.

Pup was upset that this woman would have the nerve to ask David to give her up. But she was confident he would never part with her just to suit some woman he was seeing. She had no idea how wrong she could be.

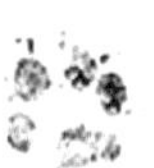

9

No time for wallowing

THE SUN WAS LOW, but still very hot as Pup lay on the roadside, abandoned, and feeling very sorry for herself. She'd been lying there for several hours and was hungry and thirsty.

Suddenly she heard a loud screechy voice. 'Better get off the side of the road before you end up a lot flatter than you already are!'

Pup found herself staring into the beady-eyed face of a yellow-crested cockatoo that had landed inches away from her.

'I don't care. My owner doesn't want me. He has just left me to fend for myself,' Pup said her eyes getting very wet.

'So now you're going to just lie here and wallow in self-pity until some stupid galah in a speeding object sends you to an early dog heaven?' the cockatoo said impatiently.

'I don't worry about humans,' the bird continued. 'They've been trying to put me in jail in their living room for years. But we have choices you know. If you ask me you're better off without them. I'm Cracker by the way.'

The bird held out a claw for Pup to sniff, but she was too

sad to notice what would otherwise have been a very enticing scent.

'All I ever wanted was to love and be loved,' Pup said, trying to stop her tears from getting onto her fur and leaving it more wet and sticky than it already was. 'How could he just abandon me like this? I was such a loyal dog.'

'Look, my mate Henry disappeared last winter,' said the feisty cockatoo. 'We were going to rob fruit trees together. He had excellent road sense. He wasn't the kind to leave me for another bird.'

'I'm sorry to hear that,' Pup said. 'You must be devastated.'

'I've got no time for this victim mentality,' Cracker screeched, pecking at a spot on her claw that was itchy. 'I intend finding out what happened to Henry. And if he's in jail somewhere, I'm going to get him out, whatever it takes. By the way do you have a name?'

'Pup.'

'Well that's an original name for a young dog,' Cracker said with a croaky chuckle.

'Hey why don't you come with me? You need to drink some water before you pass out in this heat. I know where we can find some, and yummy seeds.'

'I don't eat seeds.'

'Well how about some juicy berries? There's a tree covered in mulberries that I can't wait to rob,' Cracker added.

'I don't eat berries either.'

'Well you're a hard one to please. How about we go for a walk in the bush? That'll cheer you up. You can enjoy a good squat every time you smell something you like.'

Pup saw a human box approaching fast and, despite how

exhausted she was, her adrenalin took over and she leapt off the road into some long grass on the pavement.

'I see that you're not ready to be any flatter than you already are,' Cracker said, laughing at her own joke.

She flew on ahead and Pup wondered whether to bother to follow her. The bird seemed friendly enough, but she had such a loud voice. It was hurting her ears. She wasn't sure they had much in common either.

Pup's throat felt dry and parched. She was very thirsty and stopped by a little creek to have a long drink of cool water. Her tummy was making noises that food was very overdue, but she had no desire to eat berries. She wondered if this loud-mouthed bird would know where she could find some meat, and decided to follow Cracker.

'Come on!' Cracker squawked impatiently from a branch of a tree where she was perched. 'If you don't hurry up we could miss the best berries. I'm not the only cockatoo in the area ya know.'

'I told you I don't eat fruit. Do you know where I could find some meat?'

Cracker landed by the creek near Pup.

'Look, I don't know what tree root you've been living under, but I'm vegetarian,' she screeched. 'How you can eat that stuff is beyond me, but there might be a carcass on the side of the road. Lots of kangaroos get killed around here. They're stupid on the roads,' Cracker added.

Pup had never had to eat some old carcass that had been lying in the hot sun. The thought of it made her want to vomit.

'I'm used to eating dried dog biscuits.'

'Well you're not going to find those on any trees round

here,' Cracker said. 'If you want my advice, you'd better eat what you can find.'

Pup flopped onto the ground. 'I don't want to eat what I can find. I want to sleep on a real bed with a roof over my head, and someone to fill my bowl with tasty treats, and take me for nice walks.'

'Strike me pink! You're really into wallowing,' Cracker said pecking at Pup's tail. 'I'm *trying* to take you for a nice walk if you would just stop moaning about your life for long enough to see that. Come on, let's go and find you some dried dog biscuits.'

'Well how are you going to find those out here?' Pup asked

'Listen Pup, I know this area like the back of my crest. Follow me.'

Cracker flew ahead and Pup followed as fast as her small legs would allow. They travelled along a bush track bordered by bright yellow wattle, and fresh green ferns. The wattle scent was so strong that Pup kept sneezing and that slowed her down.

'Hurry up!' Cracker screeched.

Pup thought she was a very impatient bird. It was all very well for her. She had wings.

The track widened as the bush opened into a large grassy area. Pup could see a green-painted weatherboard house in the distance.

'You see that river gum, last tree on the right? That's where I live most of the time. It's got a good view of the fruit trees and the river.'

Pup watched as Cracker flew onto the front veranda of the house, landing on a bright red dog's bowl. The Cockatoo pecked furiously at the biscuits and flew back to Pup, dropping some biscuits under her nose. 'Here, get your beak into these,' she screeched.

Pup was so hungry she didn't even stop to smell them. She stuffed her mouth full of the tasty biscuits, and Cracker flew back and forth, dropping fresh ones in front of her.

'Bloody oath, you don't muck around. Henry said I had bad table manners. But you take the seeds. Or should I say the biscuits?' Cracker clucked at her own joke and Pup thought she was rather rude, but she was grateful for the food.

'You wait there. I'm going to get some brunch,' Cracker said. She flew off and disappeared around the back of the house.

Pup finished off the biscuits and walked up to the house. Her feet were beginning to hurt from trying to keep up with Cracker. She flopped into some soft green grass.

Cracker was in the middle of the nashi pear tree, pecking at the fruit. Pup wondered why she needed to peck only once at each nashi pear. It seemed so wasteful.

A wire door on the front veranda flung open and a middle-aged woman appeared wearing an apron, and a very angry expression.

She picked up a ball that was lying on the grass near the nashi pear tree and hurled it at Cracker, clipping her right on her yellow crest. 'Fair fluff of the feathers,' Cracker screeched.

'That'll teach you to steal my nashi pears,' the woman yelled. She picked up a stick and threw it at the bird, narrowly missing her. Cracker flew off into the distance. Pup leapt up and ran after her. She didn't want to become a target for this woman's rage. 'Hey you!' the woman screamed at Pup. She'd noticed her dog's bowl had been emptied of dried biscuits. Pup ran blind without being aware of where she was going. When she stopped running to catch her breath she couldn't see Cracker anywhere. The little dog decided to keep going. She covered many miles, but still there was no sign of the screechy bird.

After several hours she stopped in the shade. She'd been running so fast she hadn't noticed that she had left human civilisation behind. There were no houses anywhere, just a thick covering of tall eucalypts and large green ferns.

The ground was carpeted in twigs and pieces of bark. She could see blue-green mountains in the background cloaked in more eucalyptus trees. She flopped down exhausted.

Pup's survival instincts had kicked in and she no longer wanted to just lie down and die. She was feeling very dehydrated from being in the forty-six degree temperature, earlier on, without any water. Even though the thick covering of gum trees provided some good shade, her body was beginning to shake. She knew she had to find some more cool water to drink, and to lie in it for a bit. It was still very hot and she was very unused to being out in the Australian bush all by herself. Even though a loud screechy bird was not exactly the sort of friend she would choose, Cracker had a kind of confidence that made Pup feel safe. The bird was used to living in the wild and knew her way around, and where water and food could be found. She had to find Cracker or she would not survive long.

10

Bounce

BOUNCE GREW UP in a very conservative kangaroo household. She had older than usual, very conservative parents and two brothers.

She was an attractive kangaroo with pale orangey-brown fur, large dewy eyes, soft inquisitive ears, strong well-developed hind legs, and a very muscular and powerful tail.

Bounce's father was the marsupial of their personal patch of paddock and provided for the family, making sure they had enough to eat and a branch over their heads to keep them well shaded from the hot sun.

Her mother took care of the joeys. She made sure they were well-nourished. She comforted them when they got into fights. She taught them how to find food. She showed them what to do when the temperature was over thirty-five degrees Centigrade, and how to survive a bushfire.

Bounce was told that it was the female role to support the male in whatever he wanted to do. 'The female kangaroo must never think about her dreams in life,' her mother had told her.

‘She is only there to make the male happy, Bounce. I hope you realize that.

‘That’s such a pile of wombat droppings. I fully intend to have a career,’ Bounce had replied.

Bounce wasn’t clear on what that career might be, since none of her female relatives or friends had careers, but she believed deep down that she had some kind of important work to do.

One day her mother told Bounce, ‘Dear, you must stop thinking of a career all the time, or you will never find a mate.’

‘Mother, I don’t want to be like you. You live your life in dad’s shadow. You have no idea who you are. You eat the plants he tells you to eat. You jump the fences he tells you to jump. You have joeys when he wants you to have them. What about what you want?’

‘This *is* what I want Bounce. Your father is a good kanga. We have a happy union and we both love and respect each other. We understand that our roles are different. Your father is the provider, and it is my responsibility to have the joeys, and take care of the paddock-work. It’s always worked well for us this way. What you don’t seem to understand, my dear daughter, is that you’re a female and, as such, you have to be prepared to take on the tasks that are expected of you. You can’t just do what you want in life.’

‘That is such a mountain of horse dung. I don’t want to live this kind of life. I want to contribute something, other than just having babies and supporting a mate.’

And so Bounce became alienated from her immediate family. She did want to find a mate, but she didn’t want one that expected her to be a clone of her mother.

Most of the red kangaroos in their area thought Bounce was a bit odd. The females didn't like to hop over fences with her, or share their patch of grass. She made them feel insecure. The more she talked about wanting a career and not supporting the male, the more they began to question their own lives. So Bounce spent a lot of time alone.

She tried inter-paddock dating, but most of the males she met just wanted to mate with her right away. Bounce wanted to develop a friendship with them first before going the whole hop. It seemed every new male she met just wanted to find out what kind of potential mother she might be for his joeys. The minute Bounce would make any mention of having a career; they would hop off as fast as a kangaroo gets into a boxing match to protect his family or territory.

'You must put some attention on finding a mate, Bounce,' her mother told her again. 'Soon you will be too old to have joeys. There's a handsome and single red kanga living close to our patch of paddock. I can introduce you to him.'

'I'm not interested in hopping into mating with some kanga just so I can have babies. I told you mum. I'm not that bothered about bearing joeys.'

Then one day when Bounce was testing how high she could jump over fences, she heard a deafening screech. 'Hey Hoppy, wait!' She turned around and saw a yellow-crested cockatoo right near her head. She stopped and the cockatoo landed close to her tail, giving her a sharp peck.

Bounce wasn't fond of these loud birds. Their calls dominated the bush and they were such show-offs. She'd even had one land on her back and it would not get off. She still had the scars from its sharp claws. She wondered what this loud bird was doing on their personal kangaroo patch. 'What do you want?' Bounce asked crossly.

'Just wanted to let you know there's an important meeting taking place tomorrow at midday at Barn Owl's tree in the National Park. All the animals and birds are coming from miles around. Even Tasmanian devil is planning to be there. Would be good if you could make it.'

'That's a very long way from here. What's it about?'

'Dunno. I just heard on the bush vine that we should all be there.'

'Barn Owl will be awake at midday? That's a little unusual,' said Bounce.

'Apparently,' the bird responded. 'Must be really important. He's usually dead to the world at that time of day. By the way, I don't suppose you have seen a little silky-haired terrier when you've been hopping around?'

'Can't say I have. Wouldn't know one anyway if I jumped over it.'

'Well if you do see her, she's got long tan-and-silver fur, and is only a little bit bigger than me. Barks a lot and has real low self-esteem. She needs to go and see a birdocologist if you ask me. Got dumped by some stupid human. But that's nothing to be wallowing about. They just want to put you in a cage at the first opportunity. But now she has these abandonment issues.'

'I see. Well I could try and come to the meeting but that is a very large area. How would I know which tree Barn Owl will be in?'

'I heard from Bandicoot that it's at the south east corner near the edge of the river. You'll see all the animals heading there.'

‘Okay I’ll go,’ Bounce said. The Kangaroo knew this was going to upset her family but she was determined to show her father that she was not going to lead the kind of life that he expected of her.

11

So Thirsty

PUP TRIED TO DRAG HERSELF along on her stomach. She was very weak from lack of fluid and the intense heat.

Her long, tan-and-silver fur was sticky with sweat. Small pieces of bark, leaves and grit from the ground where she had been lying were attached to her clammy skin.

Pup's paws were covered in blisters from her long walk and the pieces of hot tar from the road. Some little pieces of road tar were still embedded in her feet and were pricking her soft pads, as though she were trying to walk on the back of an echidna. Her skin felt red hot as if she could burst into flames at any moment. She now knew what the expression "to be on your last legs" actually felt like. Her legs had stopped working.

Pup was clinging to the hope that Cracker would suddenly appear and lead her to some water and bring her some more dog biscuits. She was too tired to drag herself any further.

Out of the corner of her eye Pup saw something black and white swooping down. It stopped right near her face.

'Look at the state you've got yourself in,' a magpie said.

'Where is your human, little dog? Do they know where you are? You don't seem too good to me.'

Pup was too exhausted to even speak.

'Well you need to get some water into you,' the magpie said.

Pup stared at his red beady eyes that were now peering closely at her. His robust wedge shaped beak was only centimetres away from Pup's face. She remembered a time when a magpie had swooped at her aggressively when she was out on a walk with David, and she was afraid of what this bird might have in mind. She wouldn't like to connect with the dangerous looking hook on the end of his beak. Pup had heard David telling someone that people had gone to hospital with a magpie beak stuck in the back of their head that had to be surgically removed.

David always carried a stick when he had taken Pup on bush walks in the spring; this was when the magpies had young babies and were more inclined to swoop at people and their dogs.

Pup felt very vulnerable lying on the ground so close to the bird. She could smell its feathers and she didn't really like the strange oily scent. It could easily kill her if it wanted.

'You're in luck little dog. I just happen to know where there is a waterhole close by. I didn't get to be "Bird of the Year" for nothing ya know.' Magpie paused a moment. 'I'm smarter than any other bird,' he bragged. 'I'll fly you there.'

The bird grabbed hold of Pup's tail with his sharp beak. He tried to lift her off the ground. Pup had become so numb from everything she had been going through, she didn't even feel his sharp beak connecting with the skin on her tail.

'Blimey. I don't think I can lift ya. You weigh a lot for a dog that doesn't appear to have had a decent meal for a while. Fair dinkum.'

'Is it alive?' A koala was waddling slowly towards them. Pup felt sick hearing that, and being called "it". She wasn't ready to die now but she realized she was close to dropping her body if she didn't get some water soon.

'You could do with some juicy leaves,' the koala said.

'Listen, silly. Dogs don't eat leaves,' Magpie said, holding his head up high and letting out a long complaining warble.

'But young gum leaves are full of moisture. I never have to drink water at all eating them.'

'Forget the leaves. I need ya help, Koala,' Magpie said. 'I can't move her. She's too heavy for me.'

Koala came close to Pup and sat down. 'Do you think you could climb onto my back? Maybe between us we can help get you to a waterhole.'

'I'll try,' Pup said weakly.

The little dog used her last bit of strength and, with Magpie lifting her by the tail, she managed to get onto Koala's back. She hung there like waterlogged clothing on a washing line.

'Follow me. I know where there's some water close by,' Magpie said, strutting ahead on his strong black legs.

'What are you doing out here all alone?' Koala asked, waddling slowly so as not to cause her little joey to fall out of her pouch.

'I … I ran …'

'You'd better not try and speak. You must conserve your energy.'

Pup hung on with her last bit of strength. Soon she noticed they were heading to a small waterhole.

'I'll just test to see if it is cool enough,' Magpie said flying off and landing by the edge of the water. He put his beak in to feel the water temperature. He took the opportunity to have a long drink himself.

'It's quite cool,' he called out. 'That's a miracle considering how hot it's been. Maybe being so well-shaded has helped,' Magpie added.

Koala managed to carry Pup to the waterhole. She turned her back to the edge of the pool so the little terrier could just slide off. Pup fell into the water with an enormous splash. She struggled to her feet and was able to stand near the edge. She drank huge gulps of water. The little dog stood there allowing the cool water to wash all the sweat and dirt off her long fur, and float away the needles of tar that were stuck to her paws.

'I'd stay there if I were you. Until you feel strong enough to find your way home,' Koala said.

Pup was so grateful to them both for helping her. She was beginning to feel her strength coming back. The pads of her feet were feeling less sore as all the debris was washed away. It was calming standing in the water. It even helped her to feel a little stronger emotionally. She took another long drink, enjoying the sensation as it travelled down her dry and parched throat, cooling it down and helping her to breathe.

'Thank you very much for your help,' Pup said to Magpie.

'No worries. I didn't get "Bird of the Year" for no reason ya know. I am assuming once you're feeling a bit better, ya can follow ya smells home. That's what ya dogs do right? I'll be seeing ya.'

'Wait,' Pup barked. 'Could you see if you could find my friend Cracker? She's a yellow-crested cockatoo with a very loud voice. You might see, or hear her when you're flying around.'

'Listen love, all the yellow-crested cockatoos have very loud voices. They are always screeching about something. Horrible sound they make. It's nothing like our beautiful and melodious songs. Those cockatoos must be tone deaf. There's usually a bunch of them together. But if I come across one called Cracker, I will let her know where ya are.'

'Thank you for helping me,' Pup said. She felt desperate that she might never see Cracker again, and would have to fend for herself.

'No worries. Gotta fly off now and find some worms for dinner.'

Pup called after him. 'I'm sorry to bother you again, but I am really hungry. I've never eaten worms but I need to eat something. I don't eat leaves.'

'All right, I'll see what I can do, but maybe you can tell your friends to stop chasing us when we're minding our own business having our dinner,' Magpie warbled.

'Of course,' Pup said.

'And one other thing, I can't guarantee the worms won't make you feel ill. I've eaten some that must have got covered in some hideous tasting stuff those humans spray on the side of the roads. They think they're being clever killing all the weeds, but they've killed a few of my mates doing that.'

Magpie thought for a moment. 'Something has got to be done about the things the humans are doing,' he said.

'I agree. My favourite trees have been disappearing fast. But what can we do? We're just a bunch of dumb animals according to those upright beings,' Koala replied.

'We'll think of something. Gotta fly.' Magpie let out a long and melodious warble and flew off.

Pup climbed out of the water and had a good shake. She was feeling so much better. She lay down in the shade by the waterhole. Koala sat down beside her. She needed to rest as well.

'My name's Fluff,' Koala said.

'I'm Pup.'

Fluff gave Pup a hug.

'You're very kind. I don't suppose you know where I could find some dog biscuits around here?' Pup asked noticing the look of amazement on Fluff's face.

'This is the Marramarra National Park. To tell you the truth, I was rather surprised to see a dog here. Don't see them much as this place is miles from human habitation. That's what I love about it. There are none of those large human boxes ruining my views. So where did you come from?'

'Hornsby, but I don't live there anymore. I'm homeless.'

'Well stroke my fluffy ears! That's a very long way from here. No wonder you were so exhausted. But I have to be honest with you Pup; you won't find any dog biscuits around here. They don't grow on trees you know. Of course if you run into a human somewhere they might have some. They're sometimes around with their little joeys. They live in temporary homes made of some kind of material hung on long sticks they put into the ground.'

'I wish I could find Cracker. She'd know where to find me some food.' Pup flopped despondently onto the ground.

Fluff stroked Pup's head affectionately. The soothing stroke sent the little silky-haired terrier off into a deep and healing sleep. She woke up later to something tickling her. A huge earthworm was crawling over her front paws. There was no sign of Magpie or Fluff. Pup was so hungry she just gobbled the worm up. It didn't taste too bad. She stood up and noticed a couple more worms nearby. She ate them too. She went down to the waterhole and had another long drink. Pup was almost feeling her old self.

It was dusk and the temperature had dropped considerably. Pup decided to keep walking and try and find Cracker.

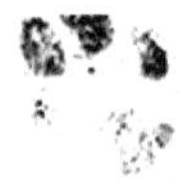

12

Chief Executive Bird

BARN OWL WAS EXHAUSTED. He'd been suffering from the worst insomnia he'd had in years. He was lucky to sleep a few hours a day. It was beginning to affect his ability to glide silently in his hunt for small mammals and rodents.

He was bumping into things and even having hallucinations. He thought he had spotted a snake for his dinner, but it was just a large stick on the ground.

His white, heart-shaped facial disc was showing signs of sleep deprivation with dark areas appearing under his eyes. His feathers had become dishevelled. Barn Owl's tiny black tear-shaped markings were hardly visible on part of his light grey-coloured body

Barn Owl wished sometimes that he wasn't so wise. If he were more like an Australian mynah bird, he wouldn't keep getting bothered by creatures wanting answers to things. It was very annoying when he was trying to sleep to have some animal or bird banging on the trunk of his tree in the middle of the day with a question. Just because most of the other birds and animals chose to sleep at night, they showed little consideration for the Owl who needed to get his daytime sleep.

Their questions were often about things they could easily figure out if they used a bit of bird or animal sense. It was ridiculous that they needed to ask him silly things like: 'Where is the nearest waterhole?' or 'Is it going to be hot today?'.

Some of the birds in the bush made it particularly hard for him to settle down during the day. The disharmonious screeching of the cockatoos often disturbed him. They would sometimes land right near his bed and let out a noise that would almost split his eardrums. The currawongs could be just as annoying with their loud repetitive chirping. It was as if they were trying to compete with the cockatoos for the bird that could most effectively project its voice.

Then sometimes a kookaburra family would move to the tree next door. He thought they were always telling stupid jokes that were simply not funny. But they thought their stories were hysterical. He didn't think their punch lines were clever or amusing.

Barn Owl's upbringing had been strict. His parents called him Barnaby. His mother wasn't interested in a career and was quite happy to be a house-bird.

His father had held the position of Chief Executive Bird (CEB) for the Australian bush for most of his life. It was a responsible position and he was well respected by the birds and animals. But Barnaby always felt pressured to take over this role when he was old enough to do so.

Barnaby's younger brother, Balthazar, lacked the wisdom of his father. A brown snake had bitten him when he was still quite young. He didn't survive long. If he had listened to his father's advice about being careful of snakes, he would still have been around, and Barnaby would not have been an only-owlet.

As he was growing up, Barnaby was taught many things about surviving in nature. He was forced to spend so much time becoming bush savvy, that the young owl didn't get much time to himself. He didn't get to do the things others his age enjoyed. While some young owls were having fun disturbing the birds that had annoyed them during the day, and hooting at people in parks at night, Barnaby was taken on serious bush surveillance trips with his father. He taught the young owl how to easily spot and catch rodents, and the best part of the tree to sleep in so as not to be seen during the day. He also taught him how to avoid being eaten by a fox, and how to achieve excellent gliding skills.

Barnaby had hoped to find a suitable mate, but he didn't seem to have much luck in love.

The first owl he dated was much younger than him and liked to stay up all day.

'Let's go and swoop on people in the park,' she'd said just as Barn Owl was getting ready to go to bed for the day.

'It's very late in the morning. I need to get some sleep,' Barnaby had told her.

'Oh come on, it's only eleven. We've got the whole day to hoot around.'

Barnaby also found her to be very fussy about her diet and she'd refused to eat the food that he had caught for her.

'I only like snakes. The king brown is especially good to eat. Prove to me you can catch one or I'm outta here,' she'd told him.

If the Owl had been anything like his little brother Balthazar, he would have taken her up on the challenge. But he had the good sense, and the knowledge from his father, not to try and catch a snake as deadly as the king brown. It was the most dangerous snake in Australia. Barnaby knew that it could kill birds, and he had even heard about humans that had a nasty encounter with a king brown and had not lived long enough to brag about it.

Although Barnaby was very taken with this pretty young owl, with her gorgeous facial disc and soft brown feathers, he wasn't prepared to risk his life for her - even if he was quite a nifty snake catcher. So she flew off to find another more accommodating owl.

Barnaby had learned how to catch less deadly snakes by watching the kookaburras. He would wait until just after dusk then glide silently towards the unsuspecting snake, and then use the kookaburra technique of repeatedly dropping the snake from a huge height until it was dead. He could then forget hunting for rodents for dinner. He'd have enough food to last for a few nights.

After his first love had rejected him, Barnaby became cynical about relationships. He dated a few owls that didn't seem to demonstrate the kind of wisdom he was seeking in a long-term mate. In the end he gave up on relationships, deciding to focus on his career.

'You will make a great CEB Barnaby,' his father told him. 'I am proud of the way you are growing in wisdom. The bush creatures will look to you for advice and guidance. I think you are old enough now to take over my position. I really am ready to retire and live out my final days in peace with your mother.'

So Barnaby became the new CEB and took over the running of the Rodent Management Program (RMP) as well as sitting on a number of committees including the Dangerous Critters Advisory Council (DCAC), the Bushfire Evacuation Group (BEG) and the Native Plant Seeding Program (NPSP).

His life was never his own as there was always something pressing that needed his wise attention. But never had he suffered from such bad insomnia.

~

It had all begun when he'd moved to his new tree near the river. Barn Owl had done everything he could think of to get to sleep easily. He'd gone to bed at the crack of dawn; he'd avoided eating too many mice close to bedtime; and he'd stopped using his vocal chords too much at things he saw in the bush close to dawn. Barnaby had found from experience that this was too enlivening and would stop him from going to sleep. He'd even tried munching on some wattle seed he'd found growing near his tree to calm him down. It was rich in magnesium, and the wise Owl knew that this would relax his muscles and help him to drift off peacefully.

Eventually he realized his insomnia problem was due to his anxiety of being woken up all day long by some bush creature. Ever since he had moved near the river he had been pestered by birds and animals to do something about the damage mankind was doing to their bush home. Of course he cared about their problem, but he just wished they would stop bothering him so early in the morning and would wait until dusk to complain. At least then he would have had a decent day's sleep. But they kept banging on the trunk of his tree just as he was drifting off to sleep. He was fed up and exhausted. If only they would give him a break. He was becoming too tired at night to even hunt for rodents and his gliding skills were not what they used to be.

After a terrible week of restless days tossing and turning, Barnaby ate a few too many wattle seeds and finally drifted off into a lovely day's sleep.

His slumber was not allowed to last long. Something very significant was about to happen.

13

Cracker – Spokesbird

PUP HAD BEEN WALKING for a good part of the night searching for Cracker. Although her feet were sore, she was able to go much further in the cool night air. The moon was full and lit her way with its soft silver light. Around midnight she finally stopped to sleep under a large leafy fern.

After a long rejuvenating sleep she was woken up by some strange sounds. She had no idea what time it was, but guessed it was around midday as the sun was high up in the sky.

She peered through the leaves of a Peppermint gum. A large number of birds and animals were gathering in a ferny gully. They collected around a river gum tree where Barnaby was peacefully sleeping.

Pup wondered what this could be about. She'd never seen so many birds and animals all together in the one place. *Would Fluff be coming to the meeting?* she wondered. She couldn't see Fluff anywhere. Magpie was nowhere to be seen either. Some of the animals she had never seen before. Tasmanian devils were not common on the upper north shore of Sydney. They normally lived in Tasmania, a large island off the south coast of Australia. Pup saw the Tasmanian devil scratching at its ear like it had a flea problem. She thought it looked like a large black rat with its pointy nose and sharp teeth and claws.

Pup had seen a kangaroo before as it hopped across a fence, and a fat wombat ambling so slowly across a road in the bush, it was a miracle it made it to the other side. Pup had also seen the pink-and-grey galahs pecking around for food on the side of the road. But she'd never seen a bilby, a goanna, a dingo, or a platypus. She wondered what this large mix of birds and animals could possibly want from the sleeping Owl. They all seemed very keen to talk to him. Perhaps there was a bushfire coming and they needed to know what to do next. Or maybe there was a plague of bush rats and they wanted Barn Owl to get rid of them. Before she could ponder any longer, her thoughts were interrupted by a loud familiar screech.

'I see you made it to the meeting.'

'Cracker! I thought I would never see you again.' Even the loud squawk did nothing to deter her happiness at re-uniting with the cocky bird. She jumped all over Cracker almost flattening the cockatoo in her excitement at seeing the bird again.

Cracker flew onto a low branch to avoid having her feathers damaged by the overly excited little terrier.

'Well I couldn't find you,' Cracker said.

'I flew away for a few minutes, and when I turned around you had disappeared like my Henry. But it's good to see ya, little dog.'

'What's going on? Why are there so many animals here?' Pup asked.

'Shoosh! I want to hear what they have to say,' Cracker squawked.

Pup watched as the Devil walked boldly up to Barnaby's tree. He shook it as hard as he could. 'Wake up, birdbrain! This is no time for shuteye.'

'He's so rude to our leader,' said a wallaby to a possum.

'What do you expect?' said the possum. 'He's not called a devil for no reason.'

'Well I wish he'd go back where he came from. He's got no business nosing around in our territory. What's he doing here anyway?'

'Probably escaped from the zoo.'

Up in the tree Barnaby opened a sleepy eye. 'What do you want?' the Owl asked.

'I want what everyone wants here. If you're so wise you've gotta do something to stop the humans from poisoning where we live. Do you realize my relatives are all gone? Tasmanian devils are heading for extinction.'

'Well that would be a relief,' the Possum told the Wallaby. 'They're nasty-tempered little things if you ask me.'

An angry goanna covered in oil dropped a note written on a gum leaf into a hole in the trunk of the tree.

'I agree with the Devil. You'd better do something about this,' he said looking up at the tired Owl.

'I'm covered in oil from some stupid human's fast moving water vehicle. It left a mess all over my river.' Goanna tried to wipe some of the thick black oil off his skin with a leaf.

A wombat waddled up to the tree and dropped a leaf into the same hole in the trunk. 'I got clocked by a flying object a human threw out the hole in their moving box. It got me right between the eyes. I've got a huge bruise. Then I tried to have a drink out of the river and it tasted nasty,' he added waddling into the centre of the birds and animals that were gathered around the tree.

'All right, All right,' Barnaby muttered, thinking for a moment.

'If I'd known this meeting had been organised for the middle of the day, I would have got to bed when it was still dark,' he said. 'It's obvious we need to do something.'

'Too right,' a crow squawked. 'I can hardly breathe from the stuff that humans dump from a flying object all over my paddock. I've had it! It's obvious from the way they treat our natural home that mankind doesn't give a hoot.'

Barn Owl sighed again. He peered down at the angry crowd.

'Doesn't give a hoot! That's pretty funny,' a galah said to a bilby.

'Not as funny as the colours you turn out in. What kind of a combination is grey and pink for a male bird?' the bilby chuckled. 'It's a bit prissy isn't it?'

The galah glared at the bilby. 'What would you know about fashion Bilby? You could do with wearing a bit of colour instead of that boring mousy brown you always turn out in. And what's with the big floppy ears? Are you trying to be a rabbit?'

'Shoosh!' said Bounce. 'I want to hear what Barn Owl has to say.' It had taken the red kangaroo a while to find where the meeting was. Cracker's directions were not that easy to follow. She was glad to have found it. *It's time all these issues were addressed*, she thought. But she knew her father would be furious about her being there.

'So what do you want me to do about this?' Barnaby asked the animals and birds.

'Well you're the one with all the answers bird brain,' said the Tasmanian devil. 'We were hoping you were going to tell us what we need to do, oh wise one.'

Barnaby thought for a moment and scratched an itchy spot on his heart-shaped facial disc.

'There is one way we will get our voices heard,' he said. 'We need to appeal to those humans that care about protecting where we live.'

'I didn't think there were any,' a platypus yelled from the bank of the creek. 'I nearly swam right into a floating object in my river. It would have choked me to death if I'd got stuck in it.'

'I know you are all very angry with the humans but, strange as it may seem, there are some who care very much about our natural bush home,' Barn Owl said.

'And how would you know that Barn Owl?' the platypus yelled from the riverbank.

'When I was a young and curious owl, I used to have a habit of flying over those human dwellings and hiding in a tree close by where I could hear them talking. There were some who seemed very distressed by what their fellow humans were doing to our natural home. I overheard a male human say once that they had to work harder if they were to save our rainforests, oceans and rivers. He was upset that their voices were not being heard by those humans who had the power.'

A wedge-tailed eagle glided down from a branch in front of Barnaby's tree. 'What makes me fly into a rage is that if human beings don't like something, they can vote on it. But no-one bothers to ask us if we would prefer our food left natural, rather than altered in some way by humans who want it to last forever, or rainforests cut down, or fast moving water objects made illegal.'

The animals put their claws, paws, wings and hooves together for a round of applause for the eagle.

Pup thought he was rather full of himself the way he fluffed up his feathers, and held his dangerous-looking beak in the air.

'We can't afford to wait any longer for things to change. The humans that are doing their best to keep our bush safe need our help,' Barn Owl continued.

'That sounds like an excellent idea,' said Bounce. 'But how can we possibly help them?'

'Well, if it is pursuit of power, greed, ignorance and politics that is running the planet, then we need to find a way to become powerful too. One sure way to do this is to become a political Party,' said the Owl.

A bandicoot that had been scratching at a flea like mad, stopped for a minute. 'That's all very well mate, but aren't we just gonna be doin' the same thing we don't like them doin?'

'I take your point, Bandicoot, but it won't be the usual kind of political Party run by politics. Our Party will set an example to the world. Not only because it will be run by us, but also because it will care for the places where we live and like to visit. The guiding principles will be the wisdom of nature,' Barn Owl added.

'Yeah we instinctively know when to wake up, when to go to bed, what to eat, when to drop our feathers,' said a kookaburra with a laugh.

'That's right Kooka. There are laws that govern nature that

we all follow. The sun never stops rising in the east and setting in the west. The Earth keeps spinning on its axis and orbiting the sun, and the sun keeps moving through our galaxy, and our galaxy keeps moving through its clusters of galaxies.' Barnaby was on a roll. His father had taught him a lot and he enjoyed showing off how wise he had become.

'Our Party will copy nature,' he went on. 'We will educate people everywhere that they need to take care of the only place they have to live.'

Goanna had been furiously trying to get oil off his head.

'Do you honestly think they're going to care about what a bunch of birds and animals have to say?'

'Those who do care will listen. They will welcome our Party and want to vote for us. Together we can become a strong voice,' said the Owl.

Pup was transfixed by what she was hearing. If she had more confidence she thought it would be great to get involved in some way with such an important political Party. She remembered how Rita never recycled anything, and how David was always picking up the human stuff they didn't seem to want on their walks and putting it into bins. One day she'd been shocked to hear David telling a friend that, before long, there would be more human rubbish in the oceans than fish. She'd hoped he was exaggerating. Pup thought back to how hot it had been when she had almost given up the will to live on the side of the road. It came back to her now that, when David was watching the news on the television, she'd seen pictures of polar bears floating around on small icebergs, because the earth was becoming so warm, their ice was melting. Pup heard that bees were dying by the millions from the overuse of nasty stuff the humans put on the plants. *Something has to be done about all of this. We can't live without the bees*, she thought.

Pup was so pre-occupied, considering how bad things had become, that she forgot that Cracker was just behind her on a branch. She almost wet herself when her cockatoo friend suddenly screeched loudly.

'This is all very well Barny, but haven't you overlooked one important thing?'

'My name is Barnaby,' Barn Owl said, gazing into the bushes to see where this loud screechy voice was coming from.

'None of the birds and animals can speak English,' Cracker said.

'Good point,' said the Owl. 'You can be the English teacher.'

'You must be joking Barn Owl,' Wombat growled. 'Cockatoo only knows a couple of phrases. "Want a cup of tea?" and "Cocky wants a cracker". That's not going to be much use to us when we're delivering our Party political platform on national TV.'

'Listen, fur ball,' Cracker squawked. 'English is for the birds. I'll soon be as good at speaking English as you are at stealing all the soil for your burrow.' Cracker swung upside down from a branch screeching with delight at the comment she had just made. Pup was embarrassed by Cracker's outlandish behaviour.

'I am sure our yellow-crested friend can expand on her knowledge of English to incorporate a few extra phrases,' Barnaby contributed with dignity. 'And once she has learned to speak perfect English, she will become the main English teacher for whoever is the leader of our Party. So, as the humans say, "without further ado", and provided of course that she accepts, I am officially declaring this yellow-crested cockatoo to be the Spokesbird for our new political Party.'

There was a raucous sound of approval from the crowd of birds and animals.

'What do you think Pup?' Cracker asked of her friend. 'Would I make a good Spokesbird for the Party?'

'You have a very strong voice,' Pup said, trying to be polite. 'I think you would be a forceful leader. And you would be making a very good contribution to the planet.'

'All right, I'll do it,' Cracker screeched, without giving it any further thought.

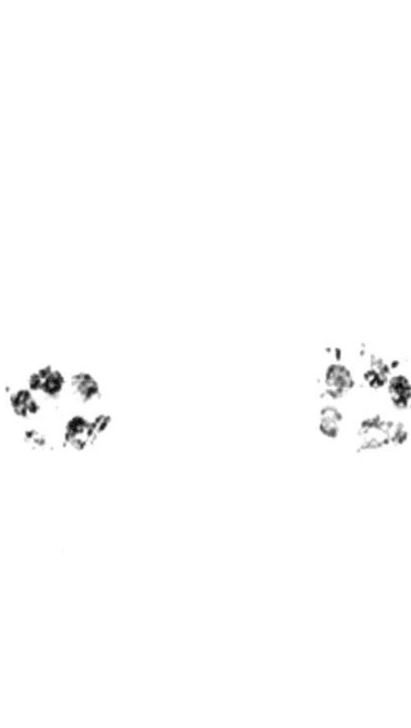

14

The Fur and Feathers Party is Born

I'VE GOT A SUGGESTION for the name of the Party,' Cracker told the Owl.

'We're not going to call it the Parrot Party,' a female goanna giggled from the steep bank where she was sunning herself.

Cracker glared at the goanna. 'I was thinking of the "Fur and Feathers Party", what about that?'

'That's an excellent name,' said the Owl. 'But we'll take a vote on it. All those in favour of the "Fur and Feathers Party", raise your paws, claws, or whatever else you have.'

The majority of the birds and animals responded positively to this new name.

'So it seems most of us agree. I declare our new Party to be called "The Fur and Feathers Party". Now I want you to take a leaf and scratch your recommendation on it for who should be our leader. Drop your suggestions into my mailbox, and I will go through them tonight. Right now I need some more shut-eye.'

The birds and animals did what Barn Owl suggested. One by

one they dropped their leaves into the dedicated hole the Owl used as a mailbox in his tree trunk.

Barnaby drifted into a deep sleep on his branch.

Pup turned around to say something to Cracker and was delighted to see Fluff slowly walking towards her.

'Am I too late for the meeting?'

'Sure are. I've seen a snail travelling faster than you lot,' Cracker giggled.

Pup was so happy to see Fluff. She raced up to her and began jumping up and down, and licking and sniffing her all over.

'I am glad you seem so much better,' Fluff said, backing away from the excited little terrier.

Pup wondered if she had bad doggy breath, but assumed Fluff was afraid that her vigorous jumping might damage the tiny Joey she could see peeping out from Koala's pouch.

'So you two know each other?' Cracker squawked.

'It's a long story,' Pup said.

'Fluff? I knew a cat called that once. It tried to have me for lunch, but I was way too large for it. It hadn't considered how big and sharp my claws were. It took one look at them and ran away in fright. I'm Cracker by the way.'

The bird held out a claw and shook Koala's little fur-covered hand. 'Blimey, ya got a lotta grey fur on ya.'

Pup thought Cracker was being rude again. By the look Fluff gave the cheeky cockatoo, she thought the Koala was a bit offended too.

'Did Magpie make the meeting?' Fluff asked.

Before Pup could answer there was a rustle of leaves and he landed on the ground near them.

'Am I too late?' Magpie asked. 'I got carried away digging for worms. I really wanted to come.' Pup tried to run up to greet him warmly, but Magpie flew onto a branch close by.

'You sure are. It's all over now,' Cracker told the bird.

'Ya lookin' better, little dog,' Magpie warbled at Pup.

'Stone the flamin' magpies Pup! What on earth happened to ya?'

'She nearly karked it ya know, wandering for miles looking for you,' Magpie said.

'Well *I* was lookin' for her. One minute she was behind me, and the next minute she was nowhere to be seen.'

'They saved my life,' Pup told Cracker. 'I was too tired to walk any further and they carried me to a waterhole.'

'Did ya like the worms I left ya?'

'Oh yes thank you Magpie.' Pup didn't want to disappoint the black-and-white bird by confessing that, compared to the dog biscuits Corrina and David used to feed her, the worms tasted terrible. But she had to admit that having something to eat had given her enough strength to keep going. This talk of food made Pup realize how hungry she still was.

'I was wondering if you could possibly find me some more dog biscuits?' Pup asked Cracker. 'I am really hungry and I've travelled a long way searching for you.'

'Well I dunno where I am going to find any round here Pup. I did see a dead carcass down by the river. Hadn't been there long.'

Pup cringed.

'We've gotta fly,' Cracker told the Koala and Magpie. 'We're gonna become a political Party. We'll be able to voice our concerns about the way mankind is stuffing up our natural home. If you have any ideas on who should lead our Party, stick your suggestion on a leaf and put it in the hollow of that tree over there where Barny lives. Just so you know, Magpie, it's been decided that I am to be the main Spokesbird for the Party,' Cracker added forcefully.

'Wait a minute! I was "Bird of the Year" ya know,' Magpie warbled.

'Yeah, well ya didn't make it to the meeting, and ya don't have the same ability to speak English. If ya ask me, ya spend too much time as a chorister in your predictable black-and-white outfit. Running a political Party is a serious business. They chose me to be their Spokesbird coz I'm gonna teach whoever becomes the head of the Fur and Feathers Party, how to speak good English.'

Pup noticed Fluff had begun to waddle away. She guessed it was because Cracker was embarrassing Koala by her rude way of speaking. But she wanted to support Cracker in her new role.

'She can already say a lot of things in the human language,' Pup said.

'Well she's gonna have to say a bit more than just "Who's a pretty boy?" Magpie said.

'Listen warble-head, in case you haven't noticed, I'm a girl bird. I've already learned to say quite a bit and I'll say this to you in English right now: go stick your head up a dead bear's bum!' Pup was shocked and she noticed Magpie's beady eyes narrowing and his beak snapping. He was ready for a fight. 'I'll be seeing ya little dog. Glad you're better, but sorry ya have to hang out with this cocky creature. Careful you don't trip over that ridiculous yellow thing on top of your head,' Magpie told

Cracker. He flew off very fast, snapping his beak in a threatening way. Cracker flew after him for a short distance screeching loudly, but Magpie had already disappeared.

Pup was worried she would lose sight of Cracker again. 'Wait, Cracker, can we get something to eat?'

Cracker turned around and swooped back down next to Pup. She pecked at her claws for a few moments trying to distract herself from the annoyance she felt at not getting the final word in before Magpie was no longer to be seen.

'Strewth. How that worm head got "Bird of the Year" is beyond me.'

'Actually I didn't think you were being very nice.'

'Yeah well, you dogs tend to like everyone. That's ya problem. Ya have to learn to discriminate, Pup.'

'I don't like everyone. I didn't like Lavinia very much.'

'With a name like that I don't blame ya. Who was she anyway?'

'Oh never mind. It was all in my past. I don't like speaking ill of others.'

'See? That's what I'm talking about, Pup. Ya need to learn how to stand up for yourself a bit better. It's a tough life. Can't let everyone just walk all over ya while ya just accept whatever they say or do, and lick them like they're ya best friend. Anyway you're a dog and I know ya see things differently. Come on Pup let's go and find ya some doggie biscuits. Then we've got lots of work to do.'

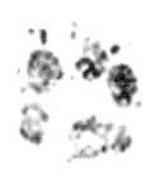

15

Elroy

CLOSE TO HIS FORTY-FIFTH BIRTHDAY Elroy Kliver was on a high. He'd done well enough in the caucuses and the state primaries, to become the chosen Vice Presidential candidate for the Party.

It was officially announced at the Party's National Convention that he was the Vice Presidential nominee. But when the votes were counted on Election Day, he didn't receive an Electoral College majority. Elroy still became the Vice President-Elect after being selected by the Senate in accordance with the U.S. Constitution.

Elroy wasn't popular with the electorate. He had a mean look about him with shifty eyes and small thin lips. His short dark hair was so full of hair grease, that it was stuck flat against his head like he had black paint for hair. His voice did nothing to improve his appeal. It was hard and scratchy as if he'd been eating carrots covered in soil.

Many voters were upset with the way Elroy had presented his views at the vice-presidential debate on television.

During the general election campaigning, it became obvious to many of the voting public that Elroy was someone who couldn't be trusted.

When he was asked about his views on climate change, all he had said was: 'That's a question for the President.'

And when the topic of gun control came up, Elroy had replied, 'Well the problem is really in our Constitution – "the right to bear alms". We will always be up against that.'

People were not happy with the way Elroy seemed to avoid talking about issues.

One night in Washington D.C., a week after the vice-presidential debate, Elroy was heading out of a very expensive French restaurant, and about to climb into his waiting car. A woman raced up to him and said: 'Excuse me sir, I watched the debate. You never mentioned anything in your address about the minimum wage. My son is struggling to survive making coffee at a café. The wage he gets each week is hardly enough to pay for the fuel to fill his car so he can get to work.'

'Well I'm sorry to hear that Madam,' Elroy said narrowing his eyes so they almost disappeared inside his head. 'Maybe he needs to go to college and get a decent qualification, so he doesn't have to rely on making coffee for a living.'

'He has a degree already,' the woman spat. 'This is the only work he can find. Living the kind of privileged life you obviously lead, you clearly have no idea how hard it is now for young people trying to find jobs. I certainly won't be voting for you,' the woman added. She walked off in a huff.

The dislike and mistrust people had for Elroy did not change once he was in office. He never looked as though he was really on side with the President's ideas and visions for

America. Right at the beginning of the Party being in government, Elroy had told the President in a private meeting, 'All this fuss about climate change. I don't think we should be wasting precious funds on it. Where is the real evidence?'

The President had been shocked by Elroy's remark and had said, 'There are many scientists concerned about global warming Elroy who consider it is very real. I don't think we can just dismiss this altogether.'

But Elroy had further exacerbated the President's view of him by saying, 'If you want my honest thoughts on this Jim, I really believe it's just a load of rubbish dreamed up by the Greens to get votes.'

'Well, I guess we are going to have to agree to disagree on that one Elroy,' the President had replied.

Elroy always had his eye on the top job. He didn't like being second best. Trying to improve his popularity, he was always stealing the President's thunder at every possible opportunity.

When Jim announced he was drawing up the plans for a low-income National Healthcare Scheme, Elroy claimed it was his idea. But when it was announced that toll road costs would be going up to pay for a new transport system, Elroy had said 'I don't agree with this decision Mr President.'

Shortly after they had been sworn in, the President had told Elroy, 'We do need to be careful. The media are constantly running snippets of us arguing about aspects of our campaign promises. It's not a good look for the Party if we want to stay in government, Elroy.'

Elroy was confident that his Vice Presidency position was safe: to oust a Vice President required a vote of the House, and two-thirds vote in the Senate.

Elroy's father was a retired property developer. He'd made a fortune buying up deceased estates and replacing their beautiful old mansions with ugly and over-priced high-rises.

His mother never had to work. But even after Elroy had left home, she still employed a cook, a cleaner, and a gardener so she could spend time playing bridge and gossiping with her friends.

Elroy was used to getting his desires fulfilled. As he was their only child, his father spent a lot of money on his son's education. But despite being handed everything on a plate, Elroy only managed to scrape into Harvard by the slimmest possible margin. Once there, his grades were ordinary.

Although he had no desire to work hard, Elroy was ambitious. His ego was the only thing larger than the people who disliked him.

Before he gave up his job to focus on his political career, Elroy became a property developer like his father. He'd managed to get away with many dodgy deals, including purchasing pristine forested areas and arranging for most of the trees to be removed to make room for his ugly buildings. Whenever there was a complaint, Elroy had an uncanny knack of shifting the blame to others.

He was not a happy man. Elroy was married to Sarah, a woman he deeply resented. Her Creative Director role at a large advertising agency brought in a fine salary, but Sarah showed little interest in politics.

It wasn't just that she earned more money than her husband: Sarah's naivety had embarrassed Elroy at official dinners. Being his wife, it was assumed by many that she would be knowledgeable about political issues. But this was not the case.

In his arrogance, Elroy felt certain that his relationship with the President would continue to be a workable one. He had a good head for finances and he was sure that Jim would not be able to fully run his campaigns without Elroy's on-going financial contribution.

But something Elroy did not realise was that things don't always go according to plan.

16

Cracker Gets a Warning

CRACKER AND BARN OWL sat together on the soft green grass under Barn Owl's tree. A large piece of bark lay in front of them.

In his wisdom, Barnaby was aware that the more successful their Party were to become, the greater the chance of a rival Party doing whatever they could to destroy them. He had learned a great deal about human activities with his habit of sneakily watching someone's television. He would hide from view on a tree branch with a thick covering of leaves, and peer at their television through an open window. The Owl was familiar with how the human political parties were constantly swinging from one side to the other, and how the opposition Party were often doing underhand things to sabotage the chances of their competition staying in government. He didn't want this to happen to the Fur and Feathers Party.

Once their leader could speak perfect English, Barnaby knew that other Parties would be keen to find out who had taught them. If they were not careful, a rival Party could use this knowledge to the detriment of the Fur and Feathers Party.

'Sign here,' said Barn Owl.

Cracker was perplexed. 'I was always told never to sign anything unless I really knew what it was.'

The Owl had a feeling that Cracker was going to be hard work. But Barnaby hoped that, by drawing up a legal agreement for the bird to sign, it would force Cracker to take her new role seriously. He hoped the feisty bird would be professional and not go around gossiping about things they needed to keep secret. He was aware that, next to destroying the fly screens on human's houses, there was nothing a cockatoo enjoyed more than a good bit of gossip. He was keen to impress upon the Cockatoo the need to keep their secret, however hard it may be.

'Since you're going to be our Spokesbird for the Fur and Feathers Party,' the Owl told Cracker, 'you need to agree in writing that you won't ever divulge to anyone outside of our Party, that you can teach the birds and animals to speak English.

'There's also a clause that states that you agree not to train any bird or animal that is not a member of the Fur and Feathers Party, no matter how tempting the offer.'

'I guess I can agree to that,' Cracker said, scratching a mark with her sharp beak on the piece of bark. 'But why all this formality?'

'This is our secret weapon, Cracker, and it must remain a secret until such time as this knowledge can be rightly used.'

'Okay, you've made ya point Barny.'

'I would prefer if you would call me Barnaby, if you don't mind.'

'Whatever' Cracker said, flying onto a nearby branch and swinging upside down. 'I'll bet you can't do this?' she added, as she threw herself into an aerobatic circle around and around the branch.

Barn Owl had no intention of trying the gymnastic feats that Cracker seemed to delight in performing. He felt dizzy watching her spinning around and around like a fly caught in a spider's web.

Suddenly there was a splintering sound as the branch broke, and Cracker fell to the ground on her head. Barnaby tried to contain his desire to laugh.

'Crikey,' Cracker screeched. 'These spindly eucalypts are a real worry. I am used to a more substantial branch.'

'Of course,' the Owl said diplomatically.

Barn Owl passed an English dictionary to Cracker who was now re-arranging her crest and feathers after her embarrassing tumble.

'Here, you will need to study this human book of words and improve your English,' the wise Owl said. 'We need our Spokesbird to speak as well as any well-educated human being.'

'No worries,' Cracker said, snatching the book in a rude manner. 'I'll have it cracked in days.' She laughed at her own joke.

Barn Owl tried to get to sleep over Cracker's muttering as the cocky bird flipped through the dictionary.

'Do you have a mate?' Cracker asked in perfect English. Barn Owl opened one eye. He was surprised at how quickly Cracker was picking up the English language.

'No. I've chosen a celibate path,' he responded.

'Blimey. I can't imagine that. Mind you, I've also chosen to be on my own since Henry disappeared. I'll never find another mate like him. Most of the birds from the bush are such a bunch of larrikins and show-offs. I've got no interest in them.'

Barn Owl stifled another laugh. *It takes one to know one*, he thought to himself. 'Maybe Henry will come back.'

'You don't come back from the dead. Before I met Henry, I went out on a few dates. Some of my failed relationships included a stupid galah with no road sense, an obsessive-compulsive parrot that checked each seed he ate five times before eating it, and a black cockatoo that was really up himself. He would have to be the worst date I ever had. Always bragging about how he could clear a field of strawberries in less than five minutes, and how many women he'd scared by appearing upside down at their bathroom window. What a featherhead.'

Barn Owl was struggling to keep his eyes open. He wasn't really listening to Cracker's constant chattering. He'd been kept awake that day with all kinds of further complaints from the birds and animals, until the early hours of the afternoon, and he had to get up as soon as it was dark.

'Well it's almost midday and I am very tired. I really have to call it a day and get back to my tree for some shut-eye,' the Owl said with a wide yawn.

'Okay Barn, but before you fly off, I was wondering if you've made a decision on who is to be the leader of the Fur and Feathers Party?'

'It's looking like Bounce, the red kangaroo, but I am still counting the votes.'

'Well, hope she gets the final vote, coz she will be hopping mad if she doesn't get picked.' Cracker said, chuckling loudly.

'Once we get the final decision, you will need to get cracking on teaching our chosen leader the English language.' Barn Owl said.

'You trying to be witty, Barn Owl?'

'No. I am trying to fly off to bed. I am very tired.

'OK Barn.'

'Barnaby, please.'

'By the way Barnaby, I don't suppose you've seen a little tan-and-silver-haired dog, have ya? She has real long silky hair. I'd got to quite like her, despite the victim mentality, which got a bit much at times.'

'I remember seeing one at the meeting,' Barn Owl said. 'She was a pretty little dog. She's probably gone home to her owner.'

'Well that's the thing Barn. She doesn't have an owner. I try to keep a watch on her but she keeps disappearing. If you do happen to see her, will you tell her where I am? Got quite fond of the little punk. Hope she found something to eat. She was a fussy little thing. Didn't like berries, or seeds. Can you believe that?'

Barn Owl yawned. He was finding Cracker's determination to abbreviate his name, plus her constant conversation, very tiring. But he hoped Cracker would find the little dog. He hated to think of her in the bush all on her own with nothing to eat.

17

Pup Meets the President

PUP DRANK WATER from a creek in the middle of the rainforest. She was disappointed to once again have found herself on her own. The little terrier was exhausted from looking for food.

A few days earlier, Cracker had forced Pup to try a bit of the carcass, but she had only been able to eat a little bit. It smelled so bad it had turned her stomach.

Cracker had also managed to find Pup some dried biscuits left on the wooden picnic table of a camping ground, but it wasn't enough to fill the little dog's tummy. Now she had not seen her yellow-crested friend for days, and had wandered deep into the bush with no idea how to find her way out.

Pup lay down to rest under a shady fern. She wished she wasn't so dependent on Cracker for her very survival. She thought about the strange set of circumstances that had brought her to this spot, and wondered what had happened to the little Maltese terrier that had been her brief companion at the animal rescue shelter. She hoped someone nice had come to give him a decent home. It was hard for Pup to understand how any human could be so cruel as to beat such a lovely dog. Maybe he had been put to sleep, and was now enjoying life in canine heaven.

Pup wondered what heaven would be like for a dog. Her mother had always told her that if she lived a good life, and was thoughtful and kind to other dogs and their owners, she would go to a very lovely place when she left her body.

'The body is simply a shell for the spirit that lives on forever,' Muffin had told the little terrier. 'It's like your wardrobe. It just gets old after a while and you need to get another one.'

She hoped her mother was somewhere nice now; eating the finest cuts of meat, surrounded by friends and maybe even with a handsome new mate.

Perhaps dog heaven was filled with an endless number of electric light poles, saturated in a tantalizing blend of fragrances that only a dog could understand and appreciate.

Pup hoped that, in dog heaven, walks would not require an uncomfortable collar and a tight lead that could pinch around the throat. Maybe all the dogs would be free to run wherever the smells took them.

A strange noise jarred Pup out of her daydreaming. It was a sound very similar to one that she had often heard when David had taken the top off a bottle of something he wanted to drink.

She sat up and looked around. There was no sign of any life and Pup was sure that the rainforest animals were not drinking the strange liquid the humans seemed to like, that often made them fall asleep or fall down.

Pup lay down again and closed her eyes. Perhaps she had

imagined the sound. But there it was again: the sound of human voices. She got up to investigate. The forest was thick with large ferns, and peppermint gums that filled the air with a delicious fresh and minty fragrance. The voices were getting louder.

Suddenly, in the distance, she could see a small timber house surrounded by trees. Four middle-aged men were relaxing in hammocks on a veranda and drinking from brown bottles. Although Pup could tell they were speaking English, they had funny accents.

Pup remembered that she had heard this accent before when David was watching television, and there was a report from another country.

The little dog was excited to see the three men and ran up to them.

'So what do we have here?' The U.S President said, as Pup jumped all over him licking his legs and trying to jump up on his lap. In her excitement, she almost tipped him out of the hammock where he was relaxing.

'What a cute little fella.'

'Actually that little fella is a girl, Mr President,' his Press Secretary said looking up from his iPad briefly.

'Oh for heavens' sake. I'm here on holiday, Mal. You're as bad as my Chief of Staff. Please stop all this formal nonsense and call me Jim.'

'Okay, Mr President, I mean, Jim.' The Press Secretary went back to checking things on his iPad.

Pup noticed another human who wasn't drinking with the other men. He was standing at the top of the wooden steps that led to the veranda. He appeared to be keeping watch. He had what looked like some kind of weapon in a belt around his waist. She wondered why he needed it. Perhaps he was going to use it to kill something for his dinner.

'I've never seen a dog like this before,' the President told one of the men.

'That's an Australian silky-haired terrier, Jim,' Hank butted in, appearing from inside the small wooden cabin. 'They're popular with the Aussies. Very lively and adventurous animals.'

'I can see you've done your Australian research Hank. She seems a little thin. Are you lost little doggie?' the President asked, rubbing Pup's silky ears affectionately.

'Yes I am, and I'm really hungry. Do you have any biscuits?' Pup barked excitedly at him. She was happy to find someone who seemed to really care about her.

'Go and get some of that leftover steak we had for lunch, Hank. The poor little dog looks like she hasn't had a decent meal in weeks. And get her some water as well. She might be thirsty.'

Pup noticed that the man didn't seem too keen to do what the other man had asked of him, but she hoped he would hurry up and get the food. She was starving, and thirsty as well.

'May I remind you Jim, that there are the daily intelligence and national security briefings to check. I have them here,' Hank said passing the President his iPad.

The President took the iPad from Hank but immediately put it down on his hammock. His focus was on his new canine friend. 'I know. Just go and get this little dog the steak, Hank.'

Pup jumped enthusiastically onto the President's lap.

'I've never had steak before,' she said, trying to lick his face.

'Well you are a friendly little dog.' The President rubbed

Pup's back. 'How would you like to come and live with me in America? I live in a big white house with one hundred and thirty-two rooms, and thirty-five bathrooms.'

Pup wondered why he would need so many rooms. She thought that maybe he got bored easily or had a massive family, or hundreds of friends who would come to stay for a while.

'You will be able to sleep on a very comfortable bed. We might even get you a special silk cushion to sit on.'

'Oh that would be wonderful,' Pup said. 'Can my friend Cracker come too?'

The President didn't answer. Pup barked her question again.

The Chief of Staff returned with a bowl of water and some large pieces of steak on a plate and put it on the ground for Pup.

Smelling the sumptuous meal, Pup lost all interest in whether or not Cracker would be joining her in America. She leapt off the President's lap and furiously gulped down the food.

'My goodness, you were a hungry little dog,' the President said.

Pup had a big drink of water. Her mouth had begun to blister and the cool water helped to make it less painful.

'Jim, this isn't the kind of dog you want in the White House. It's very excitable and clearly a barker. You know your advisors recommended a different breed,' the Chief of Staff said.

'Yes. Hank's right about that Jim,' the Press Secretary said, looking up from the iPad.

Pup felt offended by their comments. She didn't like the other two men very much.

'Don't argue with me, Hank. I'm the President and I can

have whatever dog I want. I need some company, and she is a very friendly little animal. And she has such unusual long silky hair. Since she has no collar, it would be hard for us to find the owner, even if she has one.'

'But she may have a chip on her somewhere,' Hank said.

'All right, Hank. You take her to the nearest vet or police station. If they can't find any ID, she's mine.'

The President patted Pup affectionately on her head.

18

Liar Liar Pants on Fire

HANK WAS AFRAID he would be questioned as to why he didn't insist the President choose a suitable breed of dog, like the boxer or poodle recommended by his Cabinet members. He thought, surely he could choose a dog that doesn't bark constantly, or bounce around hysterically all over the place?

He knew that, if this lively little terrier were to snag the expensive stockings of some visiting female dignitary, or leave a deposit on the Cabinet Room carpet, or snap at the legs of a foreign diplomat, all hell would break loose, and he would be the one to get the chop. But who was he to argue with the President of the United States?

Hank was not happy with the President's request either. They were miles from civilisation. Since the park was only accessible by boat or on foot, he would need to take Pup on a boat across a tributary of the Hawkesbury River to where they had left the cars.

The Chief of Staff had spent a long time researching places in Australia where the President could enjoy a very private vacation. He'd chosen the Marramarra National Park, as he'd read that it was very quiet, picturesque and all kinds of Australian native animals could be seen in the area. But what had appealed to him most of all was how rare it was to see another human being.

But there was a good reason why people didn't choose this spot for their holiday: it was teaming with mosquitoes.

Twice Hank had been asked by the President to go back on the boat, pick up the car and get him something for the insect problem.

The first time he'd been asked, the Chief of Staff had come back with an insect repellent recommended to him by the pharmacist. He was hot and exhausted from the long trip in the scorching heat. The President tried it once and asked him to go back again and get a different brand, because he hated the smell, and it was making his skin itch.

The second time Hank had come back with a more natural brand. Jim told him the next day that it didn't work and would he please go and find something else, as well as a mosquito net for sleeping.

Hank was exhausted from all these trips. He'd had to drive all over the place looking for a suitable mosquito net. He was finding this presidential vacation very stressful in the hot New South Wales summer.

If he had been at the White House, he could have delegated the job to another member of staff, but he didn't want to bother anyone who wasn't staying with them. He knew it would create more problems than it was worth.

On the whole Hank enjoyed working for the President.

He thought he was a kind man. But Jim seemed to be

thriving on the absence of air conditioning. Even Hank had found the White House too cold in the summer, and way too hot in the winter.

In their cabin, and even with the ceiling fans going at full speed, Hank was finding the heat stifling. But he couldn't say anything. It frustrated him that both the Press Secretary and the President's Bodyguard seemed to find the humidity agreeable.

Then in the morning, Jim would greet him with another one of his disgusting brown health drinks, and they seemed to be upsetting Hank's digestive system.

Hank had a look on his smart phone to see if there was a vet close by. The nearest one was a good twenty kilometres - twelve miles he supposed - away from where they had left the car.

It was all getting a bit much. He was glad this was only going to be a short vacation. Soon they would be heading to the more agreeable temperature of the U.S. Embassy in Sydney, for the rest of their time Down Under.

The Chief of Staff was relieved that at least the President's normal entourage of people, a small army of some two hundred aides, were staying at a secret location nearby. They were close enough to attend to anything he might consider urgent, but far enough away that they were not surrounded by hordes of staff. It was to be like that until he began his more formal tour of the country when they would all be together.

Hank felt sick at the thought of how he was going to explain to the rest of the President's entourage why there was a little talkative terrier now travelling with them. He hoped the dog would have an owner and that would be the end of it.

Here Hank, you can use this as a lead,' Jim said, passing the

Chief of Staff the belt from the brown cotton slacks he was wearing.

'She doesn't have a collar though, Jim.'

'I'm sure you'll be able to work it out Hank. You didn't get to be my "gatekeeper" for no reason.'

Hank went to search for something he could use as a collar.

'Where are we going?' Pup barked at the President.

'You want some more steak little doggie?'

'Oh yes please,' she barked.

'Go and get some more of that leftover steak, Mal.'

'Will do sir, ah Jim,' the Press Secretary said.

Hank was having trouble finding anything suitable for a collar. He grabbed a pair of his shoes and pulled out the laces. They seemed long enough for a small dog. He doubled them up to make them stronger.

Hank watched Mal taking some steak out of the fridge and putting it on a plate for Pup. Hank knew they were on the same page when it came to the President keeping the dog, but what could they do about it? Jim would have the final say no matter how much they protested.

Pup was standing in anticipation by the wire door and Hank wondered who owned this little dog, and why she was all by herself in such a remote place. If they found her owner, it would be the end of his having to explain anything when they re-connected with the rest of the group travelling with the President.

Hank went up to Pup with his makeshift shoelace collar while she was gulping the food down. He tested to see if it would work. It seemed strong enough. He knotted the collar at one end and grabbed Jim's belt. It was long enough to go through the collar doubled up. He held the two ends of the belt tightly and gave a sharp tug to get Pup to follow him.

'Are we going for a walk now?' I usually would love that but the pads on my feet are really sore,' Pup barked.

'Now you go with Hank little doggie,' Jim said, noticing that the little dog seemed to want to stay with him.

'She's become fond of you already Jim.'

Hank was annoyed that the Press Secretary seemed to be encouraging the President to keep the little yappy terrier. He could tell from the look Mal had given him earlier on, that he didn't approve of this decision. *He can be such a brown-noser*, he thought.

'Come on we're going for a walk,' Hank told Pup, yanking again on the makeshift lead.

They travelled a short distance and rounded a corner. The boat was suddenly visible at the end of the track.

Hank tried to get Pup to climb onto the boat but she stood firmly in one spot and would not move.

'Come on you stupid little runt.' Hank pulled harder on the makeshift lead. He tried to pick her up and she struggled and began to growl. She bit him on his arm a couple of times and he dropped her in fright. Pup ran off with the lead dragging behind her. It sent all the dried leaves on the dirt track spiralling into the air like a leafy tornado.

Hank chased after her. She was too fast for him. He started to hope that Pup had gone home to her owner. Even if she had just run away, he would be free of her. He could tell the President that he had met someone in the park, and they had claimed she was their dog who had gone missing.

He dropped down under a shady tree to catch his breath,

totally spent from all the favours the President asked of him. *The Chief of Staff is certainly not a role for the faint-hearted,* Hank thought. *It's no walk in the park managing the President's schedule and deciding who is allowed to meet with him. Not to mention negotiating with Congress on his behalf.*

This vacation was stressing Hank out. He'd had so little sleep in his hot and humid room. Now in his early fifties, and without the same stamina as the President, he wasn't able to cope so easily working a hard day with insufficient rest.

Maybe now I can have some time to myself, he thought lying down under the tree. He was soon fast asleep.

~

'Hank, are you all right?'

The Chief of Staff woke up and was embarrassed to see the President, his Bodyguard and Press Secretary staring down at him.

'What's going on? Are you ill?' Jim asked.

'No. I um, you'd never believe what happened, ah Jim.'

'Try me.'

'I ran into someone who was looking for the little dog. They were so happy to find her and they took her home with them. So I stopped to rest for a minute, and fell asleep.'

'Is that so? Well it just so happens that the dog appeared back at the cabin and was very happy to see me.'

'Oh maybe she got away from them.' Hank knew he was going to be in serious trouble now.

'I am very disappointed in you Hank. I know you didn't want me to keep the little dog, but this is just …'

Hank felt sick. He was sure he would be fired. He noticed Jim staring at his feet. When he did this he was usually devising a plan. Hank assumed it was to figure out an appropriate punishment for the way he had disobeyed him. Finally, after what seemed to him a very long time, the President spoke. 'I think we can come to an arrangement Hank. I'd never realized that you were capable of being deceitful like this. But since you have shown me this side of your nature, maybe we can stretch the truth a bit about the little dog, eh?'

Hank was relieved that he wasn't about to be removed from office. Even though he was tired and exhausted from all the President's favours, it was a well-paid job. He knew that he would never work again if Jim became too angry with him.

'Yes, Jim. I will tell everyone that we tried, but couldn't find the owner.'

The President smiled. 'Well if she does have an owner they don't deserve to have her. Judging by the way she looks, I'd say she's been on the run for a while. That's settled then. I am taking her back to America with me.'

19

Barn Owl Visits Bounce

BARN OWL HAD FINALLY finished counting the votes. It was an overwhelming majority. The birds and animals wanted a red kangaroo to be the leader of the Fur and Feathers Party, and Bounce was chosen.

The Owl was happy with this decision. He thought Bounce would be very popular with the humans, and a strong leader. He was aware there were some people who liked to shoot kangaroos, and others who even ate them. And then there were those that fed their animals with kangaroo meat, but most people liked them. They had even captured kangaroos and put them into large enclosures, so humans from all over the world could admire them, and give them scraps of food.

Barn Owl decided to glide to the paddock where Bounce and her family lived, and tell her the good news.

When Barnaby reached the Kangaroo's paddock it was almost dark. Although this was the beginning of his night, Barnaby realized that, if he didn't find Bounce quickly, she would be asleep and he would have to wake her up. He knew from his own experience of being woken up all the time, how annoying this was. With his sharp eyesight he could see Bounce in the distance. She was lying with two older kangaroos and a younger one, under a tree. They seemed to be having a discussion. He glided down to them.

'I'm sorry to bother you all,' the Owl told the family of kangaroos. 'I have some very exciting news for Bounce.'

Bounce pushed herself up with her strong tail to face the Owl. Barnaby noticed how anxious the two older kangaroos looked. He assumed they must be Bounce's mother and father. Barn Owl was a little concerned that he might get boxed around the ears when he told her family the reason he had come. He took a deep breath and, with a loud hoot, spoke to Bounce.

'The birds and animals have decided that you are to be the leader of the Fur and Feathers Party. If you accept the position, Cracker, the cockatoo will teach you to speak the human language.'

Barn Owl had to fly out of the way as Bounce almost flattened him in her excitement.

'Are you kidding me? This is so exciting! When I left the meeting at your tree the other day, I was thrilled about the Fur and Feathers Party. I wondered who would be chosen as the Party leader. I never would have dared to dream that it might be me.'

Bounce's father hopped angrily up to face the Owl.

'Now you listen to me, Barn Owl. There is no way I am going to allow my daughter to join this radical group of extremists. So you have wasted your time flying over here. You'd better go now, because it is way past our bedtime.'

'Well, I think Bounce is old enough to make up her own mind about what she wants to do with her life,' the wise Owl said. He hoped he would not be kicked backed to his tree by this male kangaroo's strong back legs.

'That's right father. This is a great honour and I couldn't be more delighted. It would be a privilege to be the leader of this Party,' Bounce told the Owl. 'I fully accept.'

'As my daughter, I forbid you to do this.'

'Well I'm sorry father, but this is my life. I know you are not used to females having a life of their own, but this is what I want. I am going to do it.'

'This is a sad moment for our family,' her father said.

'Not for me it's not,' Bounce interrupted.

'You need to know, Bounce, that if you accept this offer I will no longer consider you to be a part of this family,' her father added.

'Oh darling, I understand that you are upset but please don't be so hard on our only daughter,' said her mother.

'It's all right, mother. If this is how father feels I will leave this family now. And I will never come back.'

Barn Owl was upset that Bounce seemed to be making such a difficult decision. His own family had always supported him with his career. 'Are you sure this is what you want to do?' the Owl asked.

'I'm sure. Let's get out of here. Clearly my father is not going to budge on this, and I don't fit into this family.' Barn Owl flew behind Bounce as she hopped across the paddock. Barnaby looked back and noticed Bounce's mother staring longingly after her daughter. Bounce didn't look back.

~

Two months later, as the sun had begun to lose its summer sting, Floss yelled to her husband from their living room. 'Harry, come quickly! You won't believe this. There's a red kangaroo giving a Party political broadcast on the television. She is speaking perfect English,' the woman said with her eyes glued to the TV.

Her husband continued brewing his coffee in the kitchen of their bungalow. He didn't take any notice; he was used to his wife's imaginings. It seemed to him that Floss was slowly getting worse. Soon he would have to face putting her in a nursing home. He was not looking forward to it.

'Come on Harry, hurry up you're going to miss the English-speaking kangaroo,' Floss yelled from the living room.

Harry poured the coffee into a large mug and added his usual five spoons of sugar. He was thankful that his wife had at least stopped saying, 'Will you be having a little coffee with your sugar today dear?' She thought it was funny but it really irritated Harry. Why couldn't he have five spoons of sugar if he wanted to? He never commented on her habit of putting cream in her tea. No one puts cream in tea. He thought that it was very bad for her cholesterol levels.

Harry added some low-fat milk to his coffee mug and wandered into the living room. He almost dropped the mug when he saw a red kangaroo up on a platform speaking to camera – in English.

A long banner hung behind the kangaroo with large green words that read, "The Fur and Feathers Party for Government".

Bounce was on a podium addressing the crowd that had gathered to listen to her. 'And we will introduce a bill that prevents people from polluting our rivers with their speedboats. And man-made foods will be banned, and we will find a way to stop the bees from dying from all those deadly sprays the humans dump on the plants.'

Harry flopped onto the couch next to Floss who was transfixed to the television.

'Oh, this must be some kind of political satire dear,' he said, picking up his cup and sipping on the very sweet coffee. 'For a minute they had me fooled. This new computer animation can look very real, Floss,' he added.

Floss picked up the remote and flicked through the channels. Harry was shocked to see the red kangaroo on every channel.

'Wait a minute. They wouldn't be running the same comedy show on every network. I don't understand,' Harry said, almost dropping his cup again. 'How can a kangaroo possibly be speaking English?'

'I don't know dear, but I like her policies. We need to take more care of the environment.'

Harry began to wonder if he was catching his wife's condition. He got up and picked up the phone. He dialled a number.

'Hello Cyril, it's Harry. Look I've been watching the television and there's a red kang.....What? You have been watching her too?' he asked. 'What in heaven's name is going on Cyril? Since when can kangaroos speak English, talk about climate change and run for government?'

Harry continued to nervously gaze at the television. His hands were starting to shake as he watched the Kangaroo addressing the crowd.

'We have to put a stop to the carbon emissions that are contributing to climate change. So all cars that need oil to run will be banned, and we will further develop electric and solar vehicles,' Bounce added.

Harry's mouth dropped open as the camera panned across the large mix of birds and animals that had gathered to hear Bounce speak. He noticed some humans in amongst them, clapping enthusiastically. The noise of the crowd's excited approval would have woken even the most dead to the world critter: yelling, screeching, squawking, howling, barking, growling, warbling, stamping and crowing. Harry had to turn down his hearing aid.

'I have to go, Cyril. I'm feeling a little funny,' Harry said, putting down the phone and flopping onto the couch next to his wife. Floss had not shifted her gaze from the television.

'I think we should vote for the Fur and Feathers Party dear,' his wife said. 'This kangaroo is making a lot of sense.'

Harry pinched himself to make sure he was not dreaming. Suddenly the camera cut to another podium where Cracker was sitting. An ID came up on the television screen that read 'Cracker Yellow-Crest – Spokesbird'.

Harry and Floss watched in awe as Cracker began to speak. 'Let's put our paws; claws; wings and hooves together for Bounce,' Cracker screeched. 'Oh, and if you have hands you can use those too,' she added with a chuckle.

The camera panned again across the enthusiastic crowd and Harry suddenly looked like he was about to have a heart attack.

'That's Bob,' Harry screamed at his wife. 'He is our oldest and most sensible friend. What is he doing there?'

20

The Man-made Bird

CRACKER TAPPED HER BEAK on Barn Owl's tree trunk. The Owl opened a sleepy eye.

'You wanted to see me?' Cracker squawked.

Barn Owl had hoped that Cracker would wait until it got dark before bothering him. But he was getting used to the demands of the birds and animals. It was part of his role as Chief Executive Bird, and he realized he would just have to live with it, as his father had done.

In his sleepy state, Barn Owl tried to remember what he had wanted to see Cracker about so urgently. Then it all came back to him.

'Oh yes. I've received something in the pigeon post that is very exciting,' the Owl said with a jaw-stretching yawn. 'It seems that the birds and animals of America have got to hear about the Fur and Feathers Party, and how we are winning the hearts of voters here in Australia. They want to start their own Fur and Feathers Party there.'

'That's bonza news,' Cracker said, spitting out a seed.

The Owl frowned. He wondered what kind of an upbringing she'd had to have such appalling table manners.

'Well that's all very well,' said Cracker. 'But whoever they decide to lead their Party, needs to learn to speak English?'

'That's where you come in Cracker. I want you to fly over to the United States and teach their chosen leader.'

'Fair fluff of the feathers! I don't think my wings could take me that far. I was exhausted the time I tried to make it to Wagga Wagga in a day.'

'You'll be flying on the large human-made bird, Cracker. It can travel vast distances and doesn't get tired at all.'

'Strike me pink! What kind of seeds does it eat? I would like to be able to improve my flying.'

'It doesn't eat anything, but apparently it drinks lots of oil and people ride inside its belly.'

'Oh that's gross,' said Cracker.

'This bird doesn't have any insides, just a bunch of seats,' the Owl said.

'What a strange bird,' Cracker said.

'Well, it needs seats for people to sit on. You would get pretty tired standing up for twenty-one hours.'

'Twenty-one hours?' Cracker screeched so loudly that Barn Owl almost fell off his perch.

'It goes pretty fast when you've got movies to watch.'

'Movies?' Cracker screeched again. 'That's the funniest sounding bird I've ever heard about. It's got seats and movies inside its body? Wait a minute. How do we get inside this bird?' Cracker's body began to shake, sending some feathers into the Owl's eyes. His eyes became irritated from connecting with the feathers.

'I am not prepared to be eaten by some large bird just so some creature in America can learn how to speak English. How useful would I be over there if I'd been eaten?'

Barn Owl raised his now sore eyes to the heavens. 'I don't think you're understanding Cracker. This is not a *real* bird. It's a man-made bird that can fly long distances. It carries humans across the seas.'

'Well why didn't you say so? I thought you were talking about a real bird.'

'Made by humans?' Barn Owl sighed. 'When was the last time you saw one of those?'

'All right, you've made ya point Barny,' Cracker said feeling humiliated.

'Barnaby,' the Owl corrected.

'Now listen up. I may not be brilliant at geography, Barnaby, but I do happen to know that America is a very large place. Can you be a bit more specific about what part of the country you want me to end up in?'

'I was getting to that. You'll need to get to a place called Asheville. It's in the Blue Ridge Mountains of North Carolina. You'll have to change birds once you're in America. When you arrive in Asheville you'll need to find my distant cousin the Snowy Owl. He's very wise like me. He will know the best creature to lead their Party. I understand from the pigeon post that they haven't decided who that will be yet.'

'Wait a minute, did you say I would have to change birds? I'm not stupid Barnaby. How do I know that the American bird won't take a dislike to me invading its territory?'

Barn Owl let out another huge sigh. Clearly the Cockatoo still wasn't getting it. 'I've tried to explain to you Cracker, it's not a real bird. It doesn't have emotions and feelings, and it will take you wherever you need to go.'

'Well, I suppose it makes sense that humans would prefer to fly on a bird with no emotions or feelings. They don't demonstrate they have much in the way of feeling themselves when they put us in prison in their living rooms,' mused Cracker. And another thing Barn …'

'Barnaby,' the Owl corrected.

'Okay, whatever, how I am supposed to find this Snowy Owl? Is he going to be meeting me where the big bird lands?'

'That will be left up to nature to organise. You need to trust that this is meant to be and it will all work out as it should.'

Barn Owl was getting frustrated with Cracker. 'When will you be free to go? They want you there as soon as possible.'

'Well Barnaby, I'd have to think about this. I mean I'm a very busy cockatoo. I'm still trying to find Henry, and I've fruit to knock off trees and fly screens to destroy. And now I have all these extra responsibilities with being the Spokesbird for the Party political broadcasts on national television.'

'Well, if you can get yourself on a bird as soon as possible that would be good,' the Owl said.

'I'll have to make sure I've got enough seeds for the trip first.'

'They feed you Cracker. You don't have to worry about that. Now I really have to fly off to my nest and get some shut-eye.'

'What about Pup?' Cracker was still hoping she might re-connect with the little terrier.

'Pup?' the Owl asked.

'The little dog. She is my friend. I was hoping to find her.

I'm missing the whining.'

'I will keep an eye out for her,' the Owl said. 'She can't have gone far. She doesn't even have wings. Poor little creature.'

21

Jim Tells All

THE U.S. PRESIDENT handed the Vice President the drink he had left on the table. 'Here's your wheatgrass and prunes, Elroy.'

The Vice President took one look at the thick brownish-green mud and backed towards the exit.

'Actually Jim, I am rather full. I had a very good dinner and …'

'Go on, throw it down, Elroy. It'll put more bounce in your stride.'

Elroy resigned himself to his miserable fate.

'I might take it to my office Jim, for later.' Elroy moved towards the door. 'Perhaps as a nightcap.'

Before Elroy could escape, he noticed the President flop into an armchair, gesturing for the Vice President to join him. Reluctantly Elroy sat in another chair. He hoped Jim wouldn't keep on at him to drink the horrible health drink. Unobtrusively, he put it on the floor by his chair.

'You know Elroy, I don't have much time to myself but, when I do, the nights are long. I need some company.'

'Yes you've mentioned that before, Jim.'

Elroy gazed at the President considering whether he could be bold enough to ask. *He's a good looking man,* Elroy thought. *I just don't get it.* The Vice President decided the time had come to bring this up.

'Jim, I'm sorry if this sounds a little personal, but I've been wondering, um, why you seem so reluctant---

'Spit it out Elroy. Get it off your chest.'

'-- to um, find a partner in life?' The minute he had asked the question Elroy wished he hadn't. He watched the President examining the carpet. He had an expression on his face as if Elroy had just suggested he might think about changing his deodorant. It was a blend of surprise and embarrassment.

Elroy fiddled with a button on his jacket while he waited for Jim to say something. Finally he did.

'All right Elroy, I will tell you, but please keep this to yourself.'

'Of course Jim,' Elroy said, all ears.

The President launched into his story. 'Julie was twenty-seven when I met her. We met at a bar close to where she worked. I was twenty-four and already well into my political science studies. I was madly in love. She was beautiful, smart, warm, kind and caring. And she loved to cook.'

'Sounds like quite a catch,' Elroy said, thinking about his wife who couldn't even boil an egg.

'She was,' Jim continued. 'But I sensed that she wanted to get married, stop working and start a family.'

'There it is,' Elroy said with a smirk.

'Don't get me wrong, Elroy, I wanted to marry her. I'd have been quite happy to fully support her, but I knew I was unable to do that until I finished my studies and found the right job. That would have been years away.'

'And Julie didn't want to wait, right?'

'Well, the truth is I started to worry I might lose her if I didn't make a proper commitment. So I planned to mention the 'M' word over dinner at one of our favourite Italian restaurants.'

'Oh not the dreaded 'M' word? Don't we just love talking about that?' Elroy said with a sneer. 'I only agreed to marry Sarah coz she'd given me an ultimatum: 'Marry me Elroy, or I'll find someone else who will,' she'd told me.'

Elroy noticed that Jim was looking a little annoyed at being interrupted. 'Anyway go on with your story.'

Jim continued, 'I tried to pluck up the courage to begin the conversation we needed to have. I had a few more sips on my chardonnay to give me some "Dutch courage". I noticed Julie was moving the tortellini around and around on her plate, without actually putting anything into her mouth. She looked nervous. It was as if she knew we were about to have a serious conversation about something that maybe she would not want to hear. When I told her I wanted to talk about the relationship, she put her fork down. I could see that her hands were shaking. So I tried to reassure her that I wasn't breaking up with her. 'We get along great' I told her. 'But I think it's time for a proper commitment.'

'She would have liked that,' Elroy said. 'That's all most women want to hear. Why can't they just be happy having a nice bed companion, without all this pressure to be together for the rest of your life? You know the old saying: "Familiarity breeds contempt". That's certainly proved to be true in my marriage. I was happier as a single man with no commitments.'

'I don't have a problem with commitment, Elroy. But I regretted having this conversation with Julie, because she sat bolt upright and said 'I'm ready to start a family, Jim. I want a baby. I'll soon be thirty and my clock is ticking.'

'You see what happens when you mention the magic 'M' word Jim? That was your first mistake.'

'I was taken aback,' Jim continued. 'I knew I would not be in a position to support her for many years, and I was aware that she didn't want to become a working mother. But when I suggested that we should wait for a few more years before planning a family, she got up and said, 'Well maybe I just need to find a man who can support me sooner than later.' She stormed out of the restaurant and I never saw her again.'

'And I'll bet she met someone else, got married and had a baby?' Elroy said.

'That's exactly what happened.'

'Well, sounds like you were better off without her.' Elroy got up to leave. He hoped the President wouldn't notice the glass full of brown mud that he had left beside the armchair. He could always pretend he'd meant to take it. Maybe the cleaner would find it later without Jim ever finding out.

'If she could just have waited a few more years to start a family, we'd still be together. I never got over her.'

Elroy could see that Jim was becoming very wistful. He thought he'd better show a bit more compassion. He didn't want them to fall out with each other over this.

'Wow,' Elroy said. 'You really had it bad.'

'But what about the … you know, physical stuff, you must miss that surely? Why don't you just find someone for a good time? You don't have to spend your entire life with them.'

'I'm not like you Elroy. I want a real companion. I'd like someone who would also become my best friend. At this stage of my life, a little dog will suit me just fine.'

Elroy was frustrated that they were talking about dogs again. He had hoped the President had given up on this idea.

'Well, being the President of course, if you really want a pet dog, it's your call. Just remember though that the advice of your cabinet members was that you get either a boxer dog or a poodle. It's important that whatever dog you choose sets the right tone for your administration. It should be well behaved, friendly and quiet, and be popular with your voters. Dogs should be seen and not heard like children, especially when there are important people staying at the White House. You don't want one of those little barkers, Jim,' Elroy said, narrowing his eyes.

Elroy watched surprised as the President got up and turned towards the door that led to his bedroom.

'Well it's too late,' Jim said, whistling loudly.

Elroy tried to hide his anger as Pup suddenly appeared, barking and jumping excitedly over them both. He watched in shock as the President gave Pup a biscuit. He noticed the crumbs dropping all over the floor and the puddle of drool forming at the President's feet.

'She's an Australian silky-haired terrier. Pretty little thing isn't she? I've decided to call her Congress.'

'But my name is Pup. Will you call me that?' the little dog barked at the President.

Elroy wished that dogs could be banned in the White House. It was suddenly clear to him why the White House Christmas tree had a clay ornament of a small terrier dog, hanging in a very prominent place. He'd thought how inappropriate that was for a theme of Native American animals. He'd even spoken to the Chief of Staff about it and, although Hank agreed that it shouldn't really be there, Elroy had been firmly told the President personally put the decoration there. He knew Hank wouldn't dare remove it.

Elroy watched as Pup jumped all over the President, barking loudly.

This little yapper is going to become a problem, Elroy thought.

22

Pup at the White House

PUP WAS LIVING WITH her new owner on the second floor of the White House. As the President was not married with children, there were several spare bedrooms. The little silky-haired terrier had been given her own room. It had a connecting door to the President's private quarters.

Her bedroom had a doggie door with a covered chute that led down to the back garden. Pup thoroughly enjoyed plummeting down the plastic slide whenever she needed to do her business, or if she just wanted to hang out in the garden for a while. The President had asked Hank to install another doggie door on the ground floor at the back of the house, so she could get back into the building.

Pup was curious about what was outside the large impenetrable fence that surrounded the entire building. She had noticed some particularly intriguing fragrances wafting across from there. She hoped she would be able to find a way to enjoy them.

Some men patrolled the area, keeping an eye on her. Pup

wondered why they carried things that looked like weapons. It seemed a little unnecessary when they were just hanging out in the garden enjoying the views.

Hank was not her favourite person. Ever since he had called her a little runt, and tried to stop the President from taking her back with him to America, she'd been wary of him.

Her master asked Hank one morning to organise a regular walker for Pup.

'But there's nobody available to walk her, Jim,' he'd said.

Pup sensed he was lying and that he just hadn't bothered to ask around. Consequently, and to his obvious annoyance, this responsibility was added to the Chief of Staff's schedule.

Hank put a very tight collar on Pup that pinched her skin, and wouldn't allow her to stop and inhale the delectable fragrances that were there for her enjoyment.

When Pup had first arrived in the place her owner called Washington D.C., he had taken her on a walk. As she had stopped to sniff at each shrub and tree, he had told her the name of the plant, and how humans described its flowers.

But Hank was nothing like her owner. Pup could tell that he wanted to get the walk over as fast as possible.

Every time she'd tried to stop to inhale the sweet honey-scented white flowers on the Fothergilla shrub, or to enjoy the subtle fragrance of the rosy-lavender flowers on the Eastern Redbud tree, Hank would yank on her lead so hard she almost choked. She decided she didn't want to go out with him again.

The next time Hank tried to walk her, she just sat down and refused to move. He gave up trying in the end, and Pup overheard him lying to her master that they had been out when they hadn't.

Pup watched the President sleeping soundly. She looked out the window. The full moon had coated the White House back garden with a silvery wash.

'Now is a good time for me to do this,' Pup thought.

The little dog shot down her chute into the garden. She found a spot that was fairly well hidden by bushes. She dug a hole under the fence. She made it deep enough that, if she flattened her body and wriggled along, she would be able to get to the other side.

'This will be perfect,' she thought. 'Now I can explore outside whenever I want.' Although she was busting to get under the fence straight away, she decided it would be safer to do this some other time. If the President were to wake up and find her missing, he would be very distressed and immediately have everyone outside searching for her.

~

A day arrived when the President was busy showing a group of people around his big white house. Pup decided it might be a good day to explore what was on the other side of the back garden fence. She shot down her chute, filled with excitement at what she was about to do. She was able to easily wriggle under the fence.

She raced up to the first luscious smell and left a deposit. Pup was very happy that this was going to become her territory too. But, as she trotted down the road, she became afraid that her master would notice she was gone. She decided this would be enough for one day and shot back under the fence.

At first it hurt the little terrier's feelings to discover that she had not been missed, but Pup soon accepted that her master was just a very busy person and any insecurities she may have had, were soon washed away by his enthusiasm when he saw her again.

Pup loved her bedroom. It was filled with large cushions decorated with pictures of labradors, poodles and corgi dogs. The walls had some paintings of dogs and Pup thought her owner was so thoughtful to have done this for her.

As Pup looked around her room, she thought about the way her new owner had told her about the paintings when he first introduced her to the bedroom.

'This is a famous artist called Picasso, Pup,' he'd said. 'And this is a painting of his dachshund he called "Lump". And this painting is called "Head of a Dog" and is by the Norwegian expressionist artist, Edvard Munch.'

Pup felt so loved that he would go to so much trouble for her. It made her feel important, and so well looked after. It was doing a lot to improve her self-esteem.

Many of the people living in the huge white house paid a lot of attention to Pup. They often patted her and would stop what they were doing to watch her charging up the stairs to the President's private quarters like a lynx after a rabbit.

Pup noticed that her new master seemed to like socializing, and had many friends. Sometimes huge gatherings of people would come to the big white house where she lived. They even had men pointing large black objects at the people that were chattering together. She learned these odd-looking things were called television cameras. The little dog was meeting new people all the time and many of them had strange accents Pup found hard to understand. But they always liked to pat her. Some people had commented on her lovely long silky fur. Others had said she had soulful eyes. Pup felt very special. She thought flying on the large bird all the way from one hemisphere to another had been an adventure. But it seemed like her new owner was very keen on travelling. They'd been on the same bird at least ten times. Pup thought he must have been very wealthy to be able to afford so many holidays.

The inside of their large bird was luxurious. The little dog had a double bed to sleep on, and there was a living room that was similar to the one she'd lived in with David. But this one had dark-coloured furniture with fancy shaped legs. Judging by the way she was not allowed to go near these strange shaped chairs and tables, she sensed they must have been worth a lot of those pieces of paper the humans seemed to use all the time.

Pup enjoyed running on the staircase that went round and round in circles that led to an upstairs floor. It was full of smartly dressed men sitting on tall chairs and drinking attractive looking beverages. The oversized bird even had bathrooms. Corrina had taught her that word when she had been trying to get Pup to have a bath after she'd been rolling in the mud in her back garden.

She remembered the time when she'd been with her master to England. Pup had met an elderly female she recognized from the little silver discs that David had kept in his pockets, and that he had used to buy food and other things.

The elderly lady had funny little orange coloured dogs. Some of them only had small stubs for tails. They had short little legs that seemed out of proportion to their much larger bodies.

One of the orange dogs had tried to nip Pup's tail. He had snapped at her saying, 'Suppose you think you're better than me with your long tail. But you're not, you know. And don't pretend to be a Welsh dog either just because you come from

New South Wales.' Pup thought about how bad-tempered he was. But the elderly lady they called 'The Queen' had smiled and stroked the small dog's silky ears, inviting her to join them for afternoon tea. The Queen had given Pup a drink of water in a silver bowl and some ginger biscuits.

The little terrier thought it was strange that all the people she'd met in this place they called 'England' knew her master's name was Jim. But for some reason they called him Mr. President. She wondered why they did this. Perhaps they had just forgotten his first name. He certainly was a busy man and was always on his phone or meeting up with someone. People seemed to treat him with a lot of respect. He was obviously good at his job.

After her owner, Pup's favourite person in the White House was the Executive Chef. Pup thought she looked very nice. She was a young woman with black hair cut short, dark brown skin, and large brown eyes. She often gave Pup leftover food, including large meaty bones. Pup thought they didn't taste like anything Corrina or David had ever given her. She'd heard this food being called deer or elk. Pup thought it was odd how the woman always wore a tall white hat and all her clothes were white. She had the same outfit on every day. *Perhaps they don't pay her enough money to buy clothes,* Pup had thought.

Although she had her own lovely bedroom, Pup liked to sleep in the same room as her master. That way she could keep an eye on him and be ready to attack anyone who might be a threat in any way.

The President didn't seem to mind her being in his room and even let her get onto his bed.

One night, shortly after she had arrived at the White House, the President took off his silk robe and put it neatly across the end of his enormous bed. Pup took this as an invitation for her to jump onto the middle of the robe.

'No, come here Congress. I want you to sleep in the nice bed that daddy has made for you,' he said, patting the pink silk covered cushion that lined a large cane dog basket.

Pup was finding it hard to get used to him calling her 'Congress'. 'Will you call me Pup please?' she barked, gazing at him with her soulful eyes.

'Yes, I know you love me. And I love you too,' he said.

It was the bane of the little dog's existence that so many humans could not understand what she was saying.

She went up to her bed and jumped into it. It was nice of her master to make her such a lovely, comfy bed.

The President patted her on the head. 'Good doggie,' he said as he climbed into bed. 'It's nice to have some company at last.' He switched off his bedside lamp.

Pup lay quietly. She was afraid if she made too much noise he might get fed up with her and give her away as David had done. But she was covered in itchy bites. She wondered if she should just go into her own bedroom, but he seemed to want her in his room. She screwed up her face, trying hard not to react to the itching that was growing stronger. Unable to stand it, she scratched madly at the bites and her foot hit the side of the basket making a thumping noise.

It woke the President and he tossed and turned, trying to get back to sleep. Pup watched him switch on the light and plump himself up with large dark blue covered cushions. She saw him grab a book but, not long after he opened it, he was sound asleep again. The next thing she knew there was a loud ringing sound emanating from a small black box by the President's bed.

Pup jumped onto his bed, licking his face furiously.

'All right, that's enough,' the President said, switching off his alarm clock. He turned his head away so she couldn't lick his face anymore. Pup watched him wipe his mouth with a tissue and she hoped she didn't smell of dog food.

She turned around in circles a few times until she felt she had found the perfect spot to lie down. She was so happy to have such a nice owner. The little terrier was trying hard not to do anything that might cause him to abandon her in a strange country, without even her cockatoo friend to help her.

Pup went to sleep again and dreamed of Cracker. The bird was screeching her name loudly from the treetops. She seemed upset. Pup was at the foot of her tree barking loudly, 'Hey I'm down here.' But Cracker didn't seem to be able to see her, and kept calling out her name.

The little dog watched as Cracker flew onto the guttering of a house, hanging upside down and peering into a woman's bathroom.

'Have you seen my friend Pup?' Cracker screeched. The woman screamed and closed the shutters.

Cracker flew off and Pup ran after her, calling her name, but the bird seemed oblivious of the little dog.

In Pup's dream, Cracker flew out of sight. The little terrier dropped onto the ground and cried. *Why was she always being abandoned - even when they wanted her?*

A white pigeon walked up to her, breaking her mood. The pigeon was about to say something profound when it vanished before her eyes.

Pup woke up feeling sad to have lost track of Cracker. She

hadn't fully realized at the time what a good friend the cockatoo had been to her, even if she did seem to like the sound of her own screech.

But, if it weren't for Cracker, the little dog would have been lying very flat on a road somewhere and would never have met her lovely new owner.

She was sorry that she hadn't shown more appreciation at the time for the bird's attempts to help her. It was nice of Cracker to try and help her like that.

Pup reprimanded herself for being so thoughtless to have wandered off without looking for her newfound friend. She would have loved Cracker to meet her new master. Perhaps the cockatoo would have got an invite to visit the little dog in her big white house. Then, as if a light bulb had been switched on in her head, she had a brilliant idea.

23

Cracker Flies to the U.S.

CRACKER SLEPT SOUNDLY in her river gum tree. As the sun threw its first golden rays across the bushland, causing many of the bush birds to burst into song, Cracker remained asleep. Even the loud laughter of the kookaburras in a nearby tree did not drag this yellow-crested cockatoo from her dream.

In Cracker's dream, Henry was hanging upside down from the roof of a house. She was also on the roof looking down at him. Henry was giving her a mischievous look, and she knew he was up to something. There was never a dull moment with her Henry.

'Hey Cracker, Mrs Lander's lilly pilly bush is covered in berries. Waddayasay we go and strip it clean?'

'Oh Henry, I love the larrikin in you. I think it's a great idea, but first let's scare the woman in the bathroom by peering upside down into her window. She's in there having a shower. You do it Henry. You're better than I am in that position.'

'Okay that would be fun. We make a good team, eh Cracker?'

Cracker watched with eager anticipation as Henry flew up to the open window, and peered in.

'Yep, she's in there all right,' he clucked.

But just as Henry was about to position himself on the roof guttering, the dream turned into another dream. This time Cracker was looking up at a giant silver bird. Its mouth was wide open and there were many steep steps leading up to its beak.

In her dream, a Tasmanian devil climbed up the steps, disappearing inside the bird's mouth. She was expecting to see the gigantic creature chewing and swallowing. Cracker continued to watch horrified as Pup appeared at the foot of the steps.

'No, Pup don't go up the stairs,' Cracker called out. 'You will be eaten by this huge bird.'

Pup just looked at Cracker as if she wasn't concerned at all, and began climbing the stairs towards the bird's open beak.

She flew up to the little dog and tried to pick her up, but she was too heavy. She stood on the stair in front of Pup, blocking her way.

'Stop! You mustn't go any further unless you want to be this bird's dinner,' Cracker said in the dream.

'Excuse me, Cracker. Will you please get out of my way.' Pup pushed past her and vanished inside the giant bird's mouth.

Cracker screeched in horror, 'No!'

The nightmare woke her up. Her feathers were wet with the shock of the dream and she was trembling all over. But she was relieved it was just a nightmare. Then she remembered that soon she would be inside the belly of a huge bird flying all the way to a foreign land. She wasn't entirely comfortable at the thought of being inside this large man-made bird. But Barn Owl had reassured her it was the way people got around the world safely. So, if they could do it, so could she. There was one thing Cracker would never be; and that was a coward.

The Cockatoo wondered what kind of berries they would have over there. She hoped there wouldn't be any birds louder than her. She'd been used to ruling the roost in her bush home. *Who knows what kind of birds will live there,* Cracker thought. Then her mother came into her mind. The way Beryl always imagined the worst possible scenario about everything. Of course it would not have been easy putting up with Clancy, her bad-tempered mate, but she certainly did not want to end up a worrier like her mother.

Cracker had always believed you create your own reality. She realized she had to stop concerning herself with foreign predators, and just trust that the great bird spirit in the sky would keep her safe. *It's funny how you start believing in these spirit birds when things become scary in your life,* Cracker mused. She thought about Henry and how much she missed him. She had the strangest feeling that they were destined to meet again one day. And she thought about Pup. Once again the little dog had disappeared. She hoped she was okay. She seemed to need a lot of help when she was on her own, and Cracker was beginning to feel responsible for her.

It was odd the way humans took such an interest in having a dog in their lives. Cracker had seen humans riding horses. And on the one occasion when she did manage to peer into a woman's living room, she'd seen her cuddling a cat. But people seemed to especially bond with dogs and she wondered why this was. Maybe it was because they felt they could make a dog do whatever they wanted. Other animals would not be so easy. She'd seen a cat on a lead, but never a bandicoot, or wombat. Henry had told Cracker that he knew of a human who had a pet cockatoo but they kept it in jail in their kitchen where it couldn't stretch its wings. She thought that would be hell.

Cracker was so deep in her thoughts she hadn't noticed the white pigeon that had landed on a branch near her. It flew right up to her with a large gum leaf in its mouth.

'Stone the bleedin' crows, you could knock,' Cracker screeched at the pigeon.

'I have a message for you.'

Cracker snatched the leaf from the pigeon and it flew away. She opened the folded gum leaf and read it out loud.

'Dear Cracker, I've gone to America. Sorry I wasn't able to say goodbye in person. I miss you. Please write to me. All you need to put on the envelope is my name and care of the White House, USA and that will find me.'

The bird put down the note in an exasperated way. 'Oh come on Pup, fair stroke of the yellow crest, what kind of an address is that? The little dog is clueless. Well I'm sorry to say this Pup, but there seems little chance now we will ever meet up again,' she muttered to herself.

~

Cracker was the only bird on the plane. It had been a long trip on two planes and her feathers were all dishevelled from being strapped tightly into her seat by oversized seat belts.

Passengers kept staring at her. She'd been well fed with several trays of seeds on plastic trays, and numerous glasses of water. Cracker would have preferred the water to be delivered on eucalyptus leaves, but decided not to complain. She was tucking into the last meal of seeds before arriving in North Carolina. The seeds were spilling all over the floor and covering the passenger next to her. 'Woops, sorry,' she said to the elderly lady sitting beside her. The woman seemed shocked at the bird's grasp of English.

Cracker got a shock and suddenly stopped eating when, coming from somewhere inside the plane, a female voice said, 'Good evening ladies and gentleman and Cockatoo. The captain has just given us an update on our arrival time at Asheville. We should have you on the ground at eight-forty this evening.'

'If this giant bird knew how to flap its wings properly, we'd have been there by now,' Cracker said to the elderly lady next to her.

The lady tried to contain a laugh. 'Do you mind me asking how you learned to speak such good English?'

'Trade secret,' Cracker replied. 'My crest is on the chopping block if I tell anyone, sorry.'

The minute the plane had touched down at Asheville airport, Cracker was waiting by a rear exit door.

A flight attendant came up to her. 'You need to remain in your seat until the captain has turned off the seat belt sign.'

'Oh give a bird a break. I need to stretch me wings. They're feeling stiff from sitting so long. This is the second bird I've been on ya know, and I've travelled a long way.'

Cracker flew onto the handle of one of the aircraft doors and tried to move it with her beak. 'I don't think I can get this to move. It's about as stiff as my father was after that fast moving human box hit him. Can you open the door please?'

Cracker noticed the flight attendant's mouth tightening and she lunged at the cockatoo, trying to grab her by her tail feather.

'Catch me if you can,' Cracker screeched loudly, flying off before the woman could get a hold of her. She flew round and round the plane, dropping white blobs onto the heads of the passengers.

The plane came to a final stop and the seat belt sign was turned off. Cracker flew up to the plane's back door again and waited for it to be opened.

The minute the flight crew unlocked the door and cold air came rushing in, Cracker flew outside. She was relieved to be able to stretch her large white wings after being cooped up for so long inside the plane.

'Hey, come back! You need to go through Immigration and Customs,' a crewmember shouted. But Cracker had no idea what she was talking about and kept on going.

An icy wind was blowing across the tarmac and her wings began to stiffen with the cold.

'Fair dinkum, Barn Owl, if I'd known it was gonna be this cold, I would have grown some thicker feathers. My golden crest could snap right off in this temperature.'

Cracker landed on a big pile of snow on the outside of the airport fence near the terminal. Her claws were becoming numb. She noticed a group of people in blue uniforms, running towards her yelling loudly and holding long sticks that looked dangerous.

'Stop or we'll fire,' they shouted.

'Fair suck on the mulberry seeds! I just got here.'

For the first time in Cracker's life, she had jet lag. Her

strange incoherent flying confused the officers and they had no success in hitting hit her with any of their bullets.

'Strike me pink! What an unfriendly flock of people they have here,' Cracker muttered.

She landed on a steel fence on the very outside of the airport. The officers were no longer in sight.

From her spot on the fencepost, she had a good view of all the large man-made birds taking off and landing. Cracker thought it was odd that, even though it wasn't a real living bird, its name needed to be written on its side like that. Maybe they were afraid they would forget what the big bird was called and needed the name written down to remind them.

And these birds all had such weird names like Qantas, and Southwest Airlines. She thought whoever was in charge of naming these giant birds should have consulted with her first. She would have come up with better names than that. Even Clancy, or Beryl would have been an improvement. But she was grateful to have arrived in one piece.

After travelling all the way from Sydney on one of these huge creatures, she decided they were the weirdest bird she had ever come across. They seemed to live on airport fuel. Cracker thought this was an odd dict for a bird. Humans were certainly dumb not to know what birds like to eat, even when it was a human-made bird. But one thing was for sure; she was never going to start an argument with one of them. They were way too big.

Cracker gazed at the scene in front of her. It was blinding to look at, with the weak sun shining as strongly as it could manage, causing the snow crystals to sparkle like ocean waves twinkling in the sunshine. Everything looked like it had been saturated in bleach, devoid of even the slightest streak of colour. The snow and ice had been cleared from the tarmac leaving it a contrasting grey against the stark white landscape. She assumed the runway was kept free of the frozen water, to stop the big birds from slipping, or getting such numb feet from the cold that they couldn't run fast enough to take off properly. She'd also seen stuff being sprayed onto their wings. The frozen water seemed to melt away the minute the liquid touched it.

Just as Cracker was wondering what to do next and how she could get out of the cold, her keen beady eyes focused on a brilliant white object. It was moving on a fence not far from where she was. If it hadn't shifted slightly, it would have blended into the landscape making it almost impossible to spot. She flew closer to check it out.

24

Howl

HOWL WAS A HANDSOME red wolf. He was tawny-red with grey and black markings on his strong, muscular body. He had powerful hind legs and his tail had a smart black tip.

He was born high up in the northeast part of North Carolina and was given his name because of his exceptional ability at projecting his voice further than his brothers could do.

His father had taught Howl and his two brothers to point their heads towards the sky; this would help their voice to travel a long distance.

Howl learned to use his voice to communicate his territory to other wolves not in their pack. It was also useful for making friends, and as a way for him to find fellow pack members when they were apart.

The red wolf's father had been a fine hunter, and Howl and his young brothers always had enough to eat. He had even brought a deer home one night as a special treat.

Howl learned how to hunt for any small mammals he could find. He ate rodents and rabbits as well as insects and berries.

When Howl's mother gave birth to him and his brothers, it left her very weak. One year later, and during a very severe winter, she became sick. Their den wasn't warm enough for her, although the wolves all huddled together to try and keep her warm.

Howl had a particular attachment to his mother and, as still a young wolf, her death hit him harder than it did his brothers. He became a shy and secretive animal and preferred to hunt alone.

One day when he was out chasing a deer, he met a pretty young wolf. 'I'm Amber,' the she-wolf told Howl. 'My mother named me after the colour of my eyes. She told me they reminded her of precious stones of the same amber colour. I am her *precious* daughter,' she added.

Amber was so lovely Howl's red fur stood on end when he saw her. He thought her amber eyes were indeed like sparkling jewels. Her fur was a delicate shade of red, and was thick and glossy. She had a pretty nose, and a very voluptuous tail.

Howl was instantly smitten and wanted her as his mate. He had never been in love before, and his heart was very open. He fell deeply for this stunning wolf.

Amber became his close companion. They hunted together, and created a den in preparation for a family. But several months after he had first met the beautiful she-wolf, she disappeared and his happy time with her was over.

He called and called 'Amber!' across the mountain ranges. Many creatures could hear his call. It was a painful haunting roar. His voice soon became hoarse and all he could manage was a faint gravel-sounding whisper. Howl assumed the worst. Maybe Amber had been killed by a rival pack of wolves.

Perhaps a human hunter had wanted her fur to make a winter hat. But there was something about his missing mate that Howl did not know.

A few weeks later, he stumbled upon Amber's den. He was shocked to discover that she was vibrant and happy, and surrounded by a litter of young wolves. She had a very handsome partner that was washing her ears affectionately.

Howl was wild that he had wasted so many months grieving for her loss when she had just been unfaithful to him. He swore he would never trust another she-wolf again, and would spend the rest of his life alone.

Howl's father wanted his son to find his passion in life, and carve out a great reputation for himself in some way.

When Howl was still a pup, his father hounded him about what he wanted to do when he was a fully-grown wolf.

'You don't just have to accept a life of hunting for food, finding a mate and having a family,' his father had told the young wolf. 'Some wolves have great careers, even becoming Hollywood actors. Look at the wolves in the film "Dances With Wolves". Now, those animals have earned a lot of money, and built penthouse dens for their mates,' his father had added. 'You could do this too Howl. You just have to believe in yourself and it will happen.'

'But I don't want to be an actor,' Howl had said. 'You think those wolves have great lives? They're surrounded by all those fake creatures pretending to be superior to ordinary wolves, when actually the only thing they can cling to is their fame. They worry about their fur falling out. They jump around from mate to mate. They get dumped by one wolf, and then move onto the next one, and get dumped again. Sometimes they do the dumping. They eat too much until they become fat, and some film producer asks them to go on a starvation diet before the next movie. I don't want to live like that,' Howl had said.

'Well what do you want son?' his father had pressed the young wolf.

'I dunno. I'd like to do something where I can make a real difference to the planet. Maybe I could help the underwolf in some way. Perhaps work for a wildlife, or conservation charity catching food for them.'

His father's look had been dismissive. Howl could tell he didn't think much of his ideas. Since Amber had betrayed him, Howl had lost all desire to push himself to new heights. He remembered how passionate he had been about life when they were together. He was always trying out new things; like testing himself to climb the tallest mountains; leading his pack on food hunts, and even coming home with an elk he'd killed for food one day.

'Find your growl-power again, son. I know you have it inside that red furry body of yours.'

Howl hated to disappoint the old wolf, and he didn't enjoy being seen as a loser. A short time later, he overheard his father talking about him to Long Tooth, one of the brothers. 'Howl's been dumped by Amber, that she-wolf he was seeing.'

Long Tooth nodded his burnt-orange furry head in agreement. 'I sensed she was a bitch. Gotta feel sorry for Howl. He seems to even be losing interest in hunting.'

Ferocity, an old wolf in the pack, had upset Howl by saying, 'I think that she-wolf dumped you because you'd let an elk get away when you were out hunting.'

This kind of talk made Howl really angry. 'That's a very

unfair thing to say about me, Ferocity. I haven't seen you, or either of my brothers, or the other wolves in our pack for that matter, get even close to catching an elk. But I've caught one on more than one occasion.'

Howl felt the red fur on the back of his neck standing on end. 'You're just jealous of my superior skills,' he added.

He had even overheard Red Fur, his other brother, talking about him to his father. 'Maybe it's time Howl joined another pack. He's howled for so long after Amber left him, he's lost his powerful voice.'

Red Fur later told Howl, 'Your voice is getting weak. You're not howling properly anymore. I could hardly hear you the other day. You need to start projecting your voice a whole lot better, if you want to stay in our pack.'

Howl had been devastated by his brother's comment. He knew his voice would come back if he rested it for a while. But he had begun to feel like he didn't belong in this pack at all. So many of the wolves were speaking to him in humiliating and embarrassing ways. The wolves that didn't comment still treated him as if he didn't belong anymore. It hurt Howl's feelings that they were judging him like this. The last thing he wanted was their pity.

When Howl had been with Amber, he'd had a strong sense of self. He was courageous and strong. But since she'd left him, and his pack had been treating him the way they were, he was beginning to develop a very low opinion of himself.

Then, one bitter winter afternoon, after Howl's father had been missing for days, the old wolf re-appeared. He walked with his muzzle held low to the ground, and refused to speak to his pack for two days. Howl was worried about him.

A couple of days later, his father finally sat down next to Howl and said; 'You know, I never did tell you this son, but maybe now is the time. I met a wise elder of our pack the other day. He told me you were destined for fame and fortune. I just thought you should know this, so you don't miss a window of opportunity if it presents itself.'

Howl had no idea what his father was talking about. He'd never believed in fortune-tellers. It sounded like a load of moose dung. But he did hope that something would come along that he could get his teeth into, that wasn't another animal. What he didn't know was how soon that opportunity was going to present itself.

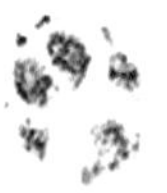

25

Snowy Owl

SNOWY OWL SAT PERCHED silently on a fencepost. He was proud of his brilliant, ghostlike white plumage. His striking yellow eyes remained focused on the snow-blanketed ground for any sign of a small mammal he could have for dinner. Snowy Owl needed to consume at least five mice a day to sustain his bulky body.

When he was growing up, the Owl had lived mainly on lemmings and ptarmigans that his father would hunt over the plains in their Arctic home. But each year in the winter, when the lemming population died down, the family would fly to the northern and central part of the U.S. where it wasn't as cold.

Now Snowy Owl was exhausted from the long trip he and his family had travelled. He waited patiently on the fencepost, hardly moving. The nest he had created was close to the ground in a richly forested area, and he felt sure that sooner or later his keen eyes would spot something his family could eat. He preferred to eat mammals, but he was also partial to some songbirds and even medium-sized geese. Snowy Owl remained hopeful that he would see a hare in the forest. That would make a substantial meal for his family.

Snowy Owl's mate, Feathery, was nesting. He didn't think she was quite as striking to look at as he was, but he wasn't the kind of owl that just went for physical appearances. Feathery had black and brown markings that gave her a kind of salt and pepper appearance. Snowy Owl had been mostly attracted to how loyal and loving she was.

Feathery had laid ten eggs, and Snowy Owl had wanted to stay close to the nest, as there were foxes and even wolves that could have his wife, eggs and all, for lunch. He was always on the ready to attack anything that threatened his family. Unlike other owls, he could be awake day and night hunting for food and protecting the nest.

Although Snowy Owl didn't think much about global warming, he had a reputation for being wise. He was tired of listening to the endless complaints from the native animals. Many of them had told the Owl that human beings were doing things that affected their lives and caused them to suffer.

'I've had to move for thousands of miles to find a new home,' Black Bear had told the Owl. 'The trees in my forest home were all cut down so the humans could move in and build their timber and brick boxes where they like to nest.'

Coyote had said, 'I've been forced to eat domestic cats and dogs because the humans have overtaken my natural habitat, and poisoned a lot of the small mammals that are my normal source of food. It didn't seem right eating these animals but what can you do? You have to survive on something.'

A racoon had stopped the Owl one day and said 'I've adapted pretty well to increased human contact. I've been able to make a temporary home for myself in roofs of those timber boxes the humans like. I was making a bit of noise one day and I was caught and put in a cage. It was terrifying. I thought they were going to eat me for lunch, or put me in those large prisons with lots of different animals, where people stare at you, and feed you things you don't want to eat,' he sighed. 'I got taken far away and let loose where there were mountain lions and black bears. They would have eaten me if they'd had the chance. I had to start all over again looking for a new home. It was very unsettling.'

Every day it seemed to Snowy Owl that there were more and more complaints. The animals and birds wanted him to solve their problems. He had no idea how he could do this. Then, one day, he met a kangaroo that had escaped from a zoo. She hopped straight up to him, and for a minute he thought he was going to be flattened by her powerful hind legs. 'Australia has a political Party set up by the native creatures. A red kangaroo is running it. She has learned how to speak English. People are voting for the Party and it has actually got into government,' the kangaroo told the Owl in an excited tone.

The bird said nothing for a few moments. He wanted to believe what the kangaroo was telling him, but it seemed so far-fetched he wondered if it was time this animal was put in a paddock for mentally-deranged marsupials. But then he thought about all the complaints he'd been hearing from the American animals. He hoped there was some truth in what the kangaroo was telling him. She seemed to be genuine. *Maybe this would solve their problems,* the Owl thought.

'That's interesting. We could start a similar Party here,' the Owl said. He noticed the look of relief on the kangaroo's face.

She must have been aware that what she was telling him might have sounded like a load of wallaby droppings.

'You need a strong leader. Maybe a red wolf would be interested,' Kangaroo continued.

Snowy Owl did not like wolves. They were quite capable of eating his family if they were given the chance. However, he knew a wolf would command the kind of respect that a Party political leader needed to be taken seriously. He shivered at the thought of getting close enough to a wolf to even begin a discussion on the subject.

'Hmmm …well, I'll have to think about that,' the Owl said at last.

~

Snowy Owl liked to hang out at airports. The wide-open spaces reminded him of the tundra where he had grown up, in the Arctic Circle.

One freezing winter morning, as he was perched on an electric light pole watching all the big human-made birds taking off and landing, something extraordinary happened. Out of the corner of his yellow eye, Snowy Owl saw something large and white moving on a telegraph wire not far from where he was. He had never seen a bird that looked anything like this before. It was covered in white plumage just like him, and he wondered what the peculiar-looking yellow thing was on top of its head.

Cracker landed a few feet from the Owl, who backed away instinctively.

'Don't come any closer. I have sharp claws,' the Owl said.

'Well I'll be a dingbat's auntie,' Cracker said, gazing in wonder at the glistening white owl. 'Ya not the only one with sharp claws ya know.' The cockatoo moved closer to Snowy

Owl. 'I must say you have a very nice white plumage. But you could do with losing a bit of weight round your bottom half, and your feet definitely need a wax,' Cracker said, noting the dense feathering on the bird's legs.

Snowy Owl thought this odd looking bird with its horrendous voice was being way too personal. 'Well at least I don't have a ridiculous yellow thing stuck on my head,' Snowy Owl said, with a haughty air.

'Don't speak about my crest in that way. It's what my partner Henry loved about me. Apart from everything else of course. But I don't want to talk about Henry. I'm not into wallowing and, when I do talk about him, it makes me feel sad.'

'Who are you? And what are you doing here?' Snowy Owl asked.

Cracker held out a claw. 'I'm Cracker from Australia. Just got off the man-made bird. Who are you?'

'I'm Snowy Owl. I'd heard there were birds like you on that great southern land, but I'd never met one before. You must be very fit, and have strong wings to have flown all that way. I only came from the Arctic Circle, and that was far enough for me.'

'Oh that man-made bird flies very fast. I didn't have to do much. I just sat and looked out through a see-through part of its body. I'd never been so far above the clouds before. That bird flew really high.'

Snowy Owl was a little envious. He'd often thought how exciting it would be to travel higher than he'd ever dared to fly before inside one of those human-made birds. But he didn't really like getting too close to the humans. He gazed at the cockatoo, deep in his thoughts. *This strange-looking bird has a lot of courage. She's travelled a very long way, and all on her own too. I wonder what happened to her partner Henry?* He thought, noticing Cracker scratching at the yellow thing on the top of her head.

'Well it's bonza that I should have met you like this Snowy, coz Barn Owl wanted me to find you. You look a bit like him, although he had a brownish appearance, like he hadn't washed for a while. And he had a funny kind of disc-shaped face. Is there somewhere we could go to talk that isn't so cold? I can hardly feel my beak.'

The Owl felt sorry for Cracker. She wasn't properly dressed for the cold winter weather of North Carolina. 'Follow me. I know where there is a cave in the forest. It's quite sheltered there.'

The Owl flew off and Cracker followed close by. 'Hey don't ya think you should fly a bit higher over this highway? I don't want to connect with one of those boxes the humans move around in,' Cracker screeched.

Snowy glided in and out of the traffic with great ease, but he climbed a bit higher to keep his new friend happy. He noticed she was struggling to keep up with his advanced flying technique.

Soon they were in a thickly forested part of the Blue Ridge Mountains. They wove in and out between the tree trunks and along dirt tracks. The Owl flew high up again over the treetops and swooped down into a ravine. He stopped by a huge cave built into the side of the mountain and went inside. 'It'll be sheltered from the icy wind here.' The Owl watched as Cracker landed beside him and began breathing on her claws to try and warm them up. She shook them a few times. Snowy thought she was a very strange creature indeed and wondered if she had a hearing problem the way she chose to screech so loudly.

'So what brings you to this part of the world?' Snowy asked.

'I already said. The big man-made bird.'

The Owl sighed. 'I know that. What I meant was, why have you come here?'

'So why didn't ya say that's what ya meant? Well, to teach the leader of your Fur and Feathers Party to speak English of course. Barn Owl said you would know who was the best creature to lead the Party.'

Snowy Owl suddenly remembered the conversation he'd had with the red kangaroo. He had been so busy hunting for food he had completely forgotten about it.

The Owl noticed the odd looking bird had suddenly stopped screeching. She'd become pre-occupied for a minute, scratching at the snow and putting some of it in her mouth. He was relieved to get a break from the loud noise she made, but it wasn't for long.

'This strange white stuff on the ground everywhere here sure is cold. I like the way it turns to water in ya mouth. I'm thirsty after all the travelling. My friend Pup could have done with some of this when I found her on the road that boiling hot day. She was a mess, poor little dog. I wonder where she is now?'

'She lives in that Southern land where you came from?'

'She did. But she's somewhere here now. But I've got no chance of finding her. If she'd left me a proper address. This is a big place. Anyway no point blubbering over lost berries is there Snow? I hope you don't mind me calling you that, but we Aussies like to abbreviate everyone's name. It's what we do.'

'Would you like me to call you Crack then?'

Cracker cringed. 'No, Cracker will be fine. Look Snow, can you please forget that I mentioned I would be teaching any creature to speak English. I will be in serious trouble for telling you that. It's meant to be a secret.'

'Your secret is safe with me, Cracker. I am not one prone to gossiping - but I would like to hear more about this political Party. Red Kangaroo told me they were doing very well in Australia, and even humans were voting for them.'

'Once we started the Fur and Feathers Party it just took off. I don't mean to brag, but I chose the name,' Cracker said fluffing up her feathers with pride.

Snowy Owl thought Cracker was a little plumped up by her own importance, but he was interested to learn about the political Party.

'You see, when we started speaking to the humans in their own language, telling them how upset we were about what they were doing to our natural home, they started seeing our point of view and voting for us. We've been able to create rules to stop them from polluting the lakes, rivers and oceans with their smelly poisonous things, and other stuff that never goes away. And we've got labels now for foods altered by humans. Of course, we're hoping they'll go back to real food eventually. And that would mean the humans would not be able to use so many poisonous substances on the plants that have been killing the bees. If those little buzzing things disappear, we're stuffed. Everything is getting so hot outside, or in your case, cold. There has been some progress but it's taking longer than we had hoped.'

Snowy Owl was very impressed. 'Well this is most fortuitous that we should have met like this.'

Cracker had no idea what *fortuitous* meant. But she assumed 'a stroke of luck'. She thought the Owl was showing off a bit using big words. 'They love to think they are so much cleverer than the rest of us birds,' she thought.

'I had a conversation with a puma a while back,' the Owl continued. 'He crept up behind me one day, giving me a terrible fright. I thought he was going to eat me but, just as I was about to fly off he said, "Can I talk with you for a minute?" '

'Strewth! Never met one of those,' Cracker said, all ears.

'I must have looked terrified,' the Owl continued. 'Because the puma then said "Relax, I'm not going to eat you. Don't like owls much. Your feathers stick in my throat." '

'That's funny,' Cracker said, enjoying chatting with the Owl.

Snowy Owl went on. 'Then the puma told me that he wanted to talk to me about the prey he'd been eating. "They've all tasted horrible, like some nasty substance the humans have made, has gotten onto them. Made me feel sick. And the road kills. I've lost most of my family that way." I felt sorry for the puma. Even though I had seen pumas eating sheep and cattle, I didn't like the way they were being treated. I had noticed how hostile some farmers had been towards these big cats, and they were being hunted and trapped so much I wondered how long it would be before they were gone,' the Owl told Cracker.

'So what does a puma look like? I should know, in case I run into one.'

'Oh they're a magnificent animal, Cracker. They have a cat-like face, a slate-grey coat and an impressive long tail. That puma wasn't the only animal that had visited me with a problem,' the Owl went on. 'I also had a mountain elk tell me how afraid it was to roam the forests because so many of its family had been hunted and killed by humans for food. There had been a time in the early nineteen-hundreds when they were almost hunted to extinction.'

'I've never seen one of those creatures either,' Cracker said, fascinated by what this brilliant white bird was telling her.

The Owl continued, 'Elks have beautiful antlers. I was glad to hear they were still around. But I wonder for how long. If we are serious about this Party, Cracker, I'll need to write a letter to the State Office and ask them about the rules for ballot access. Third parties cannot automatically stand in North America. Each state has different rules, and you have to get a certain number of signatures from the voting public. It can run into more than a hundred-thousand signatures for some states.'

'Fair crack of the gum tree branch! That doesn't seem very fair.'

Snowy Owl wanted to laugh at Cracker's strange way of speaking. 'It's how it is, Cracker. I will draft something on a leaf and give it to the pigeon post to deliver to the local State Office.'

'Well do you have any ideas about who should be the leader of your Party then?' Cracker asked.

Even though he wasn't keen on the idea, Snowy Owl said: 'I think we should find a red wolf. They are courageous and powerful. A wolf would command respect.'

'Stone the flamin' crows! They eat birds don't they?' Cracker asked with a tremble in her voice.

26

Howl Gets an Offer

HOWL THOUGHT ABOUT the conversation he'd had with his father. He hated being thought of as weak and passionless. Wolves are not like this. They are fearless creatures with a strong drive.

The wolf needed to do something that would get him motivated and keep him busy so he could forget his broken heart. But he knew that being an actor was not for him.

One day when he was out searching for food, he came upon Snowy Owl's nest. He noticed the Owl's mate was sitting on her eggs. Howl thought she'd make a good dinner for his father, who was rather fond of owl meat.

He knew that the nesting owl's first instinct would be to stay and protect her eggs. She was an easy target.

What he didn't know was that her mate, Snowy Owl, was guarding the nest from a low branch close by. Howl hadn't seen him. The Owl had kept very still, and his brilliant white body was almost invisible surrounded by the white sheets of snow. The wolf began creeping slowly towards the nest but, just as he was about to pounce, Snowy Owl glided low over his head, clipping him on the ears with his sharp claws.

Howl got such a fright he flattened himself into the snow and turned to see what had swooped at him.

'Don't even think about it,' Snowy Owl hooted as he swooped aggressively over the red wolf again. He was so close to his head that Howl could feel his hot breath contrasting against the cold air. The Wolf began to walk away, keeping an eye on the Owl. Those sharp claws could do a lot of damage, and he didn't want to make the Owl any madder than he already was.

'Wait,' Snowy Owl called after him.

Howl thought this was an odd thing for an owl to say when a wolf had come so close to killing his wife. Maybe it was a trick.

He kept on walking. Snowy Owl called after him again. 'I need to talk to you about something you might be interested in doing for the birds and animals.'

Howl wondered what he could possibly be talking about, and stopped to hear what the Owl had to say.

'It's about a new political Party called the Fur and Feathers Party. It's apparently doing well in Australia. We'd like to start one over here.'

The red wolf began to wonder if this owl needed serious birdological help. It was such a strange thing to say, given the circumstances of their meeting.

'I know this must sound odd,' the Owl continued, 'but I recently met an Australian yellow-crested cockatoo at the airport. She had flown here to try and find a suitable leader for the U.S. branch of this Party.'

'I don't know what you are talking about,' Howl said, beginning to feel sorry for the Owl. 'I apologise for trying to kill your mate. Although my father is rather partial to them, owls are not my first choice on the menu. Food has been a bit scarce lately and my father is getting old and finds hunting rather tiring. I won't bother you again. Maybe I can find a deer or a wild boar. That should keep us going for a while.'

Howl was keen to get away from the Owl. He thought he was as nutty as a walnut. He started to walk off again but Snowy Owl swooped down close to his head, startling him.

'You would be the perfect leader of this Party. You're strong and robust and people would listen to you,' the Owl persisted.

'Can we back track a bit here? You met up with some weird bird that, as far as I am aware, doesn't even live in this country, and it thinks I should run some crazy political Party?'

'Well actually, it was a red kangaroo that thought you'd make a good leader of the Party, but the cockatoo bird can teach you to speak English.'

Howl was convinced now that Snowy Owl was a needle short of a pinecone. He raced away on his powerful legs. Snowy Owl flew low, following him for a while, until the wolf could no longer see him.

~

Cracker thought about her meeting with Snowy Owl. She wondered how she was going to find a suitable red wolf to head up the Fur and Feathers Party. She'd never met a red wolf before. But when she was little, her mother had told her a story about a wolf, and a character called "Little Red Riding Hood". From what she remembered of the story, the wolf had very big eyes and ears, and vicious teeth and liked eating people.

'If a wolf was capable of eating people, it could easily polish off a yellow-crested cockatoo as a mid-morning snack. *Should they consider a less threatening leader for their Party?* Cracker wondered.

Cracker was shivering from the cold, and decided to look for a suitable hollow in a tree and make a warm nest for herself.

The trees were not like the eucalypts back in Australia. She flew for quite a distance before finally spotting an oak tree that had a large hole in its very wide trunk.

She pecked around on the ground for some useful foliage to build her nest. Cracker was so busy looking for the right materials that she didn't notice a huge, red, furry face just inches away from hers.

Cracker's feathers shot up vertically when she realized she was close enough for the huge creature to open his fearsome mouth and swallow her whole.

'I like your outfit,' Cracker said nervously, thinking that flattery might be her best option. 'It's a very nice shade of brown. Or would you call that burnt orange?'

Cracker was relieved when the large animal took a step backwards.

'I'm Cracker,' she said holding out a trembling claw.

'Howl's the name. I must say I've lived in this forest all my life and never seen or heard anything like you before.'

'Well that's because I normally live in Australia.'

'I don't suppose you are a member of a political Party run by birds and animals?' Howl asked. Could that crazy Owl really have been telling the truth?

Cracker was beginning to relax. This animal didn't seem too focused on eating her. 'Yeah. As a matter of fact, I am the

Spokesbird for the Fur and Feathers Party of Australia. It's been suggested that a red wolf would be the best leader for the Party. I've been asked to find one that might be interested, and to help the Fur and Feathers Party get on the ballot sheet in the U.S. You wouldn't happen to be a red wolf by any chance would ya?'

'Yes I am. But this is too weird! I recently met up with a Snowy Owl who told me about this. I thought he was an oak tree short of a forest.'

Cracker forgot how nervous she was, and laughed with a loud screech at the wolf's turn of phrase. She thought what he'd said was so funny, she shook from side to side, and it caused some of her white feathers to become airborne. *This wolf has a good sense of humour,* she thought. There was nothing the bird liked more than a loud throaty chuckle.

'You're one hell of a funny bugger. I didn't know red wolves had such a good sense of humour. Well waddayasay, Howl? Will you help us get this political Party off the ground in the U.S.? The Fur and Feathers Party needs a powerful animal like you to be in charge. Of course you'll need to be able to speak English. But that's why I am here. I've already taught a red kangaroo, and she's giving Party political broadcasts in Australia, and being interviewed by the media. She's become a star.'

Howl was thoughtful and said nothing for a moment. 'Well, I've never really been that interested in being in the limelight. But I have been hoping to find something I could get my teeth into.'

Cracker hoped it wouldn't be her. *Just because he had a funny turn of phrase, may not mean that this wolf would pass on trying out a little cockatoo meat*, she thought. But if he were focused on leading their political Party, he'd probably be too busy to be thinking about some new kind of delicacy to offer his dad. *I'm probably off the table so to speak*, she thought, chuckling quietly again at her choice of words.

'To be honest, I've never considered running for government before because humans run all the political parties,' Howl went on. 'But I would welcome the opportunity to talk about what needs to change to keep us animals healthy and happy. Humans have been hunting so many of the creatures that we depend on for our food. It's becoming harder and harder to survive.'

'You're right there, mate,' Cracker said.

'And the humans have done so much damage to our natural home that the summers have become unbearably hot, and blizzards in the winter get more severe every year. We're getting tornados in places where they'd never been before,' Howl said.

'Well I'm glad I bumped into you, Cracker. But you should know that I am terrible with languages.'

'We'll have it cracked in no time,' Cracker said, thinking she had used this line before. But it was a good one and Howl wouldn't have heard it.

'My father will be pleased about this new opportunity,' Howl told Cracker. 'He's been pestering me to do something useful with my life. I cannot wait to get started.'

~

For several weeks Cracker sat on a log in a thick-forested area, giving English lessons to Howl. She was perched on his head. He didn't seem that happy about it. 'Polly wants a cracker,' the bird said waiting for the Wolf's reply.

'Polly wants a cracker,' Howl repeated awkwardly. 'Would you mind getting off my head? Your sharp claws are hurting my skin, and it's rather unpleasant.' Cracker was pleased at how quickly Howl was learning English. She was also delighted that he had shown no interest in eating her.

They worked together for several weeks and, before long, Howl was speaking English almost as well as his cocky teacher.

~

Winter was turning to a lush Appalachian spring when Cracker re-connected with Howl. The Wolf had begun giving talks at new candidate meetings, and impressing everyone with his command of the English language.

'So, where will you be perching yourself next?' Cracker asked.

'I'm flying all over the place. Being the Party leader my feet are hardly touching the ground.'

'I didn't know you could fly? Where are your wings?'

'I can't fly like you. I go on planes.'

'Oh, the man-made bird. It didn't move its wings much when I was in its belly. Might have bad arthritis. I thought we would never get to America,' Cracker reminisced. She ran her eyes over Howl's lean muscular body, his beautiful thick reddish brown fur coat and his strong jaw line. *He would be quite a catch for some lucky she-wolf*, she thought.

'I'm surprised a handsome beast like you hasn't got a mate?' Cracker said.

Howl was sad and began furiously digging a hole. Cracker decided not to press this. It appeared the Wolf was using a distracting mechanism. *I wonder what happened to him?* the Cockatoo thought. *Maybe his mate went missing as well. Anyway it's not my business.* Cracker pecked at her claw. It was something she did when Henry was on her mind.

27

Howl on the Campaign Trail

HOWL SAT ON THE AEROPLANE seat next to a smart businessman who was working at his laptop computer.

The Wolf put down the book he was reading. He noticed the businessman was trying to read the title. 'It's "The Government of Nature" by Barn Owl,' Howl said. He thought the man was trying not to laugh and the Wolf felt a bit offended. *Humans always think they have the answers for everything,* he thought.

'Special meal for Howl,' the flight attendant said, passing him a meaty bone. The Wolf gnawed at the bone. He was aware that the businessman was still staring at him. He had to say something. 'I'm representing the Fur and Feathers Party of America. We're running for government. We have to get ballot access in order to be able to stand at all. We're going to need a lot of signatures in each state.'

'Ah .... might I ask how you learned to speak such good English?'

'I can't say, I'm afraid.' Howl began to feel hot with anxiety.

'I'll bet the U.S. government will be trying to find out that secret. Especially if your Party takes off,' the businessman continued. He was now busting for this Wolf to tell him more.

Howl was quiet. *Hope I haven't said too much,* he thought.

~

People had gathered to listen to Howl give a political address in a public park. He was standing on a garden seat. The red Wolf gazed with delight at his audience. He could see Snowy Owl, Wolverine and Bald Eagle busily gathering signatures from the people.

Wolverine was wearing a large placard that read "Fur and Feathers for Government – vote for the Party of nature."

Howl was thrilled at how eager most of the people seemed to be to sign for his Party's ballot access.

'If you could sign here,' Snowy Owl said, holding a large leaf under the nose of a middle-aged woman.

'I think you're doing a wonderful job and I hope the Fur and Feathers Party gets to stand for government,' the woman said.

Howl noticed a young woman, dressed smartly in a black and white outfit, approaching Bald Eagle. 'You speak such good English. You've got my vote. Where do I sign?' she asked.

Howl delivered his carefully prepared speech to the enthusiastic crowd.

'The Fur and Feathers Party will copy the government of nature. When you support natural law by respecting the planet, natural law supports you!'

People cheered and clapped and, for once in his life, Howl felt important. Finally there was something he could be passionate about. He was no longer the loser his pack had told him he was. If they could see him now, they would be proud.

When the counting of signatures was complete, Howl was delighted to discover that Snowy Owl, Wolverine and Bald Eagle had gathered enough for ballot access for New York State.

'That's great work but we're not going to stop here,' Howl said. 'We have a lot of signatures to gather right across America if we have any chance of being able to stand in the election.'

~

A few days later, Howl sat nervously next to a television presenter. He had never been on television before. He was so full of anxiety his fur was getting sweaty, and the heat of the studio lights made him look like he'd just climbed out of a river. His eyes were irritated by the thick brown pancake makeup they had plastered all over his face.

'Well I'm sure you're as surprised as everyone else at the following your Party has gained here?' a young male human interviewer asked the Wolf.

'Yes I certainly am. But people have been wanting a Party like ours that cares for the Earth.'

'I want to ask you something, Howl. Would you teach my cat to speak English? She's a Persian and I know she has a lot she wants to tell me.'

'Oh, I'm afraid I am not able to train another animal.'

'So how did you learn to speak so well?'

'Can't say. It's a secret.'

Howl could feel his skin becoming prickly with nerves as the interviewer leaned towards him with further probing questions. The Wolf could have bitten his tongue off the minute he mentioned the word 'secret'. Interviewers would not let up now until they discovered what this secret was. It was like waving a scone slathered in strawberry jam under the nose of a European wasp, and expecting it to fly away in a disinterested manner.

Everywhere Howl went he was asked how the birds and animals could suddenly speak such perfect English. He felt under a lot of pressure not to give anything away. The media were unrelenting in their quest to get to the bottom of the Fur and Feathers Party secret.

Howl spoke at several media conferences where they hounded him for answers. His standard response had become 'No comment,' or 'Can't say, I'm afraid' or 'I'll get back to you on that one.'

Fortunately, Snowy Owl had insisted that he go to media training. It had taught him a lot about how to handle the pushy reporters and television journalists.

But clever interviewers were constantly trying to trip him up by saying things like: 'The yellow-crested cockatoo has already revealed to us that *she* was the one who had taught the birds and animals to speak English.'

Howl had almost been sucked into saying 'Well she wasn't supposed to tell you.' But he stopped himself just in time.

His schedule was punishing and Howl was getting very tired, but he felt satisfied that, at last, he was doing something truly useful with his life that didn't involve killing food for his family.

Howl's father was not too well, and he had to take some time off from his campaigning to visit the old wolf in the forest.

'I'm so proud of you son,' his father had said, tucking into the wild boar carcass that Howl had brought him. 'I had a feeling you would end up making a real name for yourself. Now you've got to make sure that this Party wins the election. The present government is doing nothing to protect our wilderness areas. If this doesn't stop, we'll be forced to move even further into territories where we don't normally live. I personally hate Iowa. It's covered in corn crops and pigs,' his father said. 'It's no place for a wolf. Only yesterday I heard about a mountain lion and a black bear that had been forced to move there.'

'Don't worry, Dad. All these concerns are in my campaign portfolio.'

'I don't suppose you've met any pretty young she-wolves while on the campaign trail son?'

Howl had hoped his father would not bring up the topic of his love life. It was still a sensitive issue for him.

'Been too busy to think about those kind of things,' he said, wishing the old wolf would drop the subject.

'Well I'd hate to see you become a workaholic, son. Don't rule out the possibility of falling in love again. Now that you're becoming such a famous wolf, you never know what gorgeous hound might come into your life when you least expect it.'

But since Amber had dumped him, Howl had become afraid of opening up his heart again. He'd told himself that he was unlucky in love, and relationships were for other wolves. He'd decided he wanted to leave the opposite sex well alone. It was safer that way.

But what Howl didn't realize was that he couldn't control all the events that were destined to happen in his life. Nature often had other ideas.

28

Hank's Shock Discovery

HANK HAD NOT BEEN fully comfortable around the Vice President. He'd been amazed that their Party had managed to get into government; given how often Elroy appeared to be in disagreement with the President on major policies. But it seemed the voting public liked Jim enough, and had sufficient confidence in him to choose their Party.

It wasn't just the way Elroy often argued with Jim about policy issues, there was something else about this man that made Hank feel ill-at-ease. So, when Elroy asked Hank to fix the heating at Number One Observatory Circle, he thought this would be a good opportunity to observe the Vice President in his place of residence. Maybe he would see a better side of him.

It was snowing heavily and Hank tried not to slip on patches of black ice that were on the path. He stopped for a moment to gaze at the stately white nineteenth century house. Hank liked its Queen Ann style of architecture. He was aware the house was completed in 1893 and he loved its round turret rooms; its dark blue roof; green shutters and the way the verandas wrapped around the ground floor. He thought it looked stunning surrounded by the blanket of deep white snow. He'd done his research on the house and discovered that it was originally intended for the superintendent of the USNO. But, in 1923, the Chief of Naval Operations had loved the house so much he decided to remove the man so he could live there.

Hank thought this three storey brick house, with all its comfortable furnishings and beautiful art, would be a lovely place to live. More like a real home. He found living in the White House a little too formal for his liking. Hank was envious of Elroy being able to live for a while in such a magnificent residence.

The snow was coming down more heavily, but gazing at the front of the house made Hank think about all the other Vice Presidents and their families who had lived there since it had been named as their official residence in 1974.

He was so deep in his thoughts he didn't notice that Elroy was watching him. He was standing under the porch at the main entrance. His arms were tightly folded around a dark blue cashmere sweater, as if he was trying to stop the cold air from getting to him. He had dark grey slacks and tartan slippers outside thick grey woollen socks.

'It's a beautiful building,' Hank called out to Elroy, trying to shed some light on why he had been standing like a snow-covered statue staring at the house.

'Well you'd better come inside. It's damn cold out there,' Elroy said. The two men went through a covered porch and into the main reception area. 'Follow me. I'll show you around,' Elroy said.

'Oh no need, Elroy. I won't stay long.'

'We'll go into the sitting room. Nice comfortable seating in there. It's actually commonly known as the "library room".'

'Yes I'm aware of that.' Hank thought it was rather strange that Elroy would assume he knew nothing about the inside of the Vice President's residence. It was, after all, his job to familiarize himself with as much as he could.

Hank followed Elroy through a number of rooms connected by doors, each room having a fireplace, and many with impressive chandeliers, beautiful works of art and furniture that suited the Queen Anne style of architecture of the building.

As he passed through the rooms, Hank thought the fifty volunteers who were in charge of the Christmas decorations had rather overdone them: gold and silver baubles, Santa Claus, snowmen, and red and green glitter were wrapped around the railing of a staircase. They covered the mantles over the fireplaces. They were trailed over window frames. They were plastered over the Christmas tree that greeted important visitors on their arrival. There were so many colourful decorations on the tree, it was almost impossible to see a pine needle. *At least they had decided to leave the chandeliers alone,* Hank thought.

The Chief of Staff loved the large windows that allowed plenty of light to flood in, and enabled visiting dignitaries a pleasant outlook over the lovely manicured gardens surrounding the building.

Elroy led Hank into the library room. It was a cosy room with four comfortable leather lounges surrounding an oak coffee table. A tall crystal vase holding a single stem of orchids stood exactly in the centre of the table. The room was filled with books. It was possible to find biographies of famous political figures, essays on Democracy and the U.S. Constitution, books on U.S. Law and the history of the United States. There were even magazines on native flora and fauna. The room had everything to keep anyone who chose to be in there on their own for a while, fully occupied.

'Have a seat, Hank,' Elroy said, reaching for a decanter on the coffee table. It stood on a silver tray next to a couple of crystal glasses.

'Bourbon?' Elroy asked, half-filling one of the glasses and passing it to Hank.

'Oh just water, thanks.'

'Come on Hank, surely you'd like something a bit stronger than that?'

'I'm not a big drinker, Elroy. The water will be fine.'

Elroy raised his eyebrows and filled the second glass from a bottle of water on the table. He handed the glass to Hank, and flopped opposite him onto a beige-coloured lounge.

'How are you settling in?' Hank asked, having a sip of water.

Elroy had a large gulp of Bourbon from the glass he'd intended for the Chief of Staff. 'Oh it's been an adjustment from our house of course. I don't mind the place. It seems a lot more homely than the White House, but Sarah finds it a bit too formal. And she's suffering from the heating. Probably pre-menopausal,' Elroy scoffed.

Hank thought he was being way too personal about his wife.

'Eighty degrees does seem a tad on the warm side – even for me, and I normally like the heat,' Elroy said.

'Well I'll talk to our building maintenance man, but I'm not sure we'll be able to change the settings. There are some things, as you know Elroy, that cannot be changed in these buildings. I tried to take one of the lamps from the Lincoln room when I first arrived at the White House, and I was told nothing in that room, or the yellow room, could be touched.'

'Well, here's to your good health Hank,' Elroy said, raising his glass of Bourbon before taking another huge gulp.

'Yes cheers,' Hank said, drinking more water.

Hank noticed Elroy checking his watch. He seemed a little on edge. 'Sarah said she would be home for lunch. But it's now thirty minutes past three. Fairly typical of her I have to say.'

'Is Sarah still managing to do her job at the advertising agency?' Hank asked.

'She's finding it a bit much. Before we moved here she thought she could maintain her long hours at work. Sarah was unaware that, as the Second Lady, she might be expected to perform some official duties associated with my office. She's resented that a bit. But the fact that she hasn't turned up for lunch doesn't really surprise me. Sarah is always finding reasons to have "working lunches".' Elroy leaned towards Hank. He put his hand to cover his mouth as if he was about to share a secret and didn't want anyone else to hear it. 'Meetings with Max her lover no doubt.'

Hank was very uncomfortable. He didn't want to know what Elroy's wife might be up to, and it didn't feel appropriate that the Vice President was sharing so much personal information with him. But Elroy did not stop there: 'I wanted children you know Hank, but Sarah didn't want them. She doesn't seem to think I'd make much of a father. But really, she's the selfish one. She is used to doing exactly what she pleases. I never should have married the woman. Got pressured into it. You know how it is with women Hank? I'm choosing to ignore her shenanigans. I'd have an affair myself, but it wouldn't be a good look, now I'm the Vice President.'

Hank was keen to finish his water and leave. He was not enjoying the conversation. He thought Elroy was being very disrespectful, not just of his wife, but of women in general. He had always been a loyal and respectful husband and had gotten along well with his wife.

'You never mention your ex Hank? Did you divorce her because she was playing around?'

The Chief of Staff was shocked by this comment. 'Certainly not! It was a mutual decision that we should separate. Brought on by my political aspirations that Annie did not share. Once I became more involved in politics it began to cause her a lot of stress. We decided to go our separate ways, before we ended up enemies. It was the right decision. We are still very good friends.' Hank became aware that Elroy was now staring hard at him. He seemed to be deep in thought.

'It's strange isn't it Hank that you and I don't have children. Even the President doesn't have them. Must be really bothering our voting public that we are not, 'normal family men'.'

Hank was annoyed. Elroy knew nothing of his private life and that was how Hank wanted it. But to suggest that he wasn't a family man, when the Vice President knew so little about his personal life, got right up the Chief of Staff's nose.

'Actually I have two children, Elroy.'

'Oh, I didn't know. But you've never mentioned them before?'

'I like to keep my private life private. As much as I can in public office, Elroy.'

'But your children are not living at the White House?'

'Robert is thirty-one and lives in Seattle. He has a good job in IT and Muriel lives in London with her English husband. They're planning to start a 'normal' family soon.'

Elroy looked a bit uncomfortable and began to fiddle with a piece of cotton he discovered hanging on his slippers. 'Another glass of water, Hank?'

Hank got up. 'No I'd better get going. The President has some things he wants me to do before the day ends.'

'Can I possibly use one of the rest rooms?'

'Sure. You'll need to go through that door and' – Hank cut him off – 'Yes I know where to go Elroy, thanks.' Hank headed to the bathroom feeling irritated.

The water had gone right through him. He relieved himself and, after washing his hands, he noticed the towel rail was minus a hand towel. He opened a cupboard. It had a deep interior. Inside at the front were some lavender, and pink and green-coloured soaps neatly stacked, plus various bottles of scented body wash. Behind the bottles he could see some small blue folded towels piled high.

He went to grab one and knocked something over that was hidden from view at the back of the cupboard behind the pile of towels. He was shocked when he saw what it was, and that he had not noticed it was missing. It was the Christmas decoration, made out of clay to look exactly like Pup, that the President had asked Hank to get.

Although Hank had thought at the time that this Australian dog decoration did not really belong on a tree with a theme of Native American animals, he was obliged to do what the President had asked of him. He'd found a person who could make such a decoration, and the President had put it on the top of the tree himself. Hank suddenly felt his stomach and throat tighten with a mix of shock, anger and nerves. How dare Elroy touch something that was so important to the President, and try to hide it like this. 'He has no right,' the Chief of Staff muttered angrily to himself. He was relieved that Jim had not noticed the ornament was missing. But then again, the President was always so pre-occupied with a million things on his mind; he had obviously not been looking closely at the tree.

Hank took the clay dog out of the cupboard. He was going to have this out with Elroy. He stormed back into the library room. Elroy was lounging comfortably with another large glass of Bourbon. His relaxed mood instantly changed, and his face turned pale when he saw Hank's expression and what he was holding.

'I found this in the bathroom cupboard, Elroy when I was looking for a towel.' Hank was trying to contain his anger.

'Well I'll be darned. I have no idea what it would be doing there. Wasn't it on the top of the White House Christmas tree?' Elroy asked, feigning shock and surprise. 'Sarah must have removed it. She doesn't like dogs you know. She probably thought it was inappropriate for a theme of Native American animals. I'll definitely be having a few words with her, when she comes home.'

Hank knew Elroy was lying. He'd seen how happy Sarah was when she'd first met Pup. She'd patted the little dog most enthusiastically. And when Elroy had reprimanded her for encouraging Pup to jump all over her, she'd said 'Oh Elroy, can't we get an adorable little dog like this too?' But Hank decided it might be best to allow this lie. He didn't want to make a real enemy of Elroy, and he certainly was not going to be saying anything to the President about this. Jim had enough to worry about having a Vice President who didn't always see eye-to-eye with him on policies. He didn't need to be filled with further concerns about the man who worked so closely with him.

'All right, Elroy. If you could let Sarah know that this must never happen again. I will put the ornament back on the tree before the President notices it has gone missing. He would be very upset to discover this.'

'Well, as you know Hank, many of us are not happy about that little yapper being in the White House. I know you share my view.'

'I may not be entirely thrilled about the little dog being there Elroy, but I would never dream of removing something that the President had asked to be there.' Hank turned towards the door.

'Well thank you for coming over. I'll show you out,' Elroy said in an ingratiating tone.

'I can see myself out thank you Elroy. I will speak to the maintenance man about the heating.'

'Oh Hank, best not to mention this to Sarah when you see her. I will speak to her privately about this. And don't you worry. She will be severely reprimanded for what she did,' Elroy added, doing his best to look upset and annoyed about the discovery.

'Of course,' Hank said. He knew that Elroy would be worried and ask Sarah about it. She would be furious that she had been blamed for something Elroy had done. But Hank had been in the job long enough to know that some things were best left unsaid – especially where the President was concerned.

Hank put the dog ornament inside his coat, and left the Vice President staring after him with a look that seemed to Hank to be one of guilt more than anything else. He planned to return the dog decoration to its rightful place on top of the White House Christmas tree at the first possible opportunity. Perhaps he would say it had fallen off, and he had taken it away to clean it. It annoyed Hank that now he was the one that had to resort to telling lies. He remembered what happened when he had lied to the President about Pup when they were in Australia. That had been a close call, and he didn't want another one.

As Hank walked carefully along the slippery pathway leading back to the White House, he wondered what had motivated Elroy to do this. Was he hoping the President would find out and Elroy would have an opportunity to shift the blame to Hank? Maybe he wanted to cause trouble for the Chief of Staff. Perhaps he was annoyed that Hank had not been able to arrange for the little terrier to be removed from the building. Then he thought about the top level of security. There were always people guarding the various rooms, and cameras everywhere. Elroy must have spun a story to someone about what he was doing, and no one dared to question this because he was the Vice President.

Hank would never know Elroy's reasons, or how he had got away with it, but he was going to keep this to himself. It would only make things worse to begin asking too many questions. If the media got to hear about it, all hell would break loose. But one thing he did now know – the Vice President could not be trusted.

29

A Meeting with Congress

PUP LAY AT THE President's feet in the Oval Office. She was under his antique cherry wood desk in the west wing of the White House. The President was still in his pyjamas. He was going over his schedule for the day. Pup appreciated the way he let her stay with him as he worked. She felt very much loved.

She had never seen such a funny shaped room. There were so many doors. She knew the one at the northeast corner led to Hank's office, and the one in the west corner led to her master's private study and dining room.

Pup wondered why he needed a fireplace in the room. The whole house seemed to be at a comfortable temperature whatever the weather was outside.

The little dog's favourite place to sit was near the east door because it opened out onto the fragrant Rose Garden. Pup could inhale the delicious aroma of the flowers while she chewed on her bone.

She felt very important that her master had included her in his discussion about the decoration of the room. She'd heard him tell Hank, 'I don't like the gold drapes. Can you organise to change them please? Vermillion would be my choice. What do you think Congress?'

Hank had been privately annoyed that the President was consulting his dog over the room decorations. *'Is he going to be asking that little runt to marry him soon?'* he'd thought.

Pup had not been aware of Hank's annoyance at the time. She was happy with whatever her owner wanted and she'd barked her excited approval at his choice.

'So you agree with me Congress. I like to have red around me. It makes me feel full of energy. It seems right to have this shade in the Oval Office. It will keep me alert and focused while I work at my desk. And the drapes will work nicely with the mahogany desk. Thank you Congress. Red it is,' the President had told her.

Pup liked the large red and gold oval-shaped Persian carpet that took up most of the floor. It worked well with the curtains.

Around the walls were the special paintings the President had asked Hank to order for him. Pup remembered her master telling Hank, 'I want the picture of "Dachshunds" by David Hockney. If you can arrange that for me please.'

'Certainly Jim, but ah, wouldn't a picture of people be more appropriate? We seem to be getting rather a lot of paintings featuring dogs,' Hank had said at the time.

'If I'd wanted a picture of people I would have asked for it Hank. Now please go and source the David Hockney painting.'

'As you wish, Jim,' Pup had heard the Chief of Staff say. She thought it was touching that her master had insisted on having this animal picture. She felt he had done this so she would feel at home.

When the painting first arrived the President had told her, 'The dogs are called Stanley and Boodgie.' Pup thought they were good names.

~

The President looked up from his iPad at his Chief of Staff. Pup thought Hank looked annoyed, and wondered if it was because her master was sitting at his desk in his pyjamas and dressing gown. 'I've decided not to meet my advisors in the Cabinet Room today Hank. Can you arrange for them to come to the Oval Office now please. We have some important things to discuss.'

'Certainly Jim,' Hank said. 'Will you be getting dressed for the meeting, sir?'

'No Hank. They will just have to put up with my robe. Had a bad night's sleep and I want to get this meeting out of the way early.'

'Was the little dog keeping you awake again Jim?'

Pup was annoyed. She hated the way Hank always tried to imply that she should not be living in this big white house.

'Just tell the advisors I am ready for them now, Hank.'

The Chief of Staff ushered in the three men. They were all dressed in conservative dark blue suits with brilliant white shirts and ties of different-coloured stripes.

Pup noticed Elroy also giving her master a disapproving look at what he was wearing. She was glad he didn't dress just to please them. She went up to greet the men but the Vice President pushed her away.

'Come here, Congress, and show these nice men how you can beg for doggy snacks,' the President said. He held one far enough away that she had to do her tricks before he would allow her to take the biscuit. She stood on one leg, then rolled over and balanced on her head. The biscuit was thrown into the air and Pup did a huge leap and caught it, gobbling it up in a couple of seconds.

The little dog caught sight of Elroy's look as he raised his eyes to the ceiling. There was nothing about this man she liked. The dark aura that surrounded him reminded her of the man who came to take David's things. Although Pup had no knowledge of the ornament being removed from the Christmas tree, she also did not take to Elroy. There was something about the way he looked and acted that made her feel nervous. The other two men seemed a lot nicer. They were smiling and enjoying her biscuit-catching performance.

The men sat around the mahogany table and the meeting began. 'Whatever we might think of them Mr President, the opinion polls are showing that the Fur and Feathers Party is gaining ground,' the Chief Strategist said.

Pup was thrilled to hear this. It made her think of Cracker. She wondered if she had got her letter, and if she would ever see her cockatoo friend again.

The President didn't appear to be listening to his advisor. He was busy watching Pup finishing off a biscuit. She tried not to get crumbs on the carpet. She sensed he was concerned about that.

Elroy shifted around uncomfortably in his seat. Pup wondered if he had ants in his pants that were biting him.

'The Fur and Feathers Party now have ballot access in every state except Florida,' the Vice President said. 'If they get Florida they could win. The polls are showing they have the support of the majority of the voting public.'

Pup continued standing on her hind legs to accept the biscuits her master was offering her. He was totally focused on her. She had never felt so important and loved.

'The animals and birds learning to speak English so well took us all by surprise, sir,' the Chief Strategist told the President. 'If they can achieve this, they can achieve anything, including getting into the White House.'

Pup wondered why all the birds and animals would want to come and live in her big white house. But she remembered how many rooms the building had. She noticed the men becoming frustrated that her owner was not really listening to them. Suddenly the President stopped giving Pup biscuits as his Chief of Staff came into the room.

'This meeting is over gentlemen. Hank I need an urgent meeting with Congress,' he said, getting up and beckoning Pup to follow him. The little terrier was happy the meeting was over and ran enthusiastically after her master as he strode quickly out of the room.

The Chief of Staff called after him, 'I will organise it right away Jim.'

But the President didn't hear him. He was already in his private quarters.

~

That afternoon the members of Congress were all seated in the Capitol building on Capitol Hill, at the east end of the National Mall in Washington D.C. It was not far from Pup's lovely white house. They were wondering why this urgent session of Congress had been called so suddenly. Something important must be in the wind.

They waited and waited but there was no sign of the

President. Some of the members cleared their throats as if having a competition to see who could make the loudest noise.

One Congressman tapped his pencil in an irritated way on a lined notepad. A Congresswoman played with the combination lock on her briefcase. A man took his laptop out of its case, switching it on in the ready. But the President never arrived.

30

Howl's Heart Opens

THE PRESIDENT RELAXED in his favourite armchair with his large green health drink. Pup lay at his feet licking the drops of the drink he had spilt off the carpet of his private quarters. He gazed into her large brown eyes.

'Ya know, Congress, you could be very helpful to daddy if you could just learn to speak English.'

Pup put her head on one side. It was her way of saying, 'I understand you completely and I would do anything to please you. I adore you. You are my master, but can you call me Pup? I like that name.'

But the President didn't understand her gesture and pushed her away from him in a frustrated way. 'Oh what's the use of talking to you, Congress? You're just a dumb dog,' he said flopping back into his armchair in a resigned way.

Pup was shocked by his behaviour. All her old fears came back. Maybe he didn't want her anymore and was getting ready to abandon her. The President picked up the phone and dialled a number. 'I want an immediate meeting with Congress. Of course

I am talking about real people,' he shouted down the phone to his Chief of Staff. 'No, I am not changing the dog's name. It suits her and if you're creating so much confusion, perhaps you shouldn't be in this position.' He slammed the phone down.

Later that night the President watched Howl on television giving his Party platform speech to a huge audience.

Pup was transfixed to the screen. She was really taken with the handsome wolf; so much so that she had begun to drool on the carpet.

'Our government is the government of nature,' Howl said. 'There will be no more experiments on animals. No more fossil fuel emissions.'

'He's so gorgeous,' Pup barked. 'If I joined his Party perhaps one day we'd get to share a bowl of dog chow together.'

The President suddenly noticed Pup drooling all over the carpet and was annoyed. 'Look at the mess you've made! Go to your bed you naughty dog,' he shouted, shooing her out of the room.

Pup stared at him with her large soulful brown eyes. His tone had really hurt her feelings. 'What you don't know is that I can come and go as I please. I've dug a hole in the back garden and tomorrow I'm going to meet that handsome wolf and offer to help his Party. Maybe you will appreciate me more if I go missing for a while.'

But the President had no idea of what she was saying. Pup turned and walked out of the room, her head hung low.

That night, she lay on her pink satin cushion and thought about her friend Cracker. It was strange that she should form a bond with such an unusual creature. But there was something about Cracker's positive attitude to life that Pup liked very much. She prayed that she would see her friend Cracker again.

~

Howl stood at a podium in front of a large banner which read "The Fur and Feathers Party – Howl for President". The Wolf was nervous. But he was getting more used to doing these public speeches and the large audience of birds, animals and humans were very supportive of everything he said.

'You're no doubt wondering what a wolf is doing running for the Presidency. Normally, wolves are out howling at the moon or catching something for their dinner,' Howl said, glancing at the notes he had written on a pile of oak leaves.

The audience laughed at his turn of phrase.

'Well I'm not here because I have delusions of grandeur to be the next President of the United States. I'm also not here because I want to make pots of money so I can buy some cans of deluxe dog chow.' The audience roared with laughter.

'I am here because I am wild.'

'Yeah, we already know that,' a chipmunk whispered with a chuckle to a squirrel next to him.

'What I represent is the government of nature,' Howl continued, quickly checking his notes again. 'Because the North American birds and animals are wild about the way mankind is violating natural laws, and destroying the only home we have.'

A lynx in the audience fanned himself with a huge leaf. 'It's getting so warm I can't stand it. If only I could remove my fur coat,' he said.

A conservative-looking man in his fifties stood next to him. The man gave the lynx a strange look.

'You think you've got problems,' an elk told the lynx. 'I've been diagnosed with Chronic Wasting Disease. It's affected my brain. Some of my family members are avoiding me altogether. They think I have Mad Cow Disease,' the elk added.

'Those antlers must way a lot,' a beaver told the elk. 'I'd take them off if I were you. Give your brain a rest.'

'Well, fortunately I have enough brain cells left to realize that you are one large hole short of a lake,' the elk said.

Howl noticed a little silky-haired terrier wiggling her way through the crowds. She was almost at the front. Her arrival had caused him to stumble on his notes for a second.

'Our rivers and lakes are so full of poisons they're not fit to drink,' Howl continued. 'We have ice caps that are melting and man-made food,' he said.

The chipmunk passed the squirrel a paper bag full of acorns and offered one to him. 'Acorn?'

'I don't touch those things,' said the squirrel.

'They're organic,' the chipmunk added shoving the bag under the squirrel's nose. The squirrel took one and bit into it.

Howl continued his speech but with one eye on Pup. 'I'm pleased to say that, since the birds and animals all learned to speak English, our Party is fast gaining popularity.'

The audience of people stood up and clapped their approval.

'We're now on the ballot for presidential access in every state except for Florida and California. I will take care of California. The signature requirements are massive there. We need just one more candidate to help us with Florida. It's the second largest state for signatures. So are there any birds or animals in the audience who would like to lend a paw, or a claw to help us with the ballot access for Florida?'

Pup barked excitedly and held up her paw. Her long silver

hair tumbled in a sexy way over one of her eyes. Howl had never seen such a pretty, refined and sophisticated dog before. He became so flustered by the little dog's canine beauty, that he totally forgot what he was saying.

'The reason we called our Party the….ah, the ….'

'The Fur and Feathers Party', Snowy Owl whispered to Howl from his spot in the front row. But Howl was transfixed on Pup. He noticed the little dog was suddenly staring at the ground. Howl was so smitten by her beauty that he had temporarily forgotten where he was.

'Psst!! The Fur and Feathers Party,' Snowy Owl whispered again, this time much louder. Howl snapped out of his trance at the bird's prompt. 'Ah, the reason we called our Party the Fur and Feathers Party is because it's the first Party to be run by birds and animals. We want to follow the way nature governs the universe, perfectly and without a problem.'

Howl had one eye still on Pup who was now having an awkward scratch at her red collar. The thought of opening his heart again to another dog, caused his strong hind legs to tremble. But at the same time he knew he wasn't going to let this little dog trot off into the crowd.

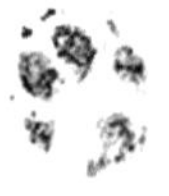

31

Head Over Paws

PUP SNIFFED NERVOUSLY around a large hollowed-out tree trunk. It didn't have the refreshing and healing scent of the eucalypts in the bush where she had grown up. It had a clean woody fragrance that Pup liked.

She noticed a sign on the trunk that read "The Fur and Feathers Party of the United States - National Headquarters".

Pup could feel herself becoming sweaty. She was as nervous as the time when Hank had tried to drag her onto the boat in the Marramarra National Park. She was about to come nose to nose with her dream dog.

She began to pant heavily, exposing her little pink tongue. She wondered if Howl had a mate already. *A handsome beast like that would not be alone for long,* she thought. But the Wolf had given her a sign that he was quite impressed with her, and she hoped he wasn't a hound dog keen on spreading his scent around.

She sniffed at her fur. The lovely woman in her big white house had given her a bath the night before, and she still had a delicate rose fragrance all over her little silky-haired body.

If she had been in the Australian bush, she would have chewed on a peppermint gum leaf to freshen her doggy breath. She had no idea about the local plants in North America.

Before she could spend any more time fretting over her appearance, Howl appeared at the entrance to the tree trunk.

'Welcome to the Fur and Feathers Party,' Howl barked nervously. 'What's your name?'

'Pup, but my owner calls me Congress.' She answered feeling her skin getting hot.

'Pup is a nicer name.' The little terrier didn't know where to look. Howl was even more handsome close up. Pup's little silky legs were shaking so much she hoped he wouldn't notice how nervous she was.

'I just need you to fill out this form and get it back to me. I am so pleased you are going to be a candidate.'

Pup took the leaf out of Howl's mouth. She could smell his delicious wild scent and it caused her to tremble even more. She gently put it on the ground by the gnarled roots of the tree trunk. 'It's such a worthwhile cause. I loved your talk. It was impressive,' she barked softly.

Howl gazed at the ground and Pup thought he was embarrassed and wondered if she'd said the right thing. Maybe he was the sort of wolf that did not take kindly to being flattered.

'Thanks. I had a very appreciative audience. When you start your campaigning you're welcome to use our national headquarters,' Howl said and retreated inside the tree trunk.

Pup followed on his tail. She was a little shocked at what she saw inside. A jutting-out piece of wood had become a desk.

There was a log for a chair, and a dirty sheepskin rug on the floor. It was nothing like the luxurious décor of her white house. There were no computers, lights or phones, and no potted plants to soften the room. One side of the tree trunk was covered with a huge map of the different states of America. Numbers had been put on each state. It had a heading that said "Ballot Access".

The map had huge leaves stuck on different states. Large black letters read; Bald Eagle – 25,000; Bandicoot – 15,000; Skunk – 10,000. Big red ticks were on each sign. Pup watched as Howl wrote something on another leaf and stuck it over Florida. It read, Pup – 119,316. She was shocked at the number of signatures she was expected to get and wondered if she had made the right decision by offering to help. The little terrier didn't want to fail miserably at the task he had set her.

A white pigeon flew in with a leaf in its mouth. Howl took the leaf, read it and scribbled a reply. He sent the pigeon off on its way. Pup felt cold. She shivered. 'Will you be installing central heating in your office?' she barked.

'Here you'd better put this around you,' Howl said, picking up the dirty sheepskin rug that had been on the ground. Pup didn't want to touch it, but she also didn't want to offend the handsome wolf. She took it in her mouth and tried to fling it over her back. Howl grabbed one side of the rug in his large teeth. He pulled it over her. Pup was flattered by his concern for her wellbeing.

'Are you planning to install phones and computers and perhaps get on the Internet?'

Howl seemed embarrassed at his lack of modern equipment and said nothing. Pup was worried again that she may have offended him. 'I'm sorry Howl. I've spent more time indoors than anywhere else. But I would like to learn about the great outdoors. You seem so big and strong. I am impressed by the way you can live in the wild like you do. Could you teach me how to hunt for food?'

'I would be happy to teach you. You'll need to take English lessons. I'm trying to communicate only in English these days so I don't forget what I have learned. There's a very good teacher that lives close by. If you want to go and see her she lives in that last tree on the left over there. There's a clause on the form you must read carefully,' the Wolf added. 'If you sign this form you will be agreeing not to divulge how you gained the ability to speak English. This is very important. You must never tell anyone who taught you.'

Pup nodded her agreement.

~

Cracker sat on a branch of a large oak tree mischievously throwing birdseed at unsuspecting passers-by. The people looked up, wondering where the shower of seeds was coming from. Cracker screeched in delight. The feisty bird always enjoyed a bit of mischievous fun, and the larrikin in her was fully on display.

She heard leaves rustling at the base of her tree. Something was moving down there. She noticed some kind of a dog through the leaves. 'Yeah come up!' Cracker screeched impatiently, raising her yellow crest at the little dog's attempts to climb the tree.

'Oh you dogs are hopeless.' The bird swooped onto the ground. But her cockiness came to an abrupt halt when she found herself face to face with her lost friend Pup.

Cracker and Pup stood like statues as they stared wide-eyed at each other. The bird waited for Pup to say something but the little silky-haired terrier was frozen on the spot, staring at Cracker with a stunned look.

All Cracker could manage was a broken squawk.

'Stone the flamin' crows! It's good to see ya Pup. Fair dinkum,' she said.

Cracker suddenly felt uncomfortable noticing that Pup's eyes had filled with tears. The bird's throat began to develop another lump, just as she had experienced when she'd told her flock that Henry was missing. She hated herself for becoming so sentimental. She looked down at her claws, trying to distract herself from showing any emotion.

'You never got in touch with me,' Pup said with a tremble in her voice. 'Didn't you get my letter?'

'Yeah, got it okay, but you didn't give me enough information Pup. All you said was you lived in a big white house. How was I supposed to find ya? Do you have any idea how many big white houses there are in America?'

'Well I'd heard this big white house was very well known in the world.'

'Anyway no use crying over spilt seeds,' Cracker added trying to disguise the emotional tremble in her voice. 'But it's really good to see you Pup. What in heavens name are you doing at my tree anyway? You could 'ave knocked me over with a feather. But you don't have any do ya?' Cracker laughed. She hoped this would lighten up this heavy moment.

Cracker could see Pup's tears were now dripping onto her silky paws. 'I want you to teach me how to speak English. I'm gonna collect signatures for the Fur and Feathers Party here,'

Pup said, with an attempt at a stronger bark. There are so many signatures to collect. I've got heaps of them. More than the others.'

'Good on ya Pup. They need all the help they can get. It won't be so easy for you to disappear on me now. What about that red wolf eh? Bit of a handsome beast isn't he?' Cracker was fishing but Pup didn't want to give anything away.

'I hadn't noticed,' she lied. 'Any sign of Henry?'

Cracker said nothing for a moment. She began to peck at her claws again. She didn't want to think about Henry. 'Been too busy to think about him, Pup. But one day, I'm gonna find out what happened to him, and if it's got anything to do with those humans, they better watch out,' Cracker said.

~

Elroy drummed his fingers on the Cabinet Room table. He was irritated that he had been waiting so long for the President to arrive. He assumed it was because he was fussing over the little dog. The Vice President did not like dogs at all. He was especially annoyed that the President had not only got himself a dog, but an overly excitable and forever-barking one. *A more suitable animal should have been chosen to suit the tone of his administration,* he thought.

Since the President had brought Pup to the White House, Elroy believed their Party had suffered as a result. He decided it was time something drastic should be done to help them survive the attention that the Fur and Feathers Party was getting. He wasn't sure what it would be, but he was determined to find a way to ruin any possible chance that this Party of animals could have of getting into government.

It also bothered Elroy that Jim didn't have a partner. The

media were always asking him about this and he was tired of making excuses for him. The President arrived with his Press Secretary, Chief of Staff and a couple of his close advisors. They all sat down.

Elroy noticed the dark circles under the President's eyes.

'So what's this all about, Elroy?' the President asked.

'You need to be aware, sir, that the Fur and Feathers Party are gaining ground. Perhaps we need to show a little interest in animal rights and environmental issues. We could mount a strong public relations or advertising campaign.'

'We don't have the funds,' said one of the advisors.

'I can arrange that,' Elroy said.

'All right, Elroy. You do what you think is best. So if that's what this meeting was about, I'm going to retire gentlemen. I'm er, having a bit of trouble sleeping at the moment,' the President said.

Elroy guessed it was Pup keeping him awake at night. He was annoyed that the President had only given them a couple of minutes of his time.

'Maybe you should add flea powder to the shopping list Jim?' Elroy commented in a tight-lipped way.

The President ignored his Vice President. He got up to leave. 'Good night, gentlemen.' He left the Cabinet Room and the minute he was gone, Elroy turned to the advisors.

'I want to know everything about the Fur and Feathers Party. Find out about that Wolf, too. What are his likes and dislikes. Most of all - what are his weaknesses?'

'He's getting a lot of media coverage but their Party will never have access to the Presidential debates so we still have an edge, Elroy,' the Press Secretary said.

‘Contact all the State Offices. Find out where they are at with the ballot access,’ Elroy said. The door suddenly opened and Pup trotted in.

‘If she could only talk I think she’d make a good candidate for our Party. What do you think?’ Elroy asked.

Pup walked up to one of the advisors and, practising the first line of English she had learned she said, ‘Wanna cup of tea?’

‘Who taught you to speak English?’ Elroy asked, amazed.

‘It’s a secret.’

‘Come on you can tell me. I won’t tell anyone,’ Elroy lied. He was determined to find out but the little dog remained silent and began to walk out of the room.

‘Look, you don’t have to tell me. But I do have ways of finding these things out, you know.’ Elroy was not a man to give up easily on anything and he was going to find out who was teaching the animals English. A plan was formulating in his devious mind.

32

Howl to the Rescue

PUP AND HOWL WALKED side by side along a narrow path in a thickly forested area. The air was crisp and cool with a delicious pine fragrance.

Pup had a large red bow tied around her neck. Howl thought she looked very pretty. He tried not to walk too fast as she seemed to be having trouble keeping up with him.

Howl knew he was lean and strong and well-toned. This was his home and he wanted to show it off to the little dog, although he felt nervous deep down about how such a city dog would take to it. *She would have led a pampered life,* he thought.

They reached a clearing and Howl stopped to show off his magnificent expansive view. A rolling mountain range swept across the horizon. It was just visible behind a soft mist that melted over the mountain like frosting on a cake.

'So this is where I live,' Howl said.

'It's such a huge back garden you have,' Pup replied.

'Well, I'm the kind of animal that needs a bit of space.'

'Do you have a house?' Pup asked.

Howl began to feel uncomfortable. It seemed already he had disappointed the little dog. He decided to stride on ahead to hide his feelings. He could sense that Pup was struggling to keep up with him, but he didn't want her to see how sweaty he had become with her questions.

'This *is* my house,' Howl called back to her.

'But what if it snows?'

'Oh I find a natural cave somewhere, or perhaps a hollowed out tree trunk.'

'But what if you need a bath?'

'I just jump in a river or a lake.'

'But what if you want to watch a DVD?' she persisted.

'Is that something you can eat?' Howl asked.

'You mean you've never seen Rin Tin Tin or Lassie?'

Howl was beginning to feel quite inadequate around this sophisticated little dog. He had no idea what she was talking about, and he was beginning to wonder how they could form a relationship when she had obviously led such a totally different life from his.

Howl's heart felt heavy. He had a strong attraction to her, but how could this relationship possibly work?

The Wolf picked up his speed as they climbed a steep grade. Pup slipped and stumbled trying to keep up with Howl. He was now quite a way ahead of her. The Wolf looked back.

'I'm sorry; do you need a helping paw?' he growled. He waited for Pup to catch up. Despite their obvious differences he was beginning to fall in love with the little dog, and he wanted this to work.

'I'm afraid I've lived rather an unsheltered life. I don't like being confined in small spaces. I was brought up in the wilderness and I mainly catch food, eat and sleep. Perhaps you can help me adjust to being a little more civilised?'

Howl thought he saw a look of relief on Pup's face and he felt a little better. Maybe he had been too over the top, pointing out what a wild beast he was. It must have freaked her. He stood still, admiring the expansive view ahead. 'I guess you city dogs have never slept in a hollowed out tree trunk?'

'No. Can't say that I have. I live in a large white house and I have my own room, and my bed is a large down-filled pillow covered in pink silk.'

Howl felt inadequate again. *I must have been crazy to think such a worldly dog would see anything in me.* He raced on ahead of her. *I'm way too wild for her. She could never live out here, and I could not put up with a pampered and protected environment. I'll have to forget about her.*

Howl didn't look back to see if Pup was following him. He just wanted to get away from the way her presence was making him feel.

The path was rocky and uneven. Howl rounded a bend and, when he looked back, he could no longer see Pup. He kept going for a while but when he turned around again she was still nowhere to be seen. He sensed something was wrong and decided to head back the way he had come. Maybe she was resting on the side of the path and he couldn't see her in the long grass. She was only a little dog. He felt bad that he had raced ahead like he had. It was easy to forget that he was more than twice her size and very fit.

~

Pup felt afraid. She had become accustomed to feeling safe

and protected and suddenly she was back in a very remote place. The little terrier was scared she could get lost without Howl to guide her home. She would have to go faster. She started thinking about the time she got lost in the Australian bush, and how she had nearly died from lack of water and food. If it hadn't been for Fluff, Magpie and Cracker, she would not have survived. She would never have been around to enjoy her comfortable life with her new master, or have met the handsome Wolf.

Pup ran so fast she was hardly aware of her little legs anymore. It was hard to even breathe. She was panting like mad and feeling very thirsty.

The path was becoming narrower and there was a steep drop off to one side plunging deeply into the valley below. But she had to keep up the pace. She rounded a bend and still couldn't see Howl. If she could just go a little faster maybe she could catch up to him.

Suddenly Pup slipped on some loose gravel and slid right off the path, tumbling over the edge and towards the ravine below. A gnarled tree growing horizontally out of the side of the cliff saved her from plunging to her death.

The terrified little dog clung desperately to the tree with her teeth and paws. Her heart was pounding like a fast drum roll. She was several feet below the path. There was no way she could reach it.

'Help!' Pup barked so loudly she felt it scratch the back of her throat. 'Help. Howl, are you there?' The wind was blowing strongly and Pup was hanging on as tightly as she could to the spindly tree that was now moving precariously from side to side. Pup didn't dare look down. She was afraid of heights and this small tree was the only thing standing between her and certain death. She had to control her shaking or she could lose her grip.

'Help!' Pup barked as loudly as she could. Her claws were getting tired from holding onto the tree branch. Howl's face suddenly appeared at the top of the cliff. Pup was overjoyed to see him.

Howl leant over the edge as far as he could. He grabbed hold of her red ribbon. Pup was afraid his sharp claws would rip it apart. His face was so close to hers she could feel his hot breath, and smell his pine scented fur. He managed to haul her back onto the path.

'Are you okay, Pup?' Howl barked anxiously.

Pup was very shaken and her little legs were trembling so much she could hardly stand on her feet. She gazed at the Wolf in admiration. 'You saved my life,' she said.

'Well I was hardly going to leave you hanging there,' he barked.

'Some of the dogs where I come from would have done just that. They're so useless they can't even remember where they've hidden their bones.' Pup could tell by the way Howl laughed that he was feeling more relaxed with her now. She had obviously freaked him out with all the earlier talk of her luxurious life.

There was an awkward moment between them. Pup sensed his desire to press his nose against hers and she badly wanted this to happen. She was a little disappointed when he seemed to be backing slightly away from her.

They walked along the path and Pup liked the way he took the side nearest the cliff edge. She felt very protected.

'You have beautiful silky hair,' he said wiping his mouth with a paw to hide the drool that was dripping onto the ground.

'Thanks. It is natural. I have been admiring your thick fur coat. It's a lovely shade.'

Pup felt the sudden warmth coming from Howl's face and she knew he was embarrassed. They stopped to rest in an open tree trunk and gazed at each other. Pup moved closer to Howl and looked into his beautiful brown eyes. She closed her eyes expecting her nose to meet his, but nothing happened. When she opened her eyes Howl was standing looking at her as if he was deep in thought.

'Well I guess we'd better get back,' he said.

Pup felt confused. He seemed to be giving her mixed signals and it was messing with her head and emotions.

~

The U.S. President relaxed in his private quarters with Pup. He was still dealing with the shock of owning a dog that could speak English. He hoped that she might open up and tell him how she managed to get outside the grounds of the White House, and where she kept disappearing to for hours at a time. He didn't really want to pry into her life. He was a private man and hated when anyone tried to get him to open up about anything. He'd resented it at the time when Elroy had pressured him to talk about why he didn't want to be in a relationship.

The first time Pup disappeared Jim had been very worried. He had asked one of the gardeners to see if they could discover how she could possibly have escaped. But no one had come up with anything and he knew the security around the gates was very tight. It was a mystery.

He had sent people out to look for her, but she returned

unharmed and Jim began to relax a bit about her increasing time away, since she always returned for her supper. He had too many other things to think about to be chasing after finding his missing dog.

Pup was now transfixed before the television screen. She was watching Howl being interviewed by a chat show host.

The President had a hunch that Pup's disappearance had something to do with this Wolf she seemed so keen on. He hoped it wasn't. He didn't like the thought of his little dog getting too friendly with such a wild animal.

Jim noticed the puddle of drool building up on the carpet, as Pup remained glued to the television. It really bothered him.

'Tell me about Howl. What is so appealing about him?'

'His big brown eyes; his angular features; his gorgeous long hair; his drive to do good for the world. He seems wild but vulnerable,' she said.

The President was astounded at her command of the English language but he resented what she was saying. He had rescued her from being abandoned in Australia, and brought her to the White House to be his pet dog. He had fed her the best-smoked salmon and allowed her to sleep in his room in her own lovely silk-cushioned bed. He had even decorated her room with famous works of art. But it seemed that he was not the centre of her world. It was Howl that she loved. He leant back in his large leather chair. He hadn't thought to pry into her life but he needed to know. 'How did you learn to speak such good English?'

'Howl taught me,' Pup lied.

'But how did he learn?' The President persisted.

'I don't know. I never asked him.'

‘And how did all the Australian birds and animals learn English?’

‘Howl went out there specially to teach them.’

But her master remained unconvinced. He flicked off the television and leant towards the little dog. ‘Would you become Howl’s mate if he asked you?’ he inquired not really wanting to hear the answer.

‘I’ve thought of nothing else since I first saw him,’ she slobbered.

The President was shocked and flopped back into his chair. He pushed her head away when Pup tried to rest her nose in his hand, and got up to find something to clean up her drool.

33

The Presidential Debates

CRACKER SAT ON A TREE branch deeply engrossed in reading 'Advanced English for the Birds'. Her command of English was already quite good. She wanted to be so familiar with the English language, that certain sayings would roll off her beak, like "A bird in the hand is worth two in the bush" and "Don't ruffle my feathers if you know what's good for you".

She didn't see herself as one to brag, but once she had told her partner Henry that, next to the Queen of England, she probably had the best command of the English language.

Although Cracker hated wallowing of any kind, this little memory caused her to feel a twinge of sadness. She remembered how much he had loved her wicked sense of humour, and how he had often complimented her on how good she was at stripping loquat and peach trees without getting caught.

Cracker was aware that Henry was a long-suffering bird and would listen to her ramblings about her feathered achievements without so much as a single squawk of protest. But when she was with Henry, she had only learned to say a few simple phrases like 'How are you?' and 'Who is a pretty boy?'

She remembered how Henry had told her that humility was not one of her strong points. But Cracker knew that he liked so many other things about her, she got away with the occasional egotistical rant.

Cracker was glad that Henry treated her with respect and was nothing like her horrible father Clancy. She hoped she would see Henry again one day. But maybe it would have to wait until they were both in bird heaven. She was aware that could be a long time, as cockatoos could live until they were forty or even fifty-years-old. There was even a case of someone's pet cockatoo living to a hundred! Cracker could not imagine being put in jail for that long, but she would wait forever if she had to in order to see her beloved Henry again.

Snowy Owl swept down onto the branch where Cracker was perched, causing her to jump out of her thoughts. 'What's the matter Snowy? You look like you've got your beak out of joint,' Cracker said, practising a new English expression she had learned from her book. 'Wanna Cup of Tea?' Cracker asked as Snowy Owl shot her an unhappy look.

The Owl passed Cracker a letter. 'I just got this. It's from the Head of the Commission on Presidential Debates.'

Cracker snatched the letter impatiently from Snowy Owl's beak. She quickly scanned it, cocked her head on one side, hung upside down on a branch and swung backwards and forwards. Then, with the ease of an Olympic gymnast, she swung right side up and ripped the letter into shreds with her claws. 'No one is more cocky than me. I'll fly over to meet with this dingbat,' she screeched. Snowy Owl removed a half chewed piece of leaf from his eye that Cracker had spat at him.

'If you're going to be a Spokesbird for the Fur and Feathers Party over here Cracker, you should try and not ruffle any feathers. You will get a lot further if you go about things in a dignified way.'

Cracker did a loop the loop on the branch and stood upright, looking down on the Owl. 'You can't hide behind a gum leaf when you're dealing with politicians,' she squawked, spitting half chewed leaves into the air. 'You've got to get off your perch and tell them how it is.'

'Well I know you will do precisely what you want Cracker. But don't say I didn't warn you,' the Owl said.

~

Cracker walked up to an immense foreboding looking wooden door. A sign on the door said 'President, Commission on Presidential Debates'. She cocked her head on one side and tapped loudly with her beak.

'Come in,' a loud voice said from behind the door. Cracker flew up to the handle and tried to open it. She swung upside down for a few moments and dropped to the floor, tapping her beak more loudly on the door.

'Yes. Come in,' the voice behind the door said again.

Cracker paced up and down outside. She flew up to the door handle and hung upside down from it, trying to peer through the keyhole.

'I can't open the flamin' door,' she screeched.

Cracker could hear footsteps approaching. The door was suddenly flung open with the Cockatoo still hanging upside down from the handle.

A very fat, tall and bald-headed man stood facing her. He wore a conservative dark blue suit at least two sizes too small for him. He glared at Cracker with a fierce expression. 'Well what do you want?' he yelled. One of the buttons on his suit flew off and landed on the floor close to where Cracker was standing.

Cracker did not like his tone of voice and, to prove her point, she placed a white deposit on the man's highly polished shoe. But he didn't notice what she had done.

'Woops, sorry,' Cracker said, hoping to draw his attention to the mess she had left on his shoe. The man gazed at the white deposit and he became really angry.

'I want to meet with you about the Fur and Feathers Party of the United States having equal access to the debates on national television,' Cracker said in her strongest screech.

'I don't meet with birds.' The man tried to close the door but Cracker was still swinging from the handle. She let go and flew past him into his office. The man followed with furious heavy strides and the door slammed behind him.

Cracker perched herself on a chair at a huge dark wooden boardroom table.

The President of the Commission on Presidential Debates plonked himself down on a chair opposite her, almost breaking it with the weight of his immense backside.

'There is nothing in the United States Constitution that says anything about birds and animals being able to form themselves into a political Party; or being part of the televised debates,' the man said with an authoritative tone.

'Then it's time for an amendment to the Constitution. I'll take this as high as I have to go until my voice gets heard.'

The man rubbed his ears as if in pain. 'What you don't seem to realize, my small feathered friend, is that you're in the minority. You're just a bird. Do you think anyone's going to take any notice of you?'

'There are a lot of birds and animals, and even humans in this country that feel the way I do. They want change. They're sick of your two-Party dominated system.'

Cracker jumped onto the boardroom table and paced up and down, leaving scratches from her sharp claws on the highly polished cherry wood. 'Have you forgotten about your American history?' Cracker continued. 'Third Parties were responsible for some of the biggest changes this country has ever known, like women getting the right to vote and the abolishment of slavery. Small voices do get heard ya know.'

'Yes but not loud screechy ones!' the man responded angrily.

Cracker landed another white deposit on the polished antique table. The man was horrified. He took a swipe at her but she flew up to swing dangerously on his chandelier.

'We, the birds and animals of the Earth, demand a clean, green environment,' Cracker continued, causing the chandelier to swing dangerously from side to side.

'It's our birthright and you cannot take this away from us.'

Cracker noticed how worried the man had become, and how his head was following her ever-increasing swing on his priceless chandelier.

'We're sick of humanity poisoning our air, water and food, and we have a right to *express* that we're sick of it too.' The cocky bird flew across to the deep red heavy curtains and hung upside down, causing them to tear from her sharp claws.

'Have you forgotten those words in your Declaration of

Independence? Something about all creatures being equal and certain *unalienable rights that, among these, are life, liberty and the pursuit of happiness?*'

'I believe the words are all *men* are created equal. It never said anything about birds and animals.'

Cracker flapped her wings in rage as a huge tear appeared in the curtain she had been hanging from.

'Yeah, and it never said anything about women, black people and poor whites either,' Cracker squawked. 'I say your democracy stinks. Just like that awful after-shave you're wearing. Give me the fresh smell of the Australian eucalypts any day.' She flew over to the door. 'I can see I'm wasting my time. But it's not going to end here. We are creatures of this planet and we have a right to be heard, and to be a part of the political debates on national television.'

'I beg to contradict you, Yellow-Crested Cockatoo. You are not a citizen of the United States. You are an Australian, and a bird to boot. Goodbye and good riddance.'

Cracker flew out the door. It slammed loudly behind her. She walked down a long corridor grumbling angrily 'anyone who is that fat must live on tubs of lard. I bet he can't swing upside down on a spindly branch whilst whistling Waltzing Matilda. The man's clearly a dingbat,' she muttered, fluttering out into the fresh air.

~

Cracker sat on her favourite branch of a large oak tree and nibbled on an acorn. She planned her next move. She was not going to allow some over fat and smelly arrogant man stifle her freedom of speech. The Fur and Feathers Party had a right to be a part of the televised debates. It was obvious by the number of people voting for them, that they had a chance to get into government. The cocky bird was determined she was not going to let this rest. She decided she would discuss their rights in a courtroom as soon as she possibly could.

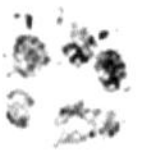

34

Cracker Goes to Court

IT WAS HOT AND HUMID in the courtroom and tempers were frayed as the air conditioning had failed to operate. Everyone sweltered in the thirty-six degree temperature and high humidity.

Belinda, the judge, wiped perspiration off her brow with a tissue. She wished she were in the pool at her apartment doing laps and getting rid of that unwanted cellulite. Since she had turned fifty, Belinda was feeling less and less like exercising, but she would have much preferred to be swimming than sitting in the stuffy courtroom with an audience of birds and animals, the likes of which she had never seen before.

Belinda had never been close to an Australian cockatoo. She didn't mind birds as long as they stayed in their trees.

Her palms began to sweat and her throat tightened as she thought about a time when she was close enough to smell a parrot's feathers.

Once, at the Chief Justice's birthday Party, her enjoyment of her glass of chardonnay had been interrupted by the resident grey and pink cockatiel landing on her shoulders, and pulling at her expensive pink diamond earrings. For a minute she had thought her gorgeous gems were going to be the parrot's appetizer. This had cured her of ever wanting to shake claws with anything resembling this kind of bird again.

Belinda watched as Cracker now paced up and down in front of her. The judge considered her case. She had one final glance at the papers, but as far as she was concerned this session would be over in time for her to make her Pilates class.

'Well waddayasay?' Cracker screeched.

'All rise,' the clerk commanded.

The judge watched Cracker fly up to the ceiling where she hung upside down from a wooden beam. Having this raucous bird directly over her head was making Belinda very nervous. She moved to her right. She did not want her smart black garment to have white spots added to it.

'Given there is nothing in the U.S. Constitution which makes any reference to birds and animals having the right to vote, or the right to form themselves into a political Party, I hereby refuse the Fur and Feathers Party any access to the televised debates,' she said, slamming down her gavel.

The judge gazed nervously up at the cockatoo, hoping it would not now plant an angry white deposit on her head.

Cracker flew down to her. Belinda leant back in her chair almost falling backwards onto the floor in her attempt to put space between herself and the angry bird.

'If you think a dingbat like you is going to stop me from getting my voice heard, you're barking up the wrong gum tree mate!' she screeched.

'I'll hold you in contempt of court,' the judge responded.

'You're not sticking me in a cage. I'll go to the highest court in the land. You haven't heard the last of me.' She flew out of the courtroom door.

The judge wiped a drop of perspiration off her chin before it landed on her papers. She was relieved this unusual court session was over.

~

Pup struggled to stay upright. She tried to control her trembling legs. The little dog hoped that Howl wouldn't notice how scared she was at making a fool of herself. Pup had never had to catch her own food before. She wished she hadn't agreed to this but maybe it would bring them closer together.

Howl was so used to being in the outdoors Pup wondered how he could be attracted to the pampered creature that she was. After all, there were plenty of attractive female wolves he could go out with. Surely they wouldn't baulk at catching their own food, or sleeping rough in a hollowed out tree trunk. *They say opposites attract, so maybe that's it,* she wondered.

She felt sick at the thought of killing her own food. But Pup realized that, if she were going to make any headway with such a wild dog, she had to get over her squeamishness and learn a few new tricks.

Pup chased after a small rodent along a path edged by thick forest. It was running very fast and she was not gaining any ground.

'Here watch me.' Pup watched as Howl pounced on the little animal in a split second. He was about to rip it apart when she barked 'No! Let it go!'

Startled by her outburst Howl dropped the animal. It ran off into the bushes. 'That was going to be our dinner,' Howl said.

Pup felt a bit foolish. 'I'm sorry. This is all very new to me.'

Howl nipped her playfully on the tail and she ran off with him in pursuit. He caught her and rolled her onto the ground and they nipped and played with each other. Pup was relieved that, despite her emotional outburst, their bond was becoming stronger by the minute.

They flopped down for a rest on some mossy ground. Howl sat close beside her. He was panting a bit and said nothing. Pup was dying to ask him something. She finally plucked up the courage. 'Have you ever had a long-term mate?'

Howl turned his head away from her. Pup immediately regretted asking him something so personal. She wished she could dig a hole and hide so he wouldn't notice her silky fur flattening on her body with embarrassment.

'I'm sorry for being so nosey. You don't have to tell me.'

The silence hung in the air between them. Pup waited patiently and finally Howl seemed to want to open up to her.

'I was close to a dog once. Her name was Amber. We were going to become mates. I thought I really knew her. She seemed so open and honest that I felt I had met a dog I could trust. So I let down my guard.'

The Wolf's bark cracked and he became wistful and silent again. Pup moved closer to him. She was so close she could feel Howl's breath ruffling her fur as he panted. She sensed that he wanted to rub noses with her.

'What happened?' Pup barked as tenderly as she could.

'Amber really let me down. She'd been leading a double life and seeing another wolf all the time we were dating.'

Pup noticed how tightly he was gritting his teeth. This confession was not easy for him.

'I've never been able to trust another female dog,' he said turning away from her.

'What a bitch!' Pup said trying to lighten things up a bit. 'Not all female dogs would behave like that.'

Howl got up and furiously dug a hole. Pup watched him and said nothing. His outburst was like rubbing over a scab with a piece of sandpaper. *He is lucky he's only had one experience of being abandoned,* Pup thought.

Although Pup had not ever had a relationship with another dog, she'd been close to two humans, only to have them dump her.

Howl was still furiously digging the hole and Pup was beginning to get annoyed. 'You're not the only one who has been hurt you know,' she barked loudly. Her bark began to falter as she fought back the tears. 'Life goes on. The way I see it, you can allow your fear to crush something wonderful. Or, you can let your painful experience make you stronger and more discerning, so you don't make the same mistake again.'

Howl ignored her and continued digging the hole.

'I believe when you meet the right dog, it just works out,' Pup added.

Howl stopped digging. 'Come on! I'll catch us something to eat,' Howl said running off ahead.

Pup leapt to her feet and raced after him. She was relieved that he still seemed to want her company. But she wondered how long this was going to last.

35

Pup Heads to Florida

PUP SAT IN THE WINDOW seat of an A380 aircraft. She wore a sun hat and sunglasses in preparation for her arrival in Florida. Pup had taken on the daunting task of helping to collect the one hundred and nineteen thousand, three hundred and sixteen signatures needed for the Fur and Feathers Party to gain ballot access.

An enthusiastic team of both animal and human volunteers had already collected the majority of the signatures. Only very few of the animals could speak English well enough to do this work. The volunteers were mainly people who supported the Party's goals and visions for a cleaner world.

Pup worked at her personal computer. She checked to see how many signatures still needed to be collected. According to the records, a skunk had joined the team of signature gatherers and had agreed to collect a further two hundred, which would have left Pup with just three hundred. Unfortunately the skunk had driven everyone away by his body odour, and had only managed to collect three signatures.

Pup would have her work cut out to reach the goal for Florida. If she was to collect the remaining four hundred and ninety-seven signatures, she would have to find some extra helpers that didn't smell like prawns which had been left a week in the sun.

The little terrier could feel the desire of the elderly lady sitting next to her to start up a conversation. Even though she had her head in a book, Pup knew she was only pretending to read it, and was busting to ask her many questions.

The Captain made an announcement from the cockpit.

'Good afternoon ladies and gentleman, and ah, silky-haired terrier. We will begin our descent into Miami in about ten minutes and should have you on the ground at 5.40pm local time. We hope you've had a pleasant flight and thank you for choosing to fly with us today.'

The elderly lady put down her book and leant towards Pup.

'Excuse me. Are you the little dog I saw on the Oprah Winfrey show the other night?' she asked excitedly.

'Yes that's me.' Pup felt her face become hot with nerves.

'Oh I am so pleased to meet you,' the elderly lady said, shaking the little dog by the paw.

Pup pulled her paw away as she felt the elderly lady's long red nails digging into her pads.

'Are you having a holiday in Florida?'

'No I'm going there to gather signatures for the Fur and Feathers Party. 'We have a huge number to collect for ballot access.'

'I hope you get into government. You have my vote.'

Pup flashed her white teeth in a wide doggy smile. She was a kind looking lady, but she thought her bright red nails looked odd on such wrinkled hands. Pup was glad she had fur that would cover up any lines, as she got older. She went back to working on her computer.

'You're a very attractive terrier. Do you have a handsome mate waiting for you at home?' the elderly lady asked.

Pup felt her skin prickling. She didn't want to let anyone know about her interest in Howl. 'Oh I'm not really in a relationship. But I have recently met someone nice.'

'And is he into politics like you dear?'

Pup was determined not to give too much away. 'He's very supportive of what I am doing.'

'Well you are a lucky dog. My husband was never supportive of my wanting a career. In the end I just stayed at home and became an ordinary housewife. But that was a long time ago. Long before you were born. I could have been an astronaut,' she added.

Pup licked the old lady's hand in a sign of appreciation. She couldn't imagine her walking around Mars. *She'd be pushing it to find that red nail stuff up there,* she thought. But she was relieved when the lady went back to reading her book.

The seat belt sign came on with a loud "ding".

Pup turned off her laptop and tightened her seat belt. She thought about what the elderly lady had asked her. It was strange that she had never had a mate, or even found a dog mildly interested in her when she was in Australia. Even the Blue Heeler had never progressed to anything more intimate than chasing a few sticks with her. But in America suddenly the most gorgeous hound on the planet seemed to be head over paws for her. Maybe because she was from another country she was more interesting with her fascinating Australian bark.

Howl seemed cautious but she could tell he was keen on her; the way he could only talk to her if he was walking around in circles; how he would dig a hole when she asked him an awkward question, and his desire to teach her to catch wild animals. Clearly he was thinking of them having a future together. No dog would put another through such a challenge, especially a city dog if he wasn't thinking of a long-term relationship.

She couldn't imagine how any female wolf could leave an animal as gorgeous as Howl. *She truly must have been a horrible bitch,* the little dog thought.

Pup wondered what kind of puppies they would have together. *They would be striking that's for sure, with Howl's gleaming red fur and my large brown eyes, our puppies would be a talking point with dog lovers,* she thought.

The plane struck some bad turbulence and the elderly lady grabbed hold of Pup's paw. 'I don't like flying,' she said.

'Oh I wouldn't worry. This is a very big and strong bird. Sometimes they like to dive in and out of the clouds. It will get us back down safely. It's probably in a hurry to get home for some seeds.'

The elderly lady stared at Pup with her mouth wide open. 'Seeds?' was all she could say.

36

Elroy's Dirty Deed

THE PRESIDENT SAT at his desk in the Oval Office drawing pictures of flowers on a notepad. It helped him to feel less stressed. He was dreading the meeting he was about to have. Given everything that was on his agenda, it seemed utterly ridiculous that he had to give a second thought to a political Party run by birds and animals.

He had no idea how he was going to address the growing popularity of the Fur and Feathers Party. It wasn't something that any past president had needed to consider. He was hoping his advisors would know what to do. He felt a tension headache coming on as the Chief of Staff entered the room.

'The advisors are waiting for you, Jim. In the Cabinet Room.'

'All right. Thank you, Hank.'

Elroy the Vice President, the Press Secretary and six other men sat silently around the large antique table that dominated the Cabinet Room. They were all dressed in neatly pressed white shirts, dark blue suits and striped ties, as if they were trying to blend in with the American flag that stood proudly in one corner.

The President entered the room. His worried expression emphasised the lines on his face. The men all stood up as he came in and he ushered them to sit down. He took a seat at the head of the table.

'I'll get straight to the point. I'm aware that some of you haven't really seen the Fur and Feathers Party as much of a threat. That is understandable. I mean, none of us have ever come across a bunch of English-speaking birds and animals before. Not to mention ones who have gone into politics.'

The President noticed his Chief Strategist was sniggering quietly. He glared at him. He did not like this kind of behaviour whatever they were there to discuss.

'I am aware there are people in this room that think the Fur and Feathers Party is a joke.' Elroy stared at his shoes. 'But you need to know that they are just a few signatures away from gaining ballot access in Florida for their presidential candidate. I don't have to tell any of you how important Florida is in the scheme of things. They now have ballot access in every other state. If they gain access to Florida, anything could happen. They could even get into government.'

'Mr President, I don't think we have too much cause for alarm here,' said one of the advisors. 'There's nothing in the ballot access rules that gives validity to signatures from birds and animals.'

'But it's my understanding that most of the signatures have come from people,' the President added.

The Press Secretary scoffed. 'I think that we could put up a case that these signatures are not to be taken seriously. I mean, people voting for birds and animals. It is ridiculous. Come on!'

'If we try to fudge anything, it could backfire on us. There will be a public outcry of such immense proportions, it could do us more harm than good,' one of the advisors said.

'Absolutely,' the President agreed. He tapped a pencil on the boardroom table as if he was suffering from a nervous twitch. The men sat in thoughtful silence.

Suddenly one of the advisors piped up 'Sir, forgive me for making this observation, but when your dog, Congress, began working for the Fur and Feathers Party, we all thought that would work in our favour. I'm a little confused as to what is happening here. She doesn't seem to be displaying the kind of loyalty to her master that one would have expected.'

This remark really touched a raw nerve for the President and he could feel his skin prickling. He had become aware that she was helping out the red Wolf. He'd seen her on the television. He'd tried to ignore the annoyance he felt about this, and how disloyal she was being to his Party, but he knew that her love interest had caused her to behave in this way.

The last thing he wanted was to involve his little dog. He was aware that she was not popular with the Vice President or the Chief of Staff. He felt a slight tinge of guilt that he had not followed the advice of his Cabinet and got a different breed of dog.

'She's crazy about Howl,' he finally said.

'Does this animal feel the same about her?' Elroy enquired narrowing his eyes.

'It seems to be a mutual attraction.'

'Our advisors have done some investigations into the character of this Wolf, sir. It seems that he is a very deep thinking, sensitive and loyal kind of a creature. He's never had a long-term mate, which is a little surprising given his handsome appearance and charismatic personality. Aren't those the qualities that appeal to most females? Could it be that this Wolf has an issue with trust?' the Vice President asked.

'What are you driving at Elroy?'

'I think we should begin to consider this bond between Howl and Pup to be our strongest weapon. That is, if we want to stay in government.'

Despite his annoyance with his pet dog, the President had a strong dislike for anything underhand. He saw himself as an honest and decent citizen. There was no way he wanted to be a part of anything that could be seen to be manipulative or dishonest in any way. He got up to leave. He was deeply disappointed in Elroy for even hinting that they should go down this road. 'Gentleman, if we have to lower ourselves to desperate measures like this, then we should not be in government. If that's the best you can come up with Elroy, I've got better things to do. Excuse me.'

The President marched out of the office, slamming the door.

'Hmm, well I think, gentlemen, it's time someone paid the Wolf a visit,' Elroy said.

'Oh, I dunno. I don't want to do something the President is not happy about,' the Chief Strategist said, fiddling with a button on his white shirt.

'He'll change his mind when he sees the polls switching to us. He's not going to turn the tables on me. I've raised more money to fund his campaign than anyone else,' Elroy added.

~

Howl sat on a log in the national headquarters of the Fur and Feathers Party. He was busy counting the signatures that had been gathered for the Californian ballot access. The Wolf heard a car pulling up outside and looked through a hole in the tree trunk. He was surprised to see it was a large black limousine. Howl watched as a well-dressed male chauffeur opened the door and Elroy stepped out. He was wearing a casual pale blue cashmere sweater, smart dark blue slacks and tan loafers.

Howl wondered why the Vice President of the United States should be visiting him. Surely the Fur and Feathers Party was the enemy, with their newfound popularity with voters. He heard a loud knock on the tree trunk and opened the oak door.

'The President himself asked me to personally pop by and pay you a visit Mr Howl. May I come in?'

'Of course,' Howl barked. His voice was scratchy from the shock of having such an important visitor.

Howl wagged his tail across the top of a tree stump to remove the dust that had collected there. He motioned with his large paw for Elroy to sit down.

'This is an unexpected honour,' Howl said, sitting down on a dustier log. 'Would you like a bowl of water or a nice old bone? I have one that still has some meat on it.'

Elroy tried to stifle a laugh. 'Ah, I'm good thanks,' he said, taking a water bottle out of his briefcase and having a drink.

'The President wished to compliment you on your extraordinary success with the Fur and Feathers Party. He's been watching you on television and listening to your Party platform, and he would like to consider adopting your policies.'

Howl could not believe what he was hearing.

'Look, it makes no sense for us to wage war with each other,' Elroy continued. 'We should join forces for the common good of the planet.'

Howl was suspicious. No political Party had ever suggested this kind of arrangement before and he thought Elroy had untrustworthy eyes.

'I see. Does this mean that you intend abandoning your Star Wars program, and the use of nuclear, chemical and biological weapons?' Howl asked.

'Well ah…'

'What about animal rights?' Howl continued.

'We….'

'And will you be addressing global warming, genetic modification of foods, sonar testing in the oceans and the destruction of the rain forests? Will you be abandoning cloud seeding, cleaning up the oceans, lakes and rivers, switching to organic and sustainable agriculture and using prevention-oriented approaches to public health? And what about consciousness-based education?'

'Well, we do aim to eventually address all these issues,' said Elroy, temporising.

'That's not good enough,' Howl continued. 'The planet will be stuffed by the time you get around to fixing everything up. Do you realize that the bees are disappearing so fast from the overuse of harmful substances on plants, that soon they may be gone forever? None of us will be able to survive for long, if the bees are gone.'

'I see your point Mr Howl. Look, on another note completely, a friend of mine is very attached to her cat. She's an old lady and she has been diagnosed with a terminal illness. She hasn't got more than about six months left. It would mean a lot to her if she could truly communicate her feelings to her pet. If the cat could learn English it could…'

'I'm sorry but I'm not qualified to teach animals to speak English. I wouldn't know how to go about it,' Howl interrupted. He sensed that the Vice President was not being honest and had an ulterior motive for his visit.

'But the President was told you were the one who taught all the birds and animals to speak English.'

Howl was shocked.

'Who told you that?'

'The President's dog, Congress. I believe she calls herself by another name. Pup I think it is. I gather that she's a candidate for your Party.'

Howl suddenly felt sick. His legs began to shake and his fur stood on end. For a minute he couldn't even bring himself to growl. His tail fell between his legs and he broke out in a cold sweat.

'Pup is the President's dog?' he spluttered in a high-pitched kind of grunt.

'Yes, but don't get me wrong. She wasn't asked to spy on the Fur and Feathers Party. She asked the President if she could be a candidate. She believes in your Party platform. I'm surprised she hasn't told you that she lives with the President at the White House. There's no reason to be so secretive about this,' Elroy added with a devious gleam in his eye.

Howl sat in stunned silence.

'Don't worry, I'll see myself out,' Elroy said. 'Let's stay in touch Mr Howl, huh?'

Howl ignored him. He was too upset to even acknowledge

that Elroy was leaving. How could Pup do such a terrible thing to him? He had trusted her and she had let him down, just like the other bitch he had loved.

'I should have listened to my instincts,' Howl growled. 'I will never allow myself to be abused like this again.' He hastily scribbled a note on a leaf. He went outside the tree trunk and put the leaf into the mouth of a pigeon that was sitting on a branch close by. He waved at the pigeon, angrily baring his teeth. It flew off quickly with the note, afraid it might be eaten.

~

Pup was busy in Florida gathering signatures. She only had about fifty to collect. She was excited, thinking how proud Howl was going to be with her.

She was just about to stop another lady in the street when the pigeon landed on the ground beside her, dropping the leaf with its message. The little terrier picked up the leaf with her paw to read the note out loud. '*Please stop gathering signatures and come back immediately. We need to talk. Howl.*'

'I don't understand,' Pup muttered to herself. 'I hope he is okay. He sounds very upset.'

37

Cocky Stew

CRACKER PACED up and down in front of the Supreme Court Justice in an agitated way. It was the last chance for the Fur and Feathers Party to be granted access to the televised debates.

The President's advisors and the Vice President sat together waiting to learn the outcome.

The Supreme Court Justice, a sickly looking man in his sixties with a very wrinkled face, leant forward to announce the verdict.

'I have considered your case and, in accordance with the rules laid down by the American Constitution, birds and animals have never been mentioned as having a right to vote. Therefore I am prohibiting the Fur and Feathers Party from access to the televised debates.' He slammed down his gavel, legally sealing the fate of the Party.

Cracker's beak dropped open and she moved close to the judge. 'Ya know what you are? You're an obsequious, fawning, grovelling excuse for a human being. Your lack of empathy for the common bird, animal or person is unprecedented.'

Cracker was pleased to see the stunned look on the face of the judge. The man was obviously surprised at her bravado and her excellent command of the English language.

'I shall hold you in contempt of court!' the judge shouted.

'You impose your bigoted views in the high court of the United States of America. It's supposed to be a democracy! That's rather ironic don't you think?' Cracker continued.

'She has an excellent command of English for a bird,' one of the President's advisors whispered to Elroy.

'Yes, doesn't she.'

~

Elroy sat with a group of men in his private quarters. He had a devious plan and he couldn't wait to get them all on side. He knew there was no point in discussing his idea with the President. He would not approve of what Elroy wanted to do. But he felt sure Jim would change his mind once Elroy's plan worked, and the threat to their Party was no longer there.

'There are two hundred and twenty million cat owners in the United States. That's a lot of potential voters,' said the Vice President. 'What if a cat suddenly learned how to speak English and could be persuaded to debunk the policies of the Fur and Feathers Party? Cats can be very persuasive when they're talking to cat lovers.'

'If only we could find out who teaches English to the animals,' said one of the advisors.

'It's not the Wolf. I'm certain of that,' Elroy said. 'I've been observing a group of candidates for the Fur and Feathers Party. I've noticed something interesting. At some point in their Party political speeches they have all incorporated the phrase 'Polly wants a Cracker'. That's rather a strange thing to say in a Party political broadcast. Perhaps that cockatoo Spokesbird, Cracker Yellow-Crest is the one who is teaching them? Maybe it is time we said 'g'day' to this cocky creature.' His shifty eyes narrowed so sharply that his eyes almost disappeared. Elroy was pleased when he saw the men all break into smiles of approval.

~

The forest was still and silent as dawn approached. The leaves were glistening with droplets of dew. The sky was coated in glorious shades of red, coral, soft pink and gold like a magnificent oil painting.

Cracker was fast asleep on her perch in an oak tree near the headquarters of the Fur and Feathers Party.

She was dreaming about Henry. They were in Australia and blissfully stripping a pear tree together and planning their honeymoon at a nearby orchard.

Henry was picking out the tastiest fruit for Cracker and she was thinking what a lucky bird she was to have a mate like Henry. Cracker was suddenly wrenched out of her nice dream by a loud voice that sounded just like her.

'Polly want a cracker?' the voice screeched.

Cracker cocked her head on one side and peered through the leaves. She wasn't able to see another bird anywhere.

'Wanna cup of tea?' the voice screeched again.

'Cracker wants a Cracker,' she squawked moving sideways along the branch in the direction of the voice.

'Here's a cracker for Cracker,' the mysterious voice said again.

Cracker moved further along the branch but still could not see a bird anywhere.

Suddenly she felt a net over her head and was pulled out of the tree and bundled into a waiting cage by a couple of men. It all happened so quickly she had not been able to see what the men looked like.

~

Cracker opened one eye. She felt very strange, as if she hadn't completely woken up from a long sleep.

The Vice President was gazing at her. His face was very close to hers, and his small, mean mouth turned up at the corners into a gratified grin. He had the look of a man who had just been told he'd won his own weight in gold. Cracker stood up, but felt very drowsy and shaky on her claws. She felt something heavy and restricting and discovered there was a solid metal chain attached to her foot.

She looked around her. She was in a small room with no windows and heavy dark blue drapes along one wall. She was standing on top of a large oak table that was devoid of anything except the surprised Cockatoo, and the thick heavy chain attached to her foot. Elroy was holding onto the other end of the chain.

She had no recollection of how she came to be in the room. The last thing she could remember was dreaming about Henry.

'You've been brought here to perform an important mission for the citizens of the United States,' the Vice President said. Cracker pulled away from him. He'd been eating garlic and his breath stank. Elroy pulled on her chain with a sharp menacing tug that almost caused her to lose her balance and fall off the table.

'As long as you co-operate, everything will be fine.'

Cracker mumbled to herself in cockatoo language.

'Did you teach all the birds and animals to speak English?' Elroy asked.

Cracker gave a parrot squeak. The Vice President pulled harder on her chain.

'Fair crack of a gum tree branch! That hurt,' Cracker said in English.

'Do you know that it's illegal to work in the United States on a tourist visa?' Elroy said firmly.

'Look here mate, I'm the Spokesbird for a political Party. It's voluntary. That's allowed.'

'And what about your work teaching birds and animals to speak English?'

'I'm not earning any money for that!' Cracker screeched. She realized she had made a terrible blunder.

'Woops.'

'So you *are* the one who is teaching English to the birds and animals?'

'I'm not allowed to say,' Cracker replied.

'Let me put it this way. We have a few kitty cats that want to learn English. We'd like you to teach them. Once they can speak well enough, you will be free to go. We'll even give you a bag of the best birdseed to take home with you, and we'll run you back to your tree. How's that for a deal?'

'No deal,' Cracker screeched.

'Okay. Let me put it another way, birdy. If you refuse to teach our kitties English, you'll be in a bit of a stew. And I am not speaking metaphorically. I'm sure you know what that word means since you're so good at English.'

Cracker didn't like the way he was narrowing his eyes. She began to babble.

'Uh Oh! Polly wants a cracker. Wanna cup of tea? I sure do!'

'I believe roast cockatoo is a delicacy in some parts of the world,' one of the advisors said, winking at Cracker. 'What you do is marinate the drumstick first in a little ginger and garlic…'

Cracker's legs began to shake. She was horrified and thought of the garlic smell on the man's breath. The cockatoo wondered if he'd already demolished some poor innocent bird for dinner.

Another man in the room produced a large cooking pot. He put the pot onto a portable stove on a long table beside the boardroom table.

'What kind of herbs would go well with cockatoo meat?' he asked Elroy.

Cracker gulped. Her throat was becoming so restricted she felt like she was being strung up with a rope around her neck. Then everything went black.

~

The next morning Cracker woke up from another deep sleep. She was back in the cage on the oak table. Something huge and furry was staring at her. She jumped back in fright. It was a large Persian cat. Its almond shaped yellow eyes were fixed on Cracker with an intense and mean expression.

'Cocky stew!' Cracker muttered to herself nervously. Every ounce of cockiness had been wrenched away from her, and she was a trembling wreck as she remembered the conversation she had with the Vice President.

Cracker sang a few shaky bars of the song 'What's New Pussycat' and stared nervously at the Persian cat who had not taken its eyes off her for a minute. 'Kitty want a cracker?' she squawked with a quavering voice

38

Abandoned Again

HOWL PACED AROUND his national Party headquarters. He was angry with himself for letting down his guard and allowing the little dog to touch his heart.

I should have known that such a pampered little creature would belong to someone important. *A dog like her could have no real interest in a wild scruffy wolf like me,* he thought. *How could I have been so blind not to see that her real interest in my Party was to find out our secrets and report it all back to her Master?*

Howl needed to let out some of his anger before he would self-combust from the level of his rage. The Wolf began attacking everything he could see. He tore into a wooden log used as a chair with his murderous teeth, reducing it in seconds to a pile of wood chippings. He grabbed one end of the dirty rug on the floor, hurling it with all his might across the hollowed-out tree trunk. It sent a meaty bone that was to be his lunch flying across the middle of the large log. It became embedded in the timber wall and stuck out like some kind of strange modern art form.

Howl noticed some movement out of the corner of his eye. Something was waiting outside. Even before he opened the door he could see a small dog, its entire body shaking violently like leaves in a hurricane. He came slowly to the entrance and opened the door.

The red Wolf stared at the frightened face gazing at him. His eyes were as cold as a midwinter day in Chicago. He was panting heavily and baring his sharp incisors in a threatening way.

'What's the matter?' Pup said with a trembling bark.

'I had a visit from the Vice President of the United States. He told me that YOU are the President's dog,' he snapped.

'Let me explain…' Pup stammered.

'Don't try and tell me that you really intended to be loyal to me and to my Party. A dog is always loyal to its master first. You know that.'

'Normally that would be true, but not in this case. You have to believe me.'

Howl didn't want to listen to anything else from her. He was too upset.

'Get out of here before I have you for dinner. I never want to see you again.'

Howl watched her run away as fast as a greyhound on a winning run. He could see she was terrified but he didn't care. 'She should have thought about the consequences before she pretended to care about me, and my Party.' he told himself out loud. He slammed the heavy oak door to his Party headquarters and flopped onto the floor.

~

The moon was full. Throwing the image of its large golden

orb into the still water of the lake that Howl had chosen to sit by. He sat hunched up on an outcrop of rock. The Wolf gazed at his sad reflection in the moonlit water. He no longer felt the same anger he'd experienced when he'd come face to face with Pup again. Now he was just deeply depressed.

There was a rustle of leaves. Howl leapt up to face where the noise came from. Pup appeared in the bushes. Howl took one look at her and began to run.

Pup barked and barked loudly after him. 'Wait, Howl please! I must talk to you.'

Howl kept running. Just seeing her again had caused the anger to rise in him. He was afraid that he might rip into her and he needed to get away. He disappeared around a bend. He was way too fast for the little silky-haired terrier.

Once he had reached his Party headquarters, he stopped outside to catch his breath. But the thoughts of Pup's betrayal were going around and around in his head. He had to do something to distract himself from thinking about her. He began to dig a deep hole with his paw. He was so busy digging the hole he hadn't noticed Snowy Owl watching him.

'Maybe you were a little hasty in getting rid of Pup,' said the Owl.

Howl took no notice and just kept on digging the hole.

'She was doing a brilliant job for Florida. You'd be lucky to find anyone to replace her. And what happened to Cracker? She disappeared just when we most needed her to train up more helpers,' the Owl sighed.

'We may lose the election now if we don't find someone quickly to do what Pup was doing for Florida. We are still a hundred or so signatures short of gaining ballot access. So many people want to know what happened to Pup. She was very popular, you know.'

Howl continued to dig furiously, trying his best to ignore the Owl's comments. But Snowy Owl would not let up.

'She adored you Howl. Perhaps you shouldn't have let her go so hastily.'

Howl stopped digging. He had heard enough.

'Well, if she adored me so much, why wasn't she honest with me? 'Females are all the same. You just can't trust them,' he snapped.

'Well, she did tell you she lived in a large white house.'

'Yes but not *THE* White House!' the red Wolf growled. 'I'm going to tell the media that the U.S. President installed his dog called Congress as a spy. That should cause a little unrest with the voters.'

'Howl, if you want a little bit of advice from a wise old bird, don't lower yourself to the level of muck-raking politics. This is not what our Party stands for. We're a little above that, don't you think? Is revenge the tack that natural law would take?'

'Oh why do you have to be so infuriatingly wise?' Howl said with a growl.

~

Pup flopped onto the ground exhausted and wept tears of utter frustration. She wasn't far from the White House but she'd been running so fast she was too tired to go on. All her issues of abandonment had come flooding back. Not only because she'd felt loved by Howl, but the work she'd been doing to help the Fur and Feathers Party had given her a strong sense of importance. She had felt worthwhile, worthy of being loved. Now everything had fallen into a heap. Her sense of self-worth had sunk so low, she felt as bad as she had when she was lying on that highway in Hornsby.

It was all over some big misunderstanding. She had no idea how she could make Howl realize that she had never betrayed him. She fell into a deep sleep and dreamed about Cracker. She was back lying on the road in New South Wales, and Cracker was doing her best to cheer her up.

'You know Pup, as dogs go you're pretty damn cute. I'll bet you've got those hounds lining up by the trees for a sniff of you. I wouldn't worry about Howl. He's got his own issues of abandonment. Don't let him get to you. You've got better things to do. What you put your attention to, grows. So, if you're gonna just lie there feeling sorry for yourself, you'll attract more misery into ya life. Look at me. I lost Henry the love of my life, but do you see me lying around feeling sorry for myself, with no will to live?'

Pup woke up from the dream. She suddenly felt guilty for dropping her bundle again. Cracker was right, even if it was just a dream. She had to believe in herself more. Just because Howl had some issues of his own was no reason to dump it all on her. She decided she was going to try and be more positive. She would stop by Cracker's tree on her way home and say hello. That would cheer her up. Maybe Cracker could shed some light on the best way to handle things with Howl.

Pup reached the base of Cracker's tree and barked loudly for her. There was no response. She yapped and yapped until a squirrel came up to her, visibly annoyed. 'Please. I am trying to enjoy my acorns, and you are making a lot of noise.'

'I'm sorry but I am looking for my friend Cracker the cockatoo bird. Have you seen her around anywhere?'

'Not heard from that loud screeching creature for days and I have to tell ya, it's a great relief. Really likes the sound of her own voice, that one!'

'Look, I can appreciate she can be quite loud, but she's been a good friend to me. Were you aware that she's the Spokesbird for the Fur and Feathers Party? She's doing a lot to help the birds and animals of America.'

'Yeah, she bored us with all of that. I'm really not a political animal.'

'I need to see her. If she comes back will you tell her I stopped by her tree, and I have to talk to her urgently about something.'

'Sure. But to be honest, after the confrontation I had with her the other day, I think she may have decided to find another tree somewhere else to screech in,' the squirrel said.

~

When Pup got back to her room in the White House she went straight into the President's quarters to let him know she was back. She knew he cared about her, as every time she had been away for a while he seemed so happy to see her again. This time was no exception and he looked very relieved when she ran up to him, wagging her tail.

'There you are Congress! I've been worried about you. You're always disappearing.'

'I had some business to attend to.'

'I hope you're not hanging out with that wild animal again?'

'I'm not seeing him anymore,' Pup said.

'Well that's good news Congress, because he could rip a little dog like you to shreds in a minute, ya know.'

'Yes I am aware of that.' The President turned on the

television and Pup was surprised to see Howl being interviewed by a female chat show host.

'Well, talk of the devil,' the President commented. Before he could take in what was being said, Jim was interrupted by a phone call. He left the room with his cell phone for a private conversation.

Pup was relieved he had disappeared and she could focus on what Howl was saying. She thought he looked sad and dejected and she felt strangely cheered up by that. Maybe he regretted cutting her out of his life.

'What I don't understand Howl is why would you get rid of the dog when she was doing such a good job?' the female interviewer asked.

'There were some issues over loyalty to the Party,' Howl answered staring at his front paw.

'Can you explain what you mean by issues? This little dog had a big following. If she wasn't being loyal to the Fur and Feathers Party, then who was she being loyal to?'

Pup watched Howl shift awkwardly in his seat. He didn't respond.

'And what about Cracker, your Spokesbird? Can you explain her sudden disappearance?'

'Not really. I….'

Pup sat upright. What did they mean she had disappeared? She knew Cracker was committed to her role teaching the birds and animals English. She wouldn't just disappear like that! Cracker loved working for the Fur and Feathers Party. Pup continued to watch, hoping some light might be shed on where her cockatoo friend had gone.

'Let's go to the studio audience,' the TV presenter said.

A middle-aged woman held up her hand. 'Ma'am,' the interviewer said.

'I've been a great fan of the Fur and Feathers Party but now I am wondering what to do. If you can't tell us what has happened to Pup and the Spokesbird, then I am sorry, you've lost my vote.'

'I can appreciate your point,' Howl told the woman. More people in the audience were putting up their hands.

'Yes, the man in the blue shirt,' the interviewer continued.

'What I don't understand is how you can just lose your Spokesbird,' the man said.

Pup was still watching the screen. Some type appeared: *Breaking News. The following is an important announcement for all those who care about their country.*

She was astonished to see a large fat Persian cat with a sinister expression speaking to the camera.

'Are you one of America's two hundred and twenty million cat owners? I'm speaking on behalf of the kitties of America. Would you honestly consider letting a wild animal run your country? Remember what the wolf did to little Red Riding Hood! Do you think he's going to care about your children, or your precious cat?'

'Oh no!' Pup barked.

'Wolves have been known to eat cats, you know. Now that we can speak English we have to take a stand. Don't waste your vote on a wolf with no clothing. Vote for the Party that has the money to take care of your needs. We've plenty of money in the kitty,' the cat hissed.

The dog biscuits that Pup had gulped on her arrival home began to churn undigested in her stomach. She knew that

Cracker was the only one who could have taught the cat English. There was no way Cracker would have chosen to do that unless she had somehow been forced. Something terrible must have happened to Cracker.

She had to do what she could to help her friend.

39

Dirty Politics

IT WAS GETTING dark and the President was still talking on the phone in another room.

Pup heard a familiar screech coming from outside and she ran to look out the window. She could see the Vice President carrying what looked like a birdcage. It was covered over with a blanket.

'Cracker,' Pup yelled and shot down her chute into the back garden. The men had already disappeared. She found her secret hole and squeezed under the fence. She hid in some bushes, waiting by the private back entrance to the White House. A large van was parked outside. She watched as the Vice President appeared from the shadows with another man.

'Let me out you creeps. You won't get away with this,' Cracker squawked.

'Shut up,' Elroy said.

'Quick, let's get her into the truck,' he said to the man helping him. 'I told you we should have drugged the stupid bird.'

Pup secretly followed the two men. She watched them loading Cracker into the back of the van. The men jumped inside and drove off.

The little dog raced after them as fast as her small legs could go. At some of the corners she thought she'd lost them, but the traffic was heavy and the little terrier was able to catch up to the men. Mercifully for Pup, the van travelled only a short distance, stopping outside a warehouse.

Pup hid in some tall bushes. She was panting furiously from her run. She watched as the two men opened the back doors of the vehicle and began unloading many cages covered loosely with blankets. A strong breeze caused one of the blankets to fly up on one side. Pup could see several Australian native birds inside the cage.

Her heart was beating as fast as a tropical downpour. She continued to watch as the men disappeared inside the old warehouse. They travelled back and forth, taking out more and more cages of wild birds from the back of the van and carrying them inside the building.

As they took out another cage, the voice inside spoke in English. 'Someone is going to find your hiding place and tell everyone how you're funding your Party,' Cracker squawked, unaware that Pup was within earshot.

The little terrier could not believe what she just heard. She watched as the man disappeared inside the warehouse only to reappear a minute later. He padlocked the door to the building. Pup watched as the man took out a large wad of money and handed it to the Vice President.

'I knew that man could not be trusted,' Pup muttered to herself. The two men climbed into the truck and drove off. Pup waited until they were well out of sight before jumping up and down at a window, trying to see inside.

She was able to see that the warehouse was filled with cages of many different kinds of Australian birds. She could just make out one cage that was rocking violently from side to side.

'Help! Get me outta here,' Cracker screeched.

'Don't worry Cracker. I will get you out,' Pup barked as loudly as she could.

'Good on ya Pup,' the bird screeched excitedly at hearing the little terrier's voice outside. Pup knew what she had to do.

~

Howl sat on a log in the hollowed out tree trunk watching the evening news on television. He blinked a few times as he watched the scene unfolding in front of his eyes.

'And thousands of demonstrators have gathered outside the White House to protest the alleged kidnapping of 'Cracker', the Spokesbird of the Fur and Feathers Party,' a newsreader reported.

'I'll bet that damn dog is behind this,' the red Wolf growled. He was about to change channels when a news flash interrupted the story.

'And we've just received news that the U.S. Vice President himself may be involved in illegally importing native wildlife from Australia to fund the President's election campaign,' the newsreader reported.

Howl sat glued to the set. He did a double take when he saw Pup at the back of the White House, surrounded by media with microphones pointed at her.

'Cracker is in a warehouse with hundreds of stolen birds.
I've seen her. It's an illegal racket,' she called out to the

assembled media. 'The Vice President is importing Australian native birds to make money for his Party,' she barked excitedly.

Howl watched amazed as the news report cut to the front of the White House where the President was answering questions from a reporter.

'Mr President, is it true that Cracker is being held hostage in the White House?' the female reporter asked.

'I can honestly tell you that I know nothing about this.'

'And what of the allegations about the Vice President? Has he been funding your campaign by illegally importing birds from another country?'

'As I said, I know nothing about this.'

Howl continued to be transfixed to the TV screen as the news report cut to Pup in the back garden of the White House.

'I can take you to the warehouse,' Pup barked excitedly to the media who had microphones all around her.

The media people jumped into their cars and Pup joined one of the reporters. 'Head up this road and then take a left,' she told the reporter. All the cars followed in pursuit.

The President was still standing in front of the White House and noticed the commotion and media people jumping into cars and driving away.

'What's happening?' he asked the female reporter, who was now off the air and clearly listening to something in her earpiece.

'They're heading to a warehouse. Quickly, come with me,' the reporter said, heading towards the news car. She opened the door for the President and he climbed inside. She leapt into the car and they drove off in pursuit of all the other cars. They pulled up outside the warehouse. The President and the female reporter jumped out of the news car. Some police rushed up to the door of the warehouse. It was open. They burst in, with members of the media crowding in behind. The warehouse was full of cages of wild native Australian birds.

Elroy was caught red handed on live television with two cages in his hands.

The President shook his head in shock. 'Oh Elroy! How could you?'

Cracker was in one of the cages, screeching loudly. 'They've got Henry. The Vice President told me I'd be cocky stew if I didn't teach a cat how to speak English,' Cracker said with a deafening screech.

Howl was still transfixed to the television screen. 'I knew there was something fishy about that man,' Howl growled.

The red Wolf continued to watch as the police pointed their guns at the Vice President.

'I'm sorry sir, but I am afraid you're under arrest.' Handcuffs were clapped on Elroy.

Cracker was let out of the cage. The Spokesbird screeched in delight at the Vice President. 'Yeah! Now *you'll* see what it's like to be in a cage.' She flew up to the cage where her partner Henry was and peered in at him. 'Henry. I thought you were dead!'

Henry screeched back in delight at Cracker in cockatoo language. 'How did you learn to speak the people's language?'

'It's a long story,' Cracker screeched. She could feel the lump developing in her throat again. She was afraid she would break down in happy bird hysterics at finding Henry again, unharmed. She gazed at her claws, trying to hide the tears that were forming in her beady eyes. 'It's a long story,' Cracker repeated. 'I'll tell you all about it over a bowl of the finest seeds.'

~

Howl continued to watch the television screen. His mouth was wide open and he drooled on the floor as he watched Pup being interviewed.

'How did you know that Cracker was being held hostage?' a reporter asked Pup.

'I was the President's dog. I joined the Fur and Feathers Party but not because I wanted to spy on them and report back to my master. I truly believed in their principles. I was deeply torn about helping my master, because this is what a dog would normally do. But I couldn't support the kind of government he wanted. The Fur and Feathers Party was set up to try and save the planet from all the damage that mankind had been doing to our natural home. I wanted to help them as best I could. It made me feel good, that I was able to contribute something of real value for the world.

~

In Melbourne, Australia, David sat glued to the television. His mouth almost met the floor as he watched Pup speaking English on the television.

Rita was lounging on the sofa, her legs draped over David.

'Rita, look! That's my little dog, Pup. How on earth did she learn to speak English? Can you believe it? She's the President's dog now. Well how 'bout that?'

'Really?' Rita said with a yawn. 'David, you can be so gullible at times. They can animate animals to make them look very real. Anyway, come on, even if it *was* her, and she had miraculously learned to speak English, how could she become the President's dog? Pup is probably living with some animal lover in Hornsby. Here can you rub my back? It's really itchy.'

David began rubbing her back but his face remained glued to the television. 'No. It's definitely Pup. She had unusual markings. I'd know that face anywhere.'

Rita sat up and gave David a long look. 'You still think this is a real dog. Darling what have you been drinking?'

'Rita don't you remember seeing the Fur and Feathers Party's kangaroo leader, Bounce on the TV? She had learned how to speak English too, remember? I'm telling you that *is* Pup my little dog. Oh, I am so relieved she's alive and happy somewhere. But living in the White House? I always thought she was a clever dog, but OMG the President's dog. Wow!'

David pushed Rita's legs off his lap and leapt up. He grabbed a pen and a piece of paper from his computer desk and began heading towards the door.

'Where are you going?' Rita asked.

'There's something I've gotta do.' David left the room leaving Rita staring after him.

~

Pup was still speaking on the television. 'But on behalf of my master, the man you call the President, I know he was not behind this. I witnessed a meeting when his Vice President wanted to do something fishy, and my master said he wanted no part of anything that was not completely above board. He would never have supported this bird trafficking. He is a good man.' Pup shed some doggie tears and stared straight into the camera. 'I was never disloyal to you Howl. I always put you and the Fur and Feathers Party before anything else, even my own master. Please forgive me. I know I should have been honest with you. It was a terrible thing I did.'

A tear ran down Howl's face. He knew he had been a fool when he had not allowed her to speak, and had thrown her out of his Party Headquarters. He had to see her again.

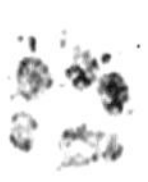

40

True Love and ....

PUP RACED THROUGH the forest along the edge of a beautiful lake. She was trying to catch a water rat that ran in and out of some long grass by the edge of a river. She wasn't having much luck. The rat was way too fast for her.

There was a rustle in the bushes and Howl appeared. He had something in his mouth. He put it on the ground by a bush.

'You'll never catch it if you go about it like that,' he told Pup. She raced up to him excitedly and they rolled about and played like old friends. Once again, they were two very happy hounds.

They stopped playing for a minute and Howl picked up the piece of paper from the ground he'd had in his mouth. He passed it to Pup. 'A boarding pass for a trip to Florida?' Pup wasn't sure what this meant. She thought for a minute that perhaps he was sending her off to get rid of her, and all her old doubts about being abandoned came flooding back.

'We'd better get going,' he barked. 'We haven't got much time and we've still got signatures to collect.'

Pup was thrilled. She ran up to him and bit him playfully on the ear. It sent ripples of pure joy across her entire body.

~

People were so happy to see the little silky-haired terrier out on the streets again collecting signatures. Pup had no idea she was so popular with the general public. She didn't have to stop a single person. They all came to her.

Pup worked her magic. In just one week she had single-pawedly collected two thirds of the signatures they needed for ballot access.

The newspapers were full of the growing success of the Fur and Feathers Party.

Howl had collected the remaining number of signatures that were required for ballot access. The Fur and Feathers Party was now a real contender in the election.

~

Howl was very pleased with Pup for all her hard work. For days he'd wanted to apologise to her properly for the way he had treated her earlier, but he had been putting off the moment.

Now that Pup had done such a wonderful job with Florida, it was time for the red Wolf to face up to what he had to do. He hoped she would forgive him.

Howl watched Pup playing with a butterfly that was dancing around her. He loved her playful and adventurous nature. He swallowed hard. He walked up to Pup, nuzzling her little silky-haired face, and inviting her to join him by a large flowering dogwood tree. The tree had beautiful, bright red flowers, fading to white in the centre. A lovely hummingbird was enjoying the flower's delicious nectar. *This is a good place for my apology,* Howl thought.

A large meaty bone waited beside him on the grass. Howl planned to share it with Pup, to celebrate the Fur and Feathers Party's success as an official third Party in the election.

Howl felt his skin prickle with nerves as he got ready to tell Pup what he had been rehearsing in his head. He hoped she would accept his apology completely, and they could get back to enjoying a happy relationship again. He took a deep breath. Pup had begun to gnaw on the bone.

'I want to apologise to you Pup,' he said.

Pup suddenly stopped eating and gazed at Howl.

'I really misjudged you. Our Party would not be where it is now if it hadn't been for all your hard work and your loyalty to me. I am so sorry I reacted the way I did.'

Pup tried to control her emotions but she couldn't stop the tear that plopped onto the bone she'd been eating. She swallowed a few times, trying to get rid of the huge lump that had formed in her throat. 'That's okay,' Pup said. I can see how it must have looked with my being the President's dog and all.'

Howl was so relieved that the little terrier had forgiven him, he didn't even notice the bone still had some meat on it after Pup had dropped it on the ground. 'We'd better get some shut-eye,' he said. 'We have a big day ahead of us tomorrow.'

~

That night, Pup watched as the red Wolf went inside a large hollow log big enough for two dogs to sleep in. He sniffed around inside the log, pulling some rough bark off and spitting it out on the ground outside.

Pup was a little apprehensive. He was obviously expecting her to lie down next to him inside this former tree trunk. She wondered if Howl had considered how he would need to adapt if the Fur and Feathers Party got into government. They would be required to move into the big white house where she had been living. Then she began to consider that they may not be successful, and she would be sleeping rough like this if she wanted to be Howl's permanent mate. Her tummy tightened with nerves. She couldn't imagine living like a wild dog all the time. But she remembered something her mother had told her once: '*Never trouble trouble, until trouble troubles you. You'll only double trouble, and trouble others too".*

Maybe her mother was with her now, prompting her to live in the moment and not worry about a future that had not arrived.

Howl gave her a gentle bark, jarring her out of her worrying thoughts. She climbed inside the log with him. He licked her head affectionately and they both fell into an exhausted sleep.

~

No one could have expected what happened on Election Day, least of all Pup's master.

Jim watched as Howl gave his inaugural address as the President-Elect in front of the West Terrace of the Capital building in Washington, D.C.

The former President was relieved that he had not been charged for being a part of the Vice President's illegal bird trafficking racket. He had Pup to thank for that.

Thousands of birds and animals gathered and millions of people watched, either in person or on television, as Howl presented his vision for America, setting forth his goals for the nation.

Even though he had lost the election, Jim had begun to take climate change more seriously, and he was glad that the Fur and

Feathers Party would be doing everything they could to clean up the planet and protect it from further damage.

He noticed how close Pup was standing to Howl, and how happy she seemed to be. He realized he'd been wrong about this Wolf. He felt sure Howl would take good care of his little dog, but he felt a twinge of sadness in his heart; he would no longer be her master.

'I want to thank everyone who voted for us,' Howl told the crowd of birds, animals and people that had gathered in front of the Capital building to watch the inaugural address. 'We are all overwhelmed by this success. Now I am going to have to get used to a more civilized way of living. No more sleeping rough. I hear they have silk cushions where I'll be living now.'

The crowd put their paws, claws, wings and hands together and made a very loud excited noise. Humans were waving their balloons and placards that read *'I voted for the Fur and Feathers Party.'* The atmosphere was so highly charged it could have powered a Ferrari.

But despite the hullabaloo there was one bird that screeched so loudly it could almost have been heard back in New South Wales. 'Good on ya Pup,' Cracker squawked turning to Henry who was beside her on the branch of an oak tree. 'She won't be wallowing anymore now.'

'I have no idea what you are talking about dear,' Henry said rubbing his ears from the piercing pain caused by Cracker's excited voice. But I am thrilled to be out of jail and back with my screechy mate. Once we are home in Australia again, we will have people to scare, and fruit trees to strip clean. We're going to be so busy,' he added.

'The planet will thank you,' a woman yelled from the crowd.

‘I’m happy about it too,’ a moose said in the background. ‘Maybe soon the rivers will be more fit to drink. The ones around my territory tasted terrible.’

‘I do have an important announcement to make,’ Howl continued. ‘I am delighted to inform you that I won’t be alone in the White House.’

The Wolf gazed lovingly at Pup and beckoned her to join him on the tree stump. ‘I’d like you to meet my “First Dog”,’ he said, putting a paw on Pup’s back. The crowd cheered. Hundreds of pictures were taken. Pup was over the moon.

~

Pup sat at a long oak table eating a plate of dog chow from a silver bowl with her beloved Howl. There was a knock on the door and a black bear entered the room. He was the newly appointed Chief of Staff to Howl.

‘There is a cockatoo here to see you Mrs Howl.’

Without waiting for an invitation, Cracker flew into the room heading straight for the chandelier. She swung precariously from it for a while, hanging upside down.

‘Just wanted to say goodbye,’ she screeched. ‘Henry and I are flying home this afternoon.’

‘But you’re our Spokesbird,’ Pup said disappointed.

‘You’ll find another Spokesbird. I think Bald Eagle is a good bet. She’s got a loud mouth just like me,’ Cracker squawked. ‘Henry and I will be officially announcing that we will be permanent mates when we get home.’

‘I’m so happy for you Cracker. But it’s a long way home. Are your wings strong enough?’

‘Don’t be a dingbat Pup. We’re going on the huge man-made bird. You know the one that never flaps its wings. Don’t know how it manages it, but it sure knows how to get there fast.'

'I'll miss you,' Pup said, with a tear rolling down her silvery cheek.

Cracker waddled up to Pup. 'Yeah, going to miss you too Pup. Thanks for saving my feathers. If it wasn't for you I'd definitely be marinating somewhere by now. Ya know, it's a funny thing but I used to know a little dog that thought she was completely worthless. Its name was Pup too. But it was nothing like you.'

If dogs could be seen to blush, Pup's furry face would have turned the same colour as the vermillion drapes in the Oval Office. She waved goodbye with her paw. 'I'll miss you, Cracker.'

Cracker flew out the door leaving a mischievous white blob at the entrance. She squawked with laughter at what she had just done. 'A token of my affection,' she screeched and disappeared out of sight.

Black Bear came back into the room and addressed Howl. 'Sir, the new Secretary for the Environment is here. Can I send him in?'

Howl glanced at Pup nervously. He knew something that she didn't. 'Yes, send him in.'

The former U.S. President appeared at the doorway. Pup was shocked. 'You're the Secretary for the Environment?' she asked.

'Well, your principles are good, and life without my Congress, I mean Pup, seemed like no life at all. Oh, I've bought you a little wedding gift. It belonged to my grandfather. It has a crest on the side. Would be nice for dog chow.'

He put a silver bowl on the ground in front of Pup. She looked awkwardly at her master and another tear ran down her silky face. Pup went up to the former President and he patted her affectionately. She noticed he was holding an envelope. He passed it to the little dog. It had an Australian stamp on it with a picture of a yellow-crested cockatoo. She turned it over to see if there was a name on the back.

When Pup saw 'David' she passed it straight back to Jim. She was upset.

'What's wrong? Don't you want to open it?' The former President asked.

'Not really. It's from my original owner. He planned to leave me with Mrs Beanie. His girlfriend Rita was more important to him than me, it seemed.'

'Let me open it, Congress. He might want to explain what happened at the time.'

Pup felt her stomach tightening again, just like when she had watched David driving off into the distance without her.

'Well, I don't want to read it but you can if you want,' Pup told Jim.

The former President tore at the envelope and began reading to Pup.

Dear Pup,

I saw you on the television and recognized you as my dog. Congratulations. You've come a long way and I am glad you are so happy, and have found true love. I want to explain why I had to leave you when I did. If I'd known that you could understand English so well, and can now even speak it, I would have communicated this to you at the time.

I started going out with Rita, remember. But you may not have understood that she was allergic to dogs. She asked me to move in with her and the only way we could be together was if I gave you up.

I want you to know how hard this was for me. I actually cried for days. Something I was a little ashamed of at the time, but I loved you more than you could imagine. I wanted you to know this and that you hadn't done anything wrong.

I will always remember the happy times we spent together, and I am so pleased that you have found your mission in life, and a wonderful partner and master who loves you. Gosh Pup, the U.S. President! You sure can pick them. Please know that I will always love you and remember you fondly.

David.

Pup couldn't hold back her tears. Soon the fur on her face was very wet. The President put the paper down and gave her a pat.

'Well, I guess I should thank him,' Pup told Howl. The red Wolf licked a tear off Pup's face.

'If David hadn't dumped me, I never would have ended up here, and with you Howl.'

'Things have a funny way of working out in life don't they?' the former President said. 'Who would have thought I would be the Secretary of the Environment of a Party of birds and animals

Their laughter was interrupted by another knock at the door and Black Bear waddled back into the room. He was carrying a report in his mouth. He placed it at Howl's paws.

'Mr President, I want to draw your attention to a problem that is developing with the gorillas. They're complaining about the unjustified use of weapons of mass destruction being used by park rangers in the tropical rainforests of central Africa.

'They've filed an official report and are threatening to take the law into their own hairy hands if nothing is done about this. They want the U.S. to intervene and help them.'

Howl looked at Pup. 'Well, First Dog, looks like we've got some work to do.'

Acknowledgements

Writing a novel can be a lonely business. This one would never have manifested if I hadn't had the help, support and encouragement from many incredible people.

I am deeply grateful to William Laing, my good friend and editor. Your expertise really helped get the manuscript into a better shape for publication.

Thank you also to Judith Rooney for the thorough copy edit and to Sally Bird, Margaret Holmes, Caroline Mullarkey, Cynthia Bartolo and Lyn Noske for reading my manuscript and providing your valuable feedback.

My very good friend and coffee mate, the late Paul Murphy, also read the manuscript and wrote some lovely words. He is so deeply missed by all of us at York's Corner café.

The Illustrators did a brilliant job on the front and back cover. I could not be happier with how it looks.

I am also very appreciative of the very thorough self-publishing training programs offered by Ingram Spark. They were incredibly helpful and gave me the confidence to proceed with publishing the novel myself.

Finally a huge thank you to Simon Creedy. Your graphic design skills really helped me get my head around so many technical publishing things. Also thanks to Shoko (Simon's lovely wife), for patiently tolerating our constant book publishing jibber jabber.

ABOUT THE AUTHOR

Maggie Lawrence grew up in Melbourne and moved to a leafy suburb of Sydney in 2001. She loves animals and at one time had a horse, a dog and a cat. She cares about the environment and has run media campaigns about developments that concerned her. When she is not cramming her laptop with creative writing, Maggie can be found enjoying a coffee with friends at her local café, singing in a modern choir, meditating, bush walking, and sometimes communicating with the whales and dolphins on the Sydney whale-watching boat.

Maggie trained in film and television production at the BBC, and has won awards in the U.S. and Australia for feature-length screenplays, and for situation and TV sketch comedy. She has written, directed and produced a short film, 'Point Blank' that was screened in several international film festivals.

The Fur and Feathers Party is Maggie's debut novel, developed from her award-winning screenplay 'PUP'.

ANOTHER BOOK BY THE AUTHOR

'An Element of Fun' – is an illustrated book for children aged 5 to 8, and written in a quirky rhyme.

Fire, water, earth, air and thunder and lightning are all bragging about being the most important element. So the wise sun decides to set them a test to see which one of them is the best. He knows in his great wisdom that they will all learn an important lesson about ego and bullying.

Both books are available on Amazon.

You can visit Maggie at: www.maggielawrence.com

ML
writing for the planet

www.ingramcontent.com/pod-product-compliance
Lightning Source LLC
Chambersburg PA
CBHW030244120726
47903CB00005B/1616

* 9 7 8 0 6 4 5 1 3 0 3 2 4 *